The Last Animal

ALSO BY RAMONA AUSUBEL

Awayland

*Sons and Daughters of
Ease and Plenty*

A Guide to Being Born

No One Is Here Except All of Us

The
LAST
ANIMAL

· · · · · · · · · ·

Ramona Ausubel

RIVERHEAD BOOKS

NEW YORK

2023

RIVERHEAD BOOKS
An imprint of Penguin Random House LLC
penguinrandomhouse.com

Copyright © 2023 by Ramona Ausubel
Penguin Random House supports copyright. Copyright fuels
creativity, encourages diverse voices, promotes free speech, and
creates a vibrant culture. Thank you for buying an authorized
edition of this book and for complying with copyright laws by
not reproducing, scanning, or distributing any part of it in
any form without permission. You are supporting writers
and allowing Penguin Random House to continue
to publish books for every reader.

Riverhead and the R colophon are registered trademarks
of Penguin Random House LLC.

Library of Congress Cataloging-in-Publication Data

Names: Ausubel, Ramona, author.
Title: The last animal: a novel / Ramona Ausubel.
Description: New York: Riverhead Books, 2023.
Identifiers: LCCN 2022023946 (print) |
LCCN 2022023947 (ebook) |
ISBN 9780593420522 (hardcover) |
ISBN 9780593420546 (ebook)
Subjects: LCGFT: Novels.
Classification: LCC PS3601.U868 L37 2023 (print) |
LCC PS3601.U868
(ebook) | DDC 813/.6—dc23
LC record available at https://lccn.loc.gov/2022023946
LC ebook record available at https://lccn.loc.gov/2022023947

Printed in the United States of America
1st Printing

BOOK DESIGN BY MEIGHAN CAVANAUGH

For
my mom
and
my sister

Before

. . . .

One

In the Age of Extinction, two tagalong daughters traveled to the edge of the world with their mother to search the frozen earth for the bones of woolly mammoths.

Eve was fifteen, reshaping herself more each day; Vera, just shy of thirteen, was a stubborn straight line. Jane, their mother, was a graduate student in paleobiology. Their father had died one year before, plunged into a shock-green mountain in a tiny car on a tiny road in Italy where he was doing research for an article. Now they were three. Girls, sad and angry and growing and trying. Mom, sad and angry and trying. Hauling their bodies across the scoop of sky to get to a bare place, a lost place where ancient beasts had once roamed. Somehow, they hoped, this trip would be the beginning of a new road. Gentler, ascending.

.   .   .

JANE'S PROFESSOR HAD GROWN a beard for the trip to Siberia, and Todd, a postdoc, wore all tan safari clothing. Everything had several pockets and zipped into different configurations. In New York, Vera watched Todd zip off the legs to his pants and jog laps around the terminal in shorts and hiking boots, his stained white athletic socks like burned-down candles. The professor plugged in a full power strip to charge his computer, tablet and two phones and then ate three kale salads out of plastic to-go containers. He said, "We're unlikely to get fresh veggies. I want to vitamin-load."

Vera wondered if the professor was someone's father.

During their five-hour layover in Moscow Jane brought blini with caviar on a real plate to the seats where her daughters were draped, sleepy and prickling.

"Airport fish eggs, Mom, I don't know," Vera said. She wanted a burrito.

"You're in junior high, what do you know? They're actually so good," Jane said, sour cream on her lips.

Eve said, "I'm in high school, but I still find this embarrassing."

Todd, in the next row of chairs, again zipped his pant legs off and slung them over his carry-on, then jogged the halls. Eve made a hand flourish and said, "Exhibit A." Vera watched the Russians watch Todd and it seemed possible that he alone might inspire a war between the two countries. Americans, if this was any indication, needed to be put out of their misery. It would have been a service.

AS THE SUN WAS going down, they boarded a plane that would take them from Moscow to Yakutsk. The stewardesses in stilettos served chicken cutlet and sweet wine. The plane crossed six time zones and they had only traveled two thirds of the way across Russia.

Eve and Vera played a favorite game, Fortunately/Unfortunately, a game that had traveled with them on buses, planes, ships, trains all over the globe.

"Once there were two sisters who wanted to run away," Eve started.

Vera said, "*Fortunately*, they had large bags full of precious gems."

"*Unfortunately*," Eve continued, "the gems were heavy and the girls couldn't carry them."

"*Fortunately*, they came upon a cave where they could hide the bags until they had a way to transport them."

"*Unfortunately*, there was a wild and ferocious bear living in the cave."

Vera smiled at her older sister. "You always put a ferocious bear."

"It's a classic."

The story was, by design, endless. Meant to carry the girls across land and sea, every piece of bad news immediately followed by the upswing of salvation.

IT WAS MORNING AGAIN when they landed, dawn a fine pink stripe on the horizon. Vera felt broken by tiredness. She was not a person anymore but a hunger for sleep. The tarmac smelled like fire and melt.

This was the coldest city on earth in winter and all the photos in the hotel lobby were of people with iced eyelashes, men in fur suits with fur hoods selling fish in the outside market and everything shimmered with frost and the fish were frozen but not because they had been in a freezer. It was summer now but Vera could sense the threat of cold.

While the travelers checked in, the professor and Todd had a loud conversation about three-pointers in relationship to wingspan in the

NBA. The professor said, "Who wants a drink?" Jane said, "It's morning and I have children."

"Go, go," Vera said. "We will sleep."

"If you sleep now you'll never get onto the right time. You'll ruin the entire trip."

The desk clerk handed Jane her key. It was old-fashioned and had a giant wooden block for a key chain. These were the moments when careers took shape. Trust was earned over jet-lag vodka.

Jane said, "Go walk, girls," and motioned her sleepy daughters outside.

"Alone? In a foreign land?" Eve said.

"It's good for you."

Outside, Eve told Vera, "I've never hated anyone so much in my life." The day cracked at them with its light.

"Dudes, ugh," Vera said, shaking her head.

"Mom abandoned us just now. Don't blame men when it was clearly her choice to make."

Vera said, "She had to. The patriarchy, and stuff?" She looked at her watch as if it could set her right, as if knowing the time would clarify the moment. The watch had belonged to her father, not fancy, a drugstore purchase, but precious because it had been on his wrist and had been a tool for mapping his life. Vera could not get the numbers to make sense.

Everyone on the street was dressed well, especially the women, all looking as if they were about to be photographed. The backdrop was bloc and bland, buildings as storage for lives.

"Americans are such slobs," Vera said. "I am basically wearing jammies and I felt proud that I brushed my teeth and hair sometime yesterday. What are we doing here again?"

Eve said, "That's easy. Mom is pretending to be a necessary part of an important project and not a token woman with both literal and emotional baggage. I can see the headline, Woman, Supposed to Be Invisible, Brings Obnoxious Children on Science Trip, Ruins Everything. Couldn't she have sent us to sleepaway camp? I'd have been a counselor and made out with boys behind the mess hall and gotten in big trouble and learned to paddle a canoe. Instead, this."

Vera said, "We won't ruin anything. Look at us being invisible and out of the way so that the adults can drink vodka in preparation to look for ancient mammoth bits to better understand the genetic code and use *that* information to edit Asian elephant cells until they act like woolly cells. Plus, tour the future home for de-extincted woolly mammoths. That's a summer well spent."

"Listen to you, little lady. You sound better than Mom."

"I have heard her say that ten thousand times. It's embedded in my brain, like a phone number."

"To making a mammoth," Eve said, holding an invisible glass aloft, toward streetlights strung up on a wire.

They cheered with their fists. "Except I think we're supposed to say 'cold-adapted elephant.'"

Eve said, "How completely lame."

"They don't want to be criticized for playing God."

"You know the professor dreams of snuggling up to a woolly of his own making."

Couples sat on benches and the girls walked across a bridge over a wide, shallow river. The bridge was covered in padlocks. Names were written on the locks. Hearts and arrows and the word "Love" in English.

At the other end of the bridge a worker in a green zip-up jumpsuit cut locks, one by one. He knelt, brought the bolt cutter into place and squeezed. The locks that did not fall into the river were kicked in by the worker, each one sounding a different note as it fell into the water.

Love and declarations of love lasted however long, and then they sank.

"Do you think the grown-ups are drunk yet?" Vera asked. "Drunk enough that we can sneak past the bar and go to sleep?" She looked to her big sister for permission.

Eve said, "All I care about is a bed. I am willing to risk my life for it."

Vera did not know what she was willing to risk her life for. Science, progress, comfort, love, sleep.

THE NEXT MORNING the expeditioners repacked and took their things back to the airport for the last Siberian flight.

The plane had had most of its seats removed to carry cargo. Vera noted cases of rice, beets, a green vegetable she did not recognize. The professor sat atop coolers with pictures of fish on them and Todd perched on a wheel of dark orange cheese. Vera kept waiting for these necessities for survival to collapse under the weight of the American visitors. "Four short hours in blissful comfort," Eve said in plastic-lady voice. "Where are you taking us?" But Jane was bright, visibly excited, and she was unbothered by her elder's skepticism.

The region below was more than a million square miles of tundra, permafrost, the earth without human intervention.

Every hour, Todd stood and did a series of stretches, hands raised to the ceiling, his shirt pulled up to reveal a thin strip of pale, furred belly. Eve mouthed, "Ew," to Vera and Vera tried not to picture her hand on that stripe of skin. She did not want to want this crush, and yet . . .

The last airport of the journey was a dirt strip lined with abandoned Soviet propeller planes that looked like a pack of grazing animals.

Thick gray beard and fisherman's hat, a man stood in the dirt beside a yellow car with no front bumper. "Dmitri," he said, squeezing each hand hard. He introduced another man so obviously Dmitri's son that he did not need to state it. "Aleksei," the younger said. Dmitri and the professor hugged and smacked each other's backs. Jane, Eve and Vera were greeted without eye contact. Aleksei took Eve's and Vera's roller bags by the handles and said, "We walk this way."

Vera liked it more than she let on, this faraway feeling, this edge-of-it-all place.

The professor and Dmitri walked together, with Todd and Aleksei behind. Eve and Vera were paired and Jane walked at the back, alone. She looked like the odd kid on a field trip, buddyless. If the girls' father had been alive he would have held Jane's hand as she walked into this mission. Or, if their father had been alive he would have stayed home with the children and Jane would have gone on her own. Either version prickled Vera. This level of parental humanity caused a very specific stomachache. She tried to catch her mother's eye but Jane's attention was toward the horizon.

Vera smelled the river before she saw it. Mud and silt and willows. To reach Dmitri's land on the northern coast of this northern land they would travel the rest of the way on water, a twenty-hour barge ride to the East Siberian Sea. The group had already gone most of the way around the globe yet they had another night and another day before they stopped moving.

The river opened so wide the banks disappeared. It was its own small, moving sea. As they traveled farther, the mosquitoes rose off the water like a living fog and found all the warm skin, this floating feast. The

Americans put their jackets on even though it wasn't cold and they wore two pairs of socks and wrapped blankets around their legs and heads, leaving spaces to breathe. Todd zipped the legs to his pants back on and hopped to confuse the insects. The professor wrapped himself tightly in blankets and lay down on the deck like a mummy. If he had died like that no one would have been able to tell the difference. Vera felt like a cocooned creature preparing to be born as a new species. Even outfitted this way, they were bitten. Vera inhaled a mosquito that had found her small air hole. She felt its soft body in her mouth but instead of risking a naked hand to fish it out, she swallowed.

Even Vera, who wanted to be up for the task at hand, now wondered if this had been too much to ask. "I'm sorry," Jane said. She could have come alone. She could have risked missing them. Could have risked them missing her.

There were enough insects that they had weight. If Vera went uncovered she would be bloodless in moments, a sheet of skin.

Dmitri swatted and he said, "You should have seen it a few weeks ago. May is worst. Lucky for you to be here in June."

There was a long sunset in the middle of the night and everything else was noon, and their bodies were so upside-downed that they rested like dogs—someone was always asleep, briefly, then hungry and disoriented. In the dawn or dusk of a day that never ended or began they pulled to a spot on the side of the river where there were two huge posts, and finally, finally tied off.

THERE WAS A SMALL wooden dock onto which Aleksei tied the boat. He stood with arms out to help the passengers down. Vera looked out at grass and brush, at the dark wet earth. She could see some small cabins down a path of mud and in the distance were pine trees. It looked like the African savanna crossed with a high meadow. She could hear the river water against the bank and from somewhere, wind or ocean—she was not sure which. Watching the people disembark was a herd of something very big, great hairy bodies and horns. The animals were chewing grass. Todd said, "Compatriots," and saluted. When Vera stepped out, the ground was spongy and dark. There was a gassy smell, the long-ago seeping out of the earth. Eve and Vera took their own bags this time because Dmitri and Aleksei had boxes of food: coffee, powdered creamer, potatoes, onions, loaves of bread, a gallon of cooking oil, a cooler of moose and a single apple balanced on top.

At home in Berkeley everyone was gluten-free or vegan or lactose-intolerant or avoided nightshades. Even the teenagers ordered cold-pressed green juice instead of coffee (or they ordered coffee but it was single-origin and fair-trade and the cup arrived with a perfect leaf in the organic, grass-fed foam). Dmitri did not ask if there were food sensitivities in the group. These were the available foods and the human bodies required their sustenance.

The large hairy creatures stared at the bald humans. Dmitri said, "Within the park where we have animals grazing the ground is flatter but you should still follow paths. Outside the park you will sink into mud immediately and get stuck. That way is the sea, everywhere else is more and more of Siberia. The size of this land is incomprehensible which is why we need all the animals to help take care of it. You have met musk oxen, we have also bison and wild horses. Grazers to save the world." One animal hoofed at the ground, eyes on Vera, who reached a hand toward her big sister. The thing was ancient and matted and seemed made-up, like a great blanket with legs. Creatures belonged to this place; humans were the obvious intruders.

"*Fortunately*," Eve said to Vera, "the beasts were vegetarians."

Vera knotted Eve's fingers in her own. "*Unfortunately*, they used their massive horns to defend themselves."

Eve said, "I've always suspected that our parents accepted the probability that we would die in the field. *Fortunately*, you won't be the victim of a mall shooting, but *unfortunately*, your mother's work has now taken you to the land of the angry yak."

Jane appeared out of nowhere and said, "That's not a yak, it's a musk ox. You'll be fine."

"Dad always told us a nervous vegetarian is more deadly than a hungry carnivore."

Vera was quiet but a blue pool sat at the bottom of her belly. Her father battered at her. This life of movement and travel and research had been his idea first and he had given it to Jane like a virus and Eve and Vera were born infected. They had grown up on the road, on the move, in countries all over the world. They had been brave, or else they had had no choice. Both felt true, in alternating moments. The summer Vera was nine and Eve eleven their family had been evacuated from Somalia when a civil war had broken out. It was four years ago but Vera remembered perfectly being driven in a bulletproof car through the deserted streets to a grass runway where a small propeller plane waited. It was only them and another white family. Their dad had said, "Life is not easy. You don't get great art without war. You don't get progress without cost. You don't get beauty without suffering." Only, the person who died wasn't the one who suffered, Vera now thought. He had been driving too fast on an Italian road but she was the one who had to live with the crash for the rest of her life. A crash that felt like it was always happening somewhere in her own mind. Vera had always wanted to be a good helper and now she bent toward tasks as a matter of survival. Heartbreak paved over with a list of to-dos.

Eve surveyed the high tundra and said, "Dear Diary, I am having the best summer ever! I have made so many fun friends at my life-guarding job and I'm getting a great tan. I think I have a crush on my boss."

At least there was Eve. At least Eve knew how to be angry out loud. As the firstborn, it was her job to be the icebreaker ship, plowing through her mother's good intentions. Fifteen was old enough to brew stronger, higher-value anger. Vera's version, at thirteen, was only a mixer.

"I do not love you," Eve said to their mother.

"You do love me and I know it. This is exactly, exactly, what love feels like."

CAMP WAS THREE WOODEN CABINS with woodstoves and tiny bedrooms, a single outhouse to share. The main house had a kitchen with a big table, coolers for the food, a counter for chopping, a propane burner, and a bucket to carry water from the well, which, at the moment and for only a moment, Dmitri told the visitors, was not frozen solid.

They ate moose meat and potatoes for lunch around a wooden table that tipped every time someone put a fork down. Eve said, "Great moose meat. Best ever. Wouldn't you say so, Vera?"

"Very tender."

"You think you know many things," Dmitri said to Eve and Vera.

Jane straightened up.

"We know some things," Eve said.

"We also don't know a lot of things," Vera added.

Vera wanted her mother to explain that they had lived all over the world. That they were resilient after loss. That they were brave and smart and competent. Maybe Jane would have said these things if Dmitri had not started to speak again. Maybe.

Dmitri said, "You girls should know the real story. Real story is a story of grass. Once upon a time, the earth was inhabited by bigger, wilder animals. Dire wolf, ground sloth, saber-toothed cats and woolly mammoths. Huge feet trudged the lands." Dmitri did not turn to tell the tale to the men in the room, kept his eyes fixed on the young females. The professor and Todd were listening passively while sipping their drinks. "It is called the Ice Age but it was kingdom of herbivores and kingdom of grasses."

Vera had never thought of it that way.

"Savannah was made by pachyderms. In Africa, elephants knocked down forests and ate leaves and spread grass seed in dung. Then they evolved to survive in cold. So did the early humans, following big animals for foods. Elephants grew into mammoths and went to northern edges of planet, thinned those forests, pounded the earth, made grasses here, too. Man and elephant evolved together, changed the land together, covered the earth. Together, they were dwellers of savannah and taiga."

"Jane worked in Africa. We lived there," Eve said, a little quietly.

Dmitri's eyes gray and serious. "Lot of people know about Africa. Siberia, only a small number of people. Arctic Circle Siberia is even less. What we see here is unique."

Vera said, "We're lucky to be here," and Eve glared at her.

"It lasted for thousands of years, these mammoths walking, humans walking, big feet and small feet. Climate shifted, grasses died, mammoth population goes down, their gene pool was less varied, not so resilient. Humans ate them. Some of them died and froze. Then humans learned to stay still and grow food, or maybe grasses were smart ones who made the humans grow them. Agriculture, after all, is story of grasses—wheat, rice, corn, sugarcane. Elephants and mammoths knocked down trees and ate brush and bush making way for vast grasslands, and other animals grazed on this green carpet. But humans killed off the mammoths and soon, the ecosystem changed forever. We believe that if we bring back megafauna we will bring back the mammoth steppe and this will protect our planet. More carbon is stored in Arctic permafrost than all the world's rain forest, and to keep ground frozen and carbon in ground we must insulate it with grasses. To make grass we need to clear trees and fertilize and spread seed. Also important is that in winter, sun is absorbed by dark trees and reflected by snow and ice. But snow can keep ground warmer, like igloo, so we also need animals to stamp snow down into ice so cold air can reach into ground. Grassland comes back and spreads, it creates blanket over soil in summer to keep cold in and makes canvas for snow, then animals stamp snow into ice, and ground gets maximum cold in winter. All we need are mammoths."

Vera's heart rose with the idea that animals in their right place could make a difference. Nature, symbiosis, systems that knew how to care for themselves. Still, it seemed hopeless. Maybe someday there would be one mammoth, but they would need thousands to cover this landscape and by the time such a thing was possible it would already be too late. But she was just a kid and here were all these adults who seemed to believe, or to want to enough that they could ride the wish.

The professor stood up dramatically, stretching and clearing his throat as if this were a stage rather than a cabin, as if he had been listening for his cue. To the girls the professor said, "To make this cold-adapted elephant–slash–woolly mammoth, we are using an enzyme/protein complex taken from bacteria called CRISPR-CAS 9 to snip out the elephant instructions in the DNA code and then we utilize the body's own repair mechanism to snip in mammoth instructions. It is like a tiny pair of scissors." Vera and Eve knew these things. They lived with these stories. But Vera was trying to be attentive because her job on this day was to be the audience and to be their mother's asset rather than her liability. She nodded and the professor continued. "The genes for fur are snipped in, the gene for hemoglobin is changed because mammoth blood is much better at carrying oxygen around the body at low temperatures. We will add genes for long, curved tusks, for that big, gorgeous square forehead. Snip by snip, more mammoth, less elephant. Rebirth by revision." The professor brought his eyes solemnly across the room. He had practiced this speech right down to the dramatic pauses.

Eve put her head on the table but Jane kicked her ankle and she sat back up straight.

Jane pasted on a smile. Vera pasted on a smile. Eve raised her eyebrows at her mother and sister.

Side by side, the professor and Dmitri were a physical argument for man against nature. They were strong men with plans and data and a moral imperative. Dmitri said, "Someday we will have a stem cell with mammoth traits, this nucleus is then zapped into an elephant egg, fertilized and grown into an embryo that grows into a blastocyst and then fetus, which is transplanted into an artificial womb in the lab. This womb will be a huge bag made of thick plastic, filled with a fluid that mimics amniotic, with a tube to the bellybutton of the fetus, a plastic umbilical cord pumping blood and nutrients. Because this womb will be transparent, we hope to watch the creature grow. And, on one miraculous day, we will be in possession of a baby animal, alive and ready to be cut out, born onto the earth." In unison, the professor, Dmitri and Todd all said, "A cold-adapted elephant."

Eve and Vera turned to each other and Eve shook her head. "Ha," she said.

Todd cleared his throat and began his part of the afternoon's impromptu speech. "After two years of work, we had a living cell in dish that was ten percent mammoth. After another year, we had a cell living in a dish that was thirty percent mammoth. Now the cell living in a dish in Berkeley is made up of seventy-two percent mammoth traits. Eventually this land *will* feel the pounding feet of megafauna. Of that I am sure."

Eve said, "Mystical beast resurrected, world saved. We are among heroes, Vera."

Jane stood up, joining the ensemble of men. She looked small and out of place. She said, "The mammoths are the heroes of this story. We just hope it's not too late." Vera, so relieved to see her mother standing with the others, clapped. Eve snapped her fingers. "Cheers to the world maybe not ending."

Dmitri took a long drink of water, then a longer drink of vodka. He closed his eyes and shook like a dog drying off. He said, "Ladies, sorry for big story. Now you have earned the tour. The first feature is permafrost. Everything depends on Arctic grounds, which holds as much carbon as all forests and rain forests in the world, and if it thaws, it warms atmosphere and a warmer planet melts more ice. And then we all die," Dmitri said, and he raised his glass of water high in the air. "Like lady said, maybe it's too late."

Eve started to laugh and Vera elbowed her in the ribs. Eve's stated position on the climate crisis was: we're screwed, might as well have fun with what's left. Vera wished she could take that medicine and have it work on her, the medicine of teenage joy and fuck-everything and you-gave-us-this-problem-why-should-we-have-to-fix-it. Vera did not know whether to think of her desire for a future as dumb or smart, as hopeful or pathetic. She wanted it. She wanted to be a grown lady with solar panels on her roof and a job on the side of good. Politics, maybe. A power suit and a briefcase full of signed documents protecting something otherwise voiceless. She wanted to help, and for this she felt half proud, half silly.

Dmitri said, "My cabin is this one. You have seen your rooms in other cabins so you need orientation to the land now." He pointed and said, "This way is north to East Siberia Sea, about two hundred meters. The cliff by water is where best bones have been found. River is to the west, to south are best permafrost caves, which we go to in a moment. Ready, yes?" Dmitri asked, and they marched south.

"Jane, would you please take the good camera and document?" the professor said. "Careful, it was expensive." The lens was wide and polished, staring out from Jane's hand. She gripped it tightly, her knuckles pale with effort.

There was a metal hatch in a hillside and when Dmitri pulled a handle on a metal door in the ground, a hole opened revealing a ladder going into the earth. "To keep snow out in winter," Dmitri said. Darkness, the smell of metal and water. The smell of a place they did not belong.

"No, thanks," Vera said.

"How deep does it go?" Eve asked.

"Twenty meters," Dmitri said. "There are deeper caves but this is simple to climb. Better for children and womens."

"We're not children," Eve said.

Each of them had a flashlight and they turned them on though the light was invisible in the sun.

"You're coming," Eve said to Vera. "Because I want to go and I won't go without you." Vera understood that this was final. She said, "You have to rescue me if I fall." She thought a second and added, "And if the earth caves in and we are trapped you must agree to hit me on the head with a rock for faster death." Eve put her hand out, "Done," she said.

Down they went, hands on the cold metal, rung by rung into the planet. At the bottom there was a cave, as big as the cabin kitchen, with a low ceiling that Vera could reach her hands and touch. All around them water dripped, but otherwise the air felt so thick it was almost alive.

Seven yellow stripes of flashlight, seven circles of light hitting the walls of the earth. The group walked into a tunnel, dark and only a little larger than they were. The path sloped downward and the tunnel sparkled when the light hit, crystalline with ice. "From here, is permafrost," Dmitri said. Earth, frozen solid.

Vera ran her hand along the wall of the cave, which was black and beautiful, and her palm came away wet. This might not be frozen in ten years. She would be twenty-three. She would have a whole life to live and the planet would be a less and less good place on which to live it. Every minute not spent solving this was a minute wasted.

Dmitri brought his light close to a chip of bone. "The most useful method for telling the difference between bone and wood is to pick it up," Dmitri said. The bones, he explained, were denser, heavier. Vera noticed that the texture was less splintery. Bone did not turn to paper-pulp when rubbed with a thumb the way wood might.

Vera pulled from the dark wall a slightly yellowed piece of jawbone with two teeth still in their sockets. It was the length of her arm and heavy. "Sir," she said, to get Dmitri's attention. "Is this something?"

"Nicely," Dmitri said, coming close. "Jawbone of a grazer, thirty thousand years old." He gave her a pat on the head like she was a child who had identified the color yellow in a daffodil and he walked away again. This was not a treasure. They were in a place so thick with bones accumulated over tens of thousands of years that most of it was not rare.

Jane said, "We could string them on a necklace for you."

"Very nicely indeed," her mother said, and they both smiled wide.

None of these mattered to science—people already knew that all these animals had lived here and when and this was only evidence of the known. Science wanted the unknown, the undone. You could not publish a paper corroborating a story that had already been proven true. You could not get a job that way. The only way to make a living was to do what had not yet been done, to show what was not yet known. To make what had never been made.

"Jane," the professor said, "you'll keep track of everything we find. Do you know how to do that? Log it all properly?"

Vera watched her mother's face do the thing where it kept from cracking. "I know how," Jane said. Vera looked at her shoes. She knew intuitively that there was no sticking up for her mother without making it worse. Jane had worried out loud for weeks about asking if she could bring her family. Her children were neon signs of her age, her widowhood, her inability to be her own kind of success. Now it made sense: she could come, the poor woman, too old to still be a student, dragging her domestic prison behind her because she was the spreadsheet keeper who could free the big minds to do the big work. Jane did not meet the eyes of either daughter.

Jane scraped at a bone trapped in the wall. "This one is a mammoth," the professor said, "probably," and took a gardening trowel from his back pocket, which he used to whack the bone free. It was a fragment, a few inches long. Something had lain down and died here and been covered by ten thousand seasons of rain, sun, snow. Vera had thought of frozen things as still and quiet, but now she saw movement—addition and subtraction, freeze and melt.

Jane reached out for the shard but the professor took it first and brought it to his nose, stuck his tongue out and licked a corner of the bone.

"Lovely," Eve said.

"I'll hold on to it," Todd said, and put his hand out like a child waiting for his piece of candy.

"Turn off the lights," Dmitri told them. Seven flashlight clicks. Total darkness. For Vera, it was a feeling of floating. Eve whispered, "I'm going to fall," and found Vera's shoulder to hold. All around them, the whine of slow and steady thaw.

Vera felt something on her back, a hard thing. It traveled up her spine. She knew what it was: the bone shard in Todd's hand. It felt as if he was marking a place to cut. When their lights clicked back on Todd was wide-eyed and stuttered, "Sorry, I thought you were . . . Never mind. Sorry." Thought she was what? Her mother? Her sister? The professor? But she was none of those things and she could still feel the line Todd had drawn up her back, the intentional marking, more knife than wand. The line was not all pain. With it there was something fizzy. Before she could squash it, a picture appeared in her mind of herself turning to Todd, him leaning down, their mouths meeting.

Dmitri said, "All over Siberia are large sinkholes where the ground is melting and collapsing in on itself. Houses fall over, trees go sideways. Locals call them gateways to underworld."

Vera's heart trotted and she imagined the ground above them softening and falling. "Maybe we could go back?" she said to her mother. Jane took Vera's hand and put it on her own cheek, an anchoring touch, skin and body heat.

THAT NIGHT IN HIS ROOM Todd chipped at the fossilized marrow from the cave and put it in a specimen jar and injected a solution. Eve and Vera, sitting on the bottom bunk side by side, watched him through both their open doors as he shook his little jar like a snow globe, as if he could see the microscopic confetti of ancient DNA. Eve whispered, "The Todds of the world, man." Vera knew what Eve meant: claiming spontaneous discovery, their arms full of prizes, their names bright and bold, humbling their way through an acceptance speech. *I looked over and there it was.* Jane glanced up from notes she was making on her laptop, her face bluelit. "Can you two stop? I'm trying to concentrate."

"Sorry for existing," Eve said.

Jane did not answer. Todd shook his bottle.

Vera could still feel the line on her back. The way one motion could divide a person in two. Desire and disgust in one body.

THE NEXT DAY the adults had a meeting, which sounded from outside the room like men yelling numbers louder than seemed necessary. From the porch outside Eve and Vera listened as their mother's softer voice said the word "yes" or the word "okay."

"Want to go for a walk?" Vera asked.

"Immediately, please."

They followed the northbound path through the scrub and patchy grass, rotted trees, climbing over logs and mudslides when they had to. They climbed carefully down a dark, sandy cliff, ten or fifteen feet tall. It was chilly but not cold and the mosquitoes were not so bad by the ocean. Vera went to the waterline and put her hand in. The sea was too salty, too thick, cold in a way that felt like a quiet threat. A person could die in minutes submerged in this water. She pictured frozen caverns ready to collapse beneath her. If she walked too far and lost sight of camp she could die on this pathless land, a little girl in a place big enough to swallow her without noticing. Eve said, "*Unfortunately*, the two beautiful sisters were sent to the edge of the world so that no one would fall in love with them."

Vera could not think of a *Fortunately* to follow this.

When they looked back the entire cliffside was full of bones and old wood and the beach was full of bones and old wood. The mud was black and everything else was pale and seaworn and ancient and Vera felt like a tiny daisy of a thing, young and fragile and out of place.

Miles from where they began Eve and Vera stopped to rest, ate a bar of chocolate Eve had in her pocket. It was soft from her heat. Vera drank and passed the water bottle.

"This place makes me want to bake," Vera said.

"Everything makes you want to bake."

It was true. Happy things and sad things and lost things all made Vera want her hands in dough. It was a small, good world she could invent by herself with the right combination of powders and liquids. In the days after news of their father's death had arrived, the counters of their home had filled with cookies. Chocolate chip and sandies and

23

peanut butter and sugar and gingersnap and tuiles and palmiers. Jane had sat outside under a bare persimmon tree alternately working down a dismal adult post-death to-do list and screaming into a dirty dish towel; Eve had kept to her room, any weeping drowned with too-loud pop music, but Vera had been riverine, her eyes a never-ending water source and around her: pain turned to pastry.

"Will our generation be the last on the planet?" Eve asked.

"Maybe not the very last. But our kids might not make it."

"I'm not having kids." Even Eve looked surprised by her own resolve.

Every person was carbon, resources. Fewer people meant a better chance for survival. Vera understood, and at the same time, this made her angry. It felt like the loss of a basic right. "My science teacher last year said the responsible thing is to have zero or one," Vera said.

"That's not why I'm not having them," Eve said. "I just don't want to. I don't want to wipe anyone else's butt. I don't want to leave anyone or have them leave me. Too much risk."

"Doesn't it kind of make you want to jump in and sink to the bottom of the sea?" asked Vera.

"Not having kids?"

"No. Being there to see the world end."

It was perfectly possible that the planet would be unlivable in their lifetime. That they were the last generation.

Vera kicked at the black dune and watched chunks of sand fall off. She wanted erosion. She wanted minor harm.

Eve joined her. They kicked and the earth gave way. It peeled away for them. Their sneakers grew sandy and wet and they held on to each other for more force. They yelled and laughed and they were furious and they were happy. No one else would have understood this desire, Vera knew. How good it felt.

They had already gone a year with no father and they would never have one again. That fact took Vera's breath away every time she remembered it—he would not be back. There was no opening at the end of this tunnel.

When Vera pictured the car crash, which she did involuntarily and often, she thought of her father putting his arm out to protect the only other thing in the vehicle with him: a cooler full of Neanderthal specimens, which he had been delivering from one lab to another. Over time she pictured not a cooler with carefully collected specimens but the iceman himself, whom her father had studied his whole career. Shorter than a modern human, scruffy beard, wise, gentle eyes, dressed in the skins of six different animals. She saw them looking at each other, a final goodbye fizzing in their eyes before flames gobbled them up.

The longer he was gone, the more Vera wanted a boy-shaped person in their family. Not for capabilities that the women lacked—their father had been bad at all the man things—but for counterpart. Difference. Vera missed him in ways both definite and indefinite. She missed the way he bit off the crusts of her toast before delivering it to her because she liked it bald and he didn't want to waste. She missed the way he fell asleep next to her when he was reading aloud. The way he knew the names of her classmates, even the inconsequential ones, and the flutter of his voice when he came home from the market with fancy mushrooms and too many kinds of berries. Sal had already softened in Vera's memory, she knew this. All his colors faded into a bluish lavender. That's how you lost someone—first in body, then their edges and furies and

mistakes went. Her father had been gone only a year. What would disappear next she did not know.

EVE KICKED AGAIN AND hit something hard. "Shit, shit," she said.
She hopped and said, "My toebones are pulsing." Vera, meanwhile, dug
at the hard spot. It was not rock, not wood. Bone. Some ancient grass
eater that had drowned, starved, been eaten. The two of them dug at
it with sticks because wasn't that why they had come to this distant
edge?

"The person I would like to drown is Todd," Eve said. "*In* his zipper
pants."

Vera did not want to admit that she had a crush on Todd. The first
plausible crush. She said, "Totally," and nicked at the sand with her
stick.

What emerged was not bone. It was fleshy, almost. Like leather, and
it had a few coarse hairs.

"What exactly is this?" Eve asked.

"Something dead. Everything here is something dead."

This was different, though. This was not another piece of decayed
skeleton.

They knew protocol would be to go get the adults and set up proper
extraction practices. They might do damage to a valuable specimen. But
it was sure to be nothing. Another juvenile discovery, brushed aside by
those in the know.

"I feel like digging."

So they dug. Eve dug in one direction and Vera dug in the other and
the thing was long and as thick as a small tree trunk. It had pores and
skin, and it had fur. Vera came to a curve and followed the shape

downward until she found the end, where there was an opening. "It's a trunk," she said. "It's a *trunk*, Evie."

They dug faster, both on Eve's side, hoping the trunk was attached to a body, a whole mammoth frozen upright in this spot.

"If there's a body we should go get help," Eve said.

But when the trunk ended more quickly than they expected and the body attached was small and they realized it was a frozen baby, it felt like a rescue mission more than a discovery and they did not stop but dug until their fingers were soaked and frozen. It was perfect. It was sad and beautiful and perfect. The size of a large dog. "Pull," Eve said, and they reached their arms around the back, Vera on the front end and Eve on the rear and they hugged it, this cold body, and they pulled hard, bracing against the cliffside until it came free with a sucking sound and both girls fell backward. The mammoth smelled of the beginnings of rot. It was starting to thaw. Vera pushed it off herself and stood. She was elated and disgusted and there was a rampage in her chest. "Is this happening?" she asked. It looked like the animal might at any time open its big eyes.

Eve nodded. She brushed her hand over the mammoth's little tail.

"What now?" Vera asked, looking at the whole now, the trunk a C, the breathing hole in the shape of a heart at the end. Tufts of almost blonde hair all around. Eyes closed and lashes thick. "We should have gotten help."

"Now we carry it back," Eve told her.

It was heavy and cold. Their clothes soaked through. It softened noticeably. They would be in trouble for not getting help and they would be praised for the find, and they did not know which would win out.

"I feel like it needs to be refrozen," Vera said, and they walked faster.

As they walked, Eve said, "Once upon a time there were two sisters but they were not enough for their mother, who wanted a giant, mythical beast. The girls bravely traveled to the edge of the world while their mother searched in vain for the animal, which was both real and made-up." Eve paused to catch her breath.

"One day," Vera said, "the brave daughters were exploring by the sea when out of the cliff's edge they saw what their mother had always dreamed of. It wasn't huge because it was a baby, but when the girls went to it and dug it out, it started to stir. They sang to it and it woke, groggy from having been asleep so long."

For a moment, the only sound was the rhythm of their footfalls on the beach, scrape of rock and wet sand.

Vera said, "In the fairy tale it always gets darker before good wins out at the last minute. And the children are often the only ones to survive."

Vera pictured the scene from Jane's perspective: mother on the cliffside with a happy-hour bottle of vodka, beginning to worry about her daughters who had been gone all afternoon. The sky faintly pink, though the sun would never ever set. Mosquitoes starting to come.

And up the beach, two girls emerge, to their mother's instant relief, and the girls are carrying something, and that something is a perfect baby woolly mammoth.

THE ADULTS WERE DRINKING and celebrating in the main cabin. Dmitri's voice was loud and the vodka was plentiful. Jane, suddenly, seemed visible to everyone. Though her daughters had found the mammoth, Jane was the reason the girls were there and she was getting credit for the baby. Dmitri, Jane, Todd and the professor talked about oocytes and nuclear transfer and carbon dating and proteomic analysis and spindle assembly. Jane said something about histone incorporation and the professor squinted in consideration. There was Jane, talking with the men, being seen as a colleague, spoken to as a scientist. She might overcome her gender, her children, after all. Vera could tell that her mother did not entirely trust this. Someone could begin to see the prize as his own anytime and there would be nothing she could do to stop it.

"We will name it Aleksei," Dmitri said. "After my father and my son."

"We should name it Dmitri," the professor said.

"What a fucking suck-up," Eve said under her breath. "We should name it Vera!" she yelled. "After the person who found it."

Jane put her finger to her lips, shushing.

"Name it Eve then!" Eve said. "Name it Veve!"

"Please be quiet," Jane said, coming close. "Let them have their fun."

Eve said, "Bullshit. You should name it. *We* should name it."

Vera wondered if this was her mother choosing her battles or quietly beginning to concede.

The sharp laughter of a roomful of men made her feel bitten.

Dmitri said, "We should take samples while the baby is here. To-morrow we will bring her to bigger lab downriver." He turned to Jane and said, "We need hairs, skins and muscles."

Everyone went out to the cabin's porch, where the mammoth lay on a table wrapped in a tarp and silver thermal emergency blankets to keep it cold. Dmitri unwrapped one corner to reveal a limb, dark and leathery and unquestionably the leg of a baby pachyderm.

"Come, lady," Dmitri said to Jane.

"Me?" Jane said.

He handed her a scalpel.

"She's just learning," the professor said. "May I?"

"I can show her," Dmitri said.

Jane looked at her daughters for a second, a look of worry and hope. Dmitri stood close while she touched the tiny scalpel to the underside of the mammoth's leg. "We're not destroying it?" she asked.

Dmitri said, "Cut."

Jane drew a sharp, straight line. "Steady," the professor said, holding his own hands out like Jane was his puppet. Vera could almost feel the heat of Dmitri's breath on her mother's neck. Could feel Todd's and the professor's envy. And beneath Jane's knife, Vera imagined the resistance of mummified flesh, the smell of mud.

Quietly, the professor said, "We need to keep our hopes in check. The specimens are highly unlikely to contain any intact cells because they will have been attacked by fungi, oxygen and enzymes. When something dies the earth immediately claims it." He sounded like someone whose home team had once again been beaten by the more strategic rivals.

"Then why?" Eve asked. "If you know there's nothing to find, why all the effort? We came here, made a miraculous find and you're telling me it'll amount to zero?"

The professor breathed in and straightened his shoulders. "Buck up. This is a profession of the slow and steady accumulation of knowledge, knowledge that eventually allows the possibility of invention and after a long time the invention bears results." Vera could picture him saying this to himself in the mirror, a mantra.

Dmitri unwrapped the mammoth the rest of the way and they all moved closer. Jane dropped the cube of flesh into a tube filled with clear solution. She put her scalpel down and smoothed the hair out of the baby's eyes. The professor ran a palm over its tufty little tail. These people could picture a living mammoth now, they had held the body and felt its weight and its texture. They believed in this creature. Wanted it. There might be incremental progress from the frozen baby, but what Vera saw now: a kind of heat rose off the scientists, her mother included. Love, or something like it.

"Let's go," she said to Eve. She nodded at a half bottle of vodka by the door. The mammoth had been her victory first, hers and Eve's.

Eve said, "How fun are you, lil' sis?" and they went out into the clouded evening. Once out of sight they peed behind a short bush. On the horizon they could see the outline of wild horses and in the branches there was a fish eagle, its white face feathers reddened with blood. It looked at the girls as if assessing whether they were edible, and turned away. Vera slapped a mosquito on her arm; now she matched the bird, only the blood on her arm was her own.

They walked to the bone pile at the cliff's edge, the collection of discards, non-valuables, nothings. It felt like a familiar place. A real-life representation of what their hearts looked like. They passed the vodka back and forth. It tasted awful but they wanted it in their bodies. "Doesn't it feel good to be bad?" Eve said, looking out at the northern sea, at the world's forgotten waters.

"But how are we ever going to get kissed with this as our life?" Vera asked.

"What about Aleksei?" Eve said. Aleksei who had a haircut like a sergeant and wore a tank top. Who had a tattoo of a wolf on the side of his neck.

"Ha," Vera said. She took a sip of the drink. She sifted through the dirt and discard. She knew to look for the yellower, the larger, knew the honeycomb of bone.

"Maybe we should run away and take the train to some Siberian city and go clubbing."

"(A) We are days and days from anything and we need to take that barge to get anywhere. (B) Clubbing?"

"I want darkness and loud music and sweaty people. Doesn't that sound delicious?" Eve said.

It did not. Vera thought of being kissed by Todd on a park bench in Berkeley. She thought of cupcakes cooling on a rack. She thought of an air-conditioned mall, slick and clean, the floors polished. She thought of the windows full of promises—mannequins in seasonal colors, rows of lipsticks, racks of fake diamond studs, the plastic smell of a cheap shoe store, all the choices white or gold. Vera pulled a thin bone out of the pile. It was needle-sharp, from something small and insignificant, short-lived. A creature born in a litter, hunted from the instant it appeared on earth. She poked the shard into her palm until it stung.

"Tell me a Dad story," Vera said. "Tell the one about when Mom and Dad met."

Eve slapped a mosquito on her ankle. "Do you want the beeped version or the unbeeped version?"

"Unbeeped," Vera said. "You know it?"

"I asked once and now I'll never not know."

"Sal, Dad, was still Professor Drake to Jane when she took his class on ancient humanoids in college. Jane was a senior and she fell immediately in love with all those ancient people. One Friday she was with her roommate at a party where a lot of people seemed to be wearing wigs—there must have been a theme—and Jane said, 'Don't you just feel like you want to meet the people or creatures or whatever they are that we grew out of?'

"'You mean like your grandparents?' the roommate asked.

"'No, like our ancestors.'

"The roommate said, 'My cousin studied abroad in Ireland and she felt at home and everyone assumed she was from there. You could do that.'

"Jane was like, 'No, further back. Ancestors, ancestors. Like, evolutionary.'

"'Cavemen?'

"'They were not all troglodytes. That's a myth,' Mom said.

"She drank some of the beer in her red plastic cup.

"The roommate said, 'Oh, I know why. You have a crush on your professor. That's always why.'

"It felt like the opposite of that to Jane. She had a crush on human evolution, on adaptation. The professor was a doorway. 'Nope,' she said. 'That's backward.'

"But when her professor wrote an email the day before spring break and told her about a dig in Kenya that he was writing about, a summer internship where they needed someone smart and organized, she was so excited. She also could not help but note what a good answer this would be to all the what-will-you-do-after-graduation questions. She sent her résumé and a cover letter explaining her new but keen interest and within the hour had been hired. The roommate said, 'Have fun fucking the anthropologist.'"

Vera cut in. "Yuck," she said. Now that professor was her dad, but also her absent dad, the swirl of these facts made her seasick.

"You said you wanted the unbeeped version," Eve said.

"I know. Sorry. It's just . . . never mind," Vera said.

"So the roommate goes, 'Okay, Jane. He's a man in khaki. I bet you one million dollars that you sleep with him.' She pulled up the professor on the school's website. 'He's not *not* hot. I'm going to go ahead and approve the affair. Let me know if you need any paperwork around this.'"

"She sounds like you," Vera said. "You would be friends with her."

"I think in real life she's got like five kids and lives in St. Louis now."

"Anyway," Vera prompted. "So Mom goes to Kenya . . ."

"Sal—no longer Professor Drake—turned out to be funny and had good stories and listened when Jane talked, unlike the boys she'd dated at school, and he brought her coffee from the camp kitchen each morning before the anthropologists started digging. They worked bones out of the dry earth with tiny, precise tools. They were like dirt dentists. In the evenings they sat on stumps by a fire. They talked about their families. Jane told him how her parents were being preserved by the Florida sun and he told her how his parents had died when he was a teenager. First his mother, of cancer, then his father of addiction and misery. Neither of them had siblings. One morning, a ginormous herd of zebra surrounded the camp at dawn and Jane and Sal stood together and watched them. Jane knew that when Sal wrote the chapter in his book, this would be its final scene. When the herd dispersed, they were holding hands. He asked her to marry him the next day."

"It's not really fair," Vera said. "How are we supposed to live up to that?"

"I know. Other people make out in the car. But it's cool. We still have lots of chances to fall in love with older, more powerful men."

Vera wanted to be one half of a balanced equation but for this she had no model.

The fact of the girls had not been what made their parents' life a success. Breeding was never the marker because humans were not rare and therefore not valuable. They had often talked about feeling like a curiosity, a side project in a petri dish. Sal and Jane together, their love story, had been the first great endeavor, then Sal's work, then Jane's. When he died, grief and fury and responsibilities had hurricaned across their lives until nothing else stood. The daughters did not know how much their mother dreamed of them or didn't, longed for them even when they were all in the same room. They might never know. Maybe these markers were not what mattered anyway. Jane took care of them and did not abandon them when she had work on the other side of the globe. Though Vera sometimes wished for weeks spent in a dark burrow where she could simply be sad, she knew the world did not provide such spaces.

THEY HEARD THE SOUND of someone in the distance calling their names. Eve and Vera did not call back, but they did stop talking to listen. Soon, the voice came closer and the two girl-forms on the bone pile must have been spotted in the nighttime sunlight because Jane jogged over with camp cups and a plate of meat and bread. She waved and called, "There you are! I brought dinner!" Jane had a water bottle in her back pocket and circles under her eyes. She said, "You smell like booze?" and Eve said, "We had a nip." How did she know this word, Vera wondered? Eve was two years older but seemed far ahead of that, like a person who had been alive once already, been through the loop the loops of all this before. Sometimes she seemed older than the grown-ups. It was disarming even to her mother. Jane did not yell or grab the bottle and dump it dramatically onto the grass. She had been drinking, too.

She sat down, said, "You girls are so weird sometimes." She took a piece of bread and bit it.

Vera said, "You made us a plate," as if Jane had handed her something of tremendous value. She had, in fact. A meal assembled by the hands of a mother with the intention to nourish the two children in her care. "Thanks, Mom," Vera said. This gesture should not have meant so much to her but it did.

"No, thank you," Jane said. "For finding him." Her girls had made their mother much more important to this mission. Before she had been a graduate student secretary, now she was something approaching a colleague.

"Him?" Vera asked. "Do we know that now?"

"We do. A little guy."

"I'm sorry I shushed you about the name," Jane said. "But it really isn't important to me, okay? I don't care what they name it, as long as I get some credit. And a male mammoth named Veve would, you have to admit, be weird."

Vera said, "Fair enough. But you don't think you claim credit by putting a stamp on it?"

"By naming it after your glorious daughters who found it?" Eve added. "We can totally come up with a masculine version. Evo. No, Vero. Doesn't that mean truth in Latin or something? Are you kidding? That's perfect."

"I don't want them to take this away," Vera said.

Jane said, "It's Aleksei now. That's done. I won't forget who found it, though. That's the *vero*."

Eve shrugged. She took a tangle of meat and ate it with her fingers, a piece of dark bread. "To life," she said, raising her bread. "To Vero Evo Aleksei, the baby mammoth of Siberia."

Vera could not remember feeling this purely happy. The three of them exploring together, creating together, bound and beloved.

She was a little buzzed and she watched the scene like she was floating above it all. She did not want to eat and get sober but wanted instead to observe with this distance: the family's behaviors while eating, their behaviors while drinking, the way they all three lay down on this pile of bones, the nighttime sun pale and cold, put their arms over their faces and let themselves go soft.

Two

Home again, so jet-lagged that her brain was its own fog machine, Vera wanted to disappear into her bed and never sit or stand again but it was summer and Jane did not want her daughters to rot away so she made them get up, eat fried eggs, drink tea, walk around the block, wave at the old man who always sat at the same window in the big blue Victorian on the corner.

"I could happily die of tiredness," Eve said. "I really wouldn't even mind."

"You can't die of being tired," Jane said.

"Sure you can," said Eve. "Sleep deprivation is dangerous. You could fall asleep driving and roll off the road. A person can only survive a few days on no sleep."

"Obviously you can't be left alone today," Jane told them. "You are in no condition to make sound choices. You're coming to work with me."

Eve stopped walking and shouted, "We came to work with you in Russia and that is why we are now experiencing life-threatening exhaustion. We're staying home and sleeping all day."

Vera said, "Mom, we'll be fine. We'll just watch TV. If you let us stay home we can make you dinner, just like good little house-daughters."

"Sorry," Jane said. "You'll never get on the right time and you'll be maniacs and I can't deal with two girl-children awake at all hours. Pack books, you're coming."

THE PALEO LAB was all glass and wood and polished steel. It was sheen and order. They were the first people in and it felt vaguely like entering an uninhabited planet. Vera pointed to machines and made Jane tell her what they were and how much they cost. "Fluorescence microscope, four thousand dollars," Jane said. "Sixty thousand for that DNA particle gun. A laminar-flow polymerase chain reaction workstation for amplifying RNA and DNA with air-velocity meter."

Eve asked, "What do you do with that?"

"It's for monitoring airflow. To stay within specifications."

"What's that?" Vera asked, pointing at a small vial on a shelf.

"Tube of powdered gold. I think about six hundred dollars."

"For?" Eve and Vera asked at the same time.

"No idea. I've never been asked to use it."

The three of them continued their walk around the room and Jane named things as she had when her girls were little. Then it had been ball, dog, garbage truck, bicycle. Now it was rapid thermal cyclers, microplate incubators, mega centrifuge, mini centrifuge, micro centrifuge, vacuum concentrator, freeze-dry systems, cryogenic storage systems, ultra-low-temperature freezers, liquid nitrogen containers, handheld homogenizers, sonicators and cell disruptors (designed, Jane said, for cell lysis and tissue grinding), a thermocycler, micropipettes, constant temperature shakers, an autoclave, glassware, molecular biology enzymes, reagents and consumables.

"This is the most expensive place we've ever been," Eve said. "I never thought of the university as being rich before. You always picture the corduroy jacket with elbow patches, not the thermocycler nuclear whatever machine."

Jane said, "CRISPR patents equal millions or billions of dollars. This will eventually cure cancer, muscular dystrophy, Huntington's disease, heart disease, every deadly virus, who knows what else. A team has eradicated HIV from mice. Another can slow cancer growth. People will make superbugs that kill themselves. Mosquitoes that can't reproduce. It's limitless."

"Will we be rich, maybe?" Eve asked.

"Only the inventors get really rich. The patent owners. I'm just a plebe. Do you know what a plebe is?"

The girls nodded because they got the idea. "But someday? Could you win the Nobel Prize?" Vera asked, almost in a whisper.

"The professor could. If cancer is cured, someone will. If someday we have a living woolly mammoth . . ." Her voice fizzled to smoke.

Eve's eyes were slippery with hope. She said, "Is this a near-future-ish thing? Like, maybe soon enough that we get to have fun with some prize money?"

Vera imagined house hunting, not having a landlord, her own room, a dog.

"Evie, there is no prize money. We're years away, decades probably. Even if the lab did it and won something, it would be the professor who got the prize. I'd get a steak dinner and an anonymous quote in an article at best. And anyway, we're not the only ones working on it. Someone will probably beat us."

Jane explained that discoveries were made and published as quickly as possible because similar labs dotted the globe, the technology cheap now, cheap enough that a child could have his own gene-editing set for fifty dollars and though he was able to experiment only on mold, in a decade or two, maybe he would be able to send those tiny scissors into a fern genome, edit out the piece that told it to remain small, plant himself a jungle in his backyard, everything dinosaur sized, his little world shadowed by the fringe of leaves.

Presiding over the laboratory room, over all that potential, was a huge poster of a herd of mammoths traveling across a snowy world, their tusks curled high, their fur red and frozen. Vera looked at them and she felt the buzz in her arms of the baby they had carried along that rocky shore. She knew this animal. There was no money in it, but it felt like another kind of treasure, too.

"I need to get to work," Jane said. She pulled out two stools at a long metal table and gave the girls a twenty-dollar bill. "There's a vending machine downstairs and you can get lunch at the café. Sit and read for a while first."

The door opened and the professor stood there, his whole body filling the frame, and said, "Jane, would you mind?" Her mother jumped up and jogged to hold the door, put a hand out for the coffee cup the professor was finished with, went to place this cup in the sink without being told to. She must have done this before. This was a routine.

"Ladies," the professor said. "My little mammoth hunters. What a nice surprise."

"Professor," Eve said, and offered a fake salute.

"Have we looked at the slides yet?" the professor asked Jane.

"I was about to," she said.

"Then let's." She went back to her stool and he pulled another close and watched her as she put a slide with bits of her mammoth, their mammoth, under the microscope.

The girls watched for a clue. They took only shallow breaths, hoping for news whose details they did not understand.

"What do you see?" Vera asked.

The professor said, "A confetti parade. No intact cell. We won't be the first people in the world to clone a mammoth."

"Was that the dream?" Vera asked.

"It might have been someone's dream but not mine."

Jane was still looking into the lens, not moving.

"Don't fret, kiddo," he said to Jane. "We'll keep cutting mammothness into elephantness, just like we planned. Your mummy will prove useful still, even if it's just good PR."

In the distance: a mostly mammoth cell, ready for implantation into an artificial womb. Not a clone, but something else. An invention and a memory at the same time.

Vera looked at the rows and beakers. She had wanted the breakthrough to be her mom's. She wanted the animal she and Eve had found to reveal as-yet-unknown information, and for their mother to be the scientist who made it possible. A woman, achieving alongside her family, not in spite of it.

Jane said, "I had a thought." She waited for the professor to look at her before she spoke. "The baby has milk tusks, right? And I noticed that the chipped one is completely smooth inside while specimens of adult mammoths where the tusks are broken show a ring pattern, like tree rings. It made me wonder if we could discover information about the animals' lives by looking at those rings."

The professor made his fingertips into a tent. "That," he said, "is a very interesting question, Jane."

Todd opened the door carrying a bike helmet and a thermos and took the buds from his ears, though his music was loud enough that it was audible across the room. Something unjustly upbeat, for happy people to feel yet happier.

"Hello, party people," Todd said. "Or should I say *Zdravstvuyte*."

"Toddster," Eve said, nodding.

Vera looked fast at her book and the words were scrambled and she couldn't read them.

"Jane," the professor said. "I want you to keep working on the embryos. We've already changed the forty-five most important gene pairs. That cold-adapted elephant is on its way. If we didn't have to follow the rules we could grow one right now."

Todd laughed. "Let's do it," he said.

"You have a new research project this week," the professor said to him. "I want you to look into all the literature about ring patterns in tusks."

Jane said, "That was my idea."

"Tusks?" Todd said, dismay a blue thread in his voice. "I want to work on gene editing."

The professor reached into his pocket and took out two spiral peppermint candies, which he dropped in front of each of the girls. He said, "It's a real project, Todd. A hypothesis worth exploring. Janey, there's a gala at the Academy of Science tomorrow," he added. "It's for the Cross Lab. You should be there. It's good networking."

Todd, putting on his lab coat, looked up. Desire for the same invitation dripped from his face. He might have thought that it was easy to be a beautiful woman, doors opening.

"What time?" Jane asked.

"Eight. Your name will be on the list."

"I have to find someone to keep an eye on the girls."

"Can I?" Todd said.

"Babysit?" Jane said. "Sure, pal. I'll leave a box of mac and cheese on the counter. You can have my ideas and my responsibilities."

"No, obviously not babysit and I never wanted your idea. Can I come to the party? If Jane can't?"

"*We're* the ones who found the mammoth," Eve said. She just wanted to dress up, Vera knew. Vera would rather have stayed home and watched a man on TV fall simultaneously in love with many different women even as he dismissed one of them each week.

"You can go, Mom. It's really fine," Vera said. "We are not kids. We don't need a babysitter." Vera did not want Todd to go in her mother's place.

"This is ridiculous. Everyone's name will be on the list. Can we work now?" the professor said.

Vera unwrapped a candy and put it in her mouth. She thought of Todd in a suit, Todd with a red rose in his lapel. She crunched hard, her teeth sugar-stuck and aching.

THE GALA WAS IN the science museum, sharks swimming overhead, the big-lipped suck of a bottom feeder behind the head of a young human beauty. Jane wore a long black dress and pearls. She looked good, still young enough to be convincing in an evening dress. Eve wore a plaid skirt that made her feel infantilized and furious and Vera wore a corduroy skirt and button-down that she liked fine for school but made her feel worthless among so much satin.

"We don't even own dresses," Eve said. "We might as well be in onesies."

"Babies wear dresses all the time," Jane said. "Quit complaining. We're not spending a fortune on fancy dresses for kids."

Eve said, "We are, once again, not children. It's because Dad is dead and we don't have enough money." This knife was always ready for cutting.

"Because you have a mother who is following her dreams. If you're not a kid then you can get a job if you want new clothes."

Vera allowed herself a brief flash of a fantasy: Mom in a power suit and blow-dried hair, her hand on the gold door handle of an international bank, but before going in to work she turns to blow two kisses to the black limousine outside in which two daughters will soon be whisked away to prep school.

The three of them stood in the atrium, fishes tanked and swimming, intermittent shock of laugher, clink of glass, the noise of hundreds of people speaking at the same time.

Someone in a white button-down appeared suddenly with a silver tray of tiny corn pancakes sprinkled with fish eggs (fish swimming in the next tank). Vera and Eve stood back, arms linked, while Jane rotated between conversations, each identical to the last: insincere compliments, talking up the speaker's own research and flirtations between people who should not be flirting. The professor saw her and he looked at her like she was a lovely object he had forgotten he owned. Then he looked at Eve and Vera and his nose wrinkled.

"Professor," Eve said. "Good evening."

"Girls."

Vera leaned to whisper to her sister, "He *loves* that we're here."

Eve laughed and said, "Let's go see if they'll serve us alcohol."

They went to the bar and waited for their turn. Across the big room Vera saw Todd. Todd was wearing crisp jeans, now with a jacket and tie. She imagined him playing a video game on his phone on the train over, thinking ahead to free snacks. Vera's chest hummed.

Eve said, "Ugh, there's Todd. Todds assume they belong everywhere."

They watched as the professor approached Todd and they hugged the hug of men, backs patted and chests thumped together. Vera went warm. They might have been talking about basketball or experiments, their needy girlfriends or the price of real estate. It didn't matter. The men understood and trusted each other without explanation or question.

Vera scrunched her eyes tight and said, "Stop it," to her dumb heart, pittering in her chest at a boy who she knew deserved none of her affection. He was terrible, obviously and clearly so.

Jane appeared, hands on each daughter's shoulder, and said, "A round of Shirley Temples?"

"I was thinking of a beer," Eve said.

"It isn't funny, you know. Lives are ruined."

"Not mine. I'll ruin it in a more interesting way, if I decide to go that direction. I want to try a beer for the same reason every single other person in this room has a drink in their hand."

Vera said, "Can I have a Coke? No cherry, just the soda?" She wanted to grow up incrementally, while Eve, already older, attempted to leap over the years.

Jane ordered three, one with whiskey, and they put their glasses together and Eve said, "To Dad," and Jane looked at her feet and Vera tried to radiate okayness to both sister and mother, the only two people she loved in the entire world, who knew all the secret codes to break one another's hearts.

The professor came over to the bar with another man, smiled at Jane. The professor introduced her and said, "Jane was there when we found the mammoth."

Todd trotted over with his casual pants and persistent confidence and the professor said, "And this is Todd Markstram. Todd is about to start work on some interesting research on mammoth tusks."

The man shook hands with Todd and looked at Eve and Vera, unsure what children were doing here. Eve curtsied. Another girl-blur.

Jane said, "They were the ones who found it, actually. My daughters."

"Do you always bring them to work with you?" the man asked.

Todd said, "My theory is that the cross sections of a mammoth tusk could give a window into the life the animal lived, like a tree ring might," and the man turned to him with full attention.

Jane looked to Vera like she might spit. Like she wanted to kick a hole in the shark tank and watch the room flood. "Girls," she said. "Now." Her hands full of alcohol, her daughters trailing like streamers, Jane cut a path through the party.

In the center of the museum was a three-story enclosed rain forest and Jane beelined for it, an actual different world in the middle of the party, a true escape. Jane pulled the doors and it was warm and wet inside. It smelled like soil, like growth. There were birds with bright purple heads sitting in the branches. It did not feel like a real rain forest—too neat, too sculpted—but the air felt good. Dirty and sticky.

Jane stopped and drank, breathed and finished it. "Mom?" Vera said. "Are you all right?"

"Nope," Jane said. "I'm supposed to tell you that it's all okay. My entire job is to tell you that it's all okay, but it's not. I'm not. I am expected to wear a dress with a low neckline and I am dismissed for wearing a dress with a low neckline. I hate that I like the way the dress looks. I hate that Dad is not here to appreciate me in it. I hate that I have dragged you here to see me humiliated. Again. I hate that the house is a mess and will be when we get home. I hate that my job as a woman is to disappear any evidence of our lives, of the passing of time and be pretty and tidy all the time. Twice as capable and half as appreciated."

Eve glowed at her mom. "Wow, yes, Mom, yes."

Vera did not say that she needed Jane to be the caretaker, to be sturdy so that Vera could be a kid.

Jane said, "Soon Todd and I will both go on the job market and he will suffer over all the positions he has to choose from and I will be told that I am lucky if I get one nibble at a shit school located hours from civilization with a heavy teaching load and a paycheck that will need to be supplemented." She looked at her obviously fearful daughters. "I shouldn't have said that out loud. I'm sorry."

Vera held a question in her throat for the ten millionth time: will we be all right? She had kept it there, unvoiced, for so long that it had solidified. A sharp gem she wore on the inside.

Eve kept glowing and Vera kept quiet. "I want to walk," Jane said, and they began to spiral upward. "I'm sorry. I may have come to the end of this little career attempt, huh? I may have reached the pinnacle. We found a baby mammoth and I should be happy about that. Maybe it should be enough."

Eve almost yelled, "Aren't you supposed to teach us not to settle?"

Electric blue butterflies landed on meaty green leaves. Orchids tangled around branches. Jane took deep breaths and tried to let her anger drift upward and away. She said, "I'm very, very tired."

Vera said, "Eve is right. Don't give in. Don't stop."

Outside of this glass rain-forest bubble the rest of the party played on, a movie on mute. Jane leaned on the railing and peered down through the fat, leathery leaves to the bottom of the exhibit—a freshwater pool full of carp, slow shadows in the lit blue.

Up the rain-forest walkway came another woman. She was dressed exactly like Jane except her black gown moved like it was made of water and her neck was draped in shimmering teardrops of diamonds. Her hair was also blonde and twisted back and all three of them watched her ascend like she was a version of Jane, several decades older, richer. A better, luckier model of the same woman. She looked at the family and said, "More escapees," and stopped to lean nearby. "This place makes me want to smoke," she told them. "I love to smoke in humid climates." From her accent it was clear she was from a good English family because her letters were crisp and clean.

"How is everyone tonight?" she asked.

"Lovely?" Vera said.

"The world is shit, but what else is new," Eve added.

"Please excuse my daughters," Jane said. "I should not have made them come."

Humidity settled on their skin. Real moisture, imaginary place.

"I never got to have children so I have a lot of extra goodwill stored up for all sorts of outbursts." The woman explained she was visiting a friend who was a donor to the university. "But I live in Italy. I don't know how you all survive this fog. I need sunshine."

Jane said, "I spend a lot of time in Italy, in the north, near Bolzano.

Spent, I should say. My husband used to write about an ancient humanoid there." Usually these were not things she told people upon meeting them.

"The iceman, of course. I like to visit him sometimes. He's famous." The woman smiled.

"My husband was sort of the official biographer."

"Then you know how hard Italy fought to consider him ours. We almost had a small war with Austria. Did I learn that from your husband's book?"

"Very likely."

Vera felt her father zigzag through her bloodstream like a fast-moving ghost. Like he was there with them, conjured by the woman who had read his words. Vera was balanced between loud weeping and crazed joy and she did not know which direction she would tip.

"I'm Helen," the woman said.

They all shook hands and Helen's shake was hard, but her skin was the skin of expensive creams and regular manicures. Eve said, "My mom was just saying that she might quit trying to be a scientist because of a bunch of assholes down there who don't get how brilliant she is."

Jane elbowed her elder daughter hard in the ribs and said, "Your concerns have been noted."

Helen said, "You can't give them the satisfaction. We're all counting on you to prove them wrong."

Vera wanted rescue for everyone. "Italy is nice," she said.

"Very. We're on Lake Como. We live on a fifty-acre animal preserve that my husband's great-great-great-grandmother started."

"Wow," Jane said. "We live in a shitty two-bedroom rental with a lot of deferred maintenance."

Helen laughed. "Oh, we have plenty of deferred maintenance."

Jane took her pearls off as if they were trying to strangle her. Vera could almost feel the warm weight of them as Jane held them, passed them hand to hand while Vera asked what animals Helen kept on her preserve and pictured what Helen described: ibex, monkeys, kit foxes, zebras, giraffes, an elephant.

"You have an elephant? Like, as a pet?" Eve asked.

"She's my husband's pet. He is a retired veterinarian with a special love of pachyderms. She's a good girl. A little feisty, but good."

"We're not even allowed to have a dog," Eve said.

Jane told her, "We've talked about this. We'll get a dog when it's time."

"My mother," Eve said, "doesn't want to replace our dad with a dog. It's a sticking point."

"Pets are a big responsibility. You should see our food bills. That elephant alone has probably cost us twenty thousand euros over the fifteen years we've had her."

"Is that old?"

"It's breeding age. The males want to be in their forties and fifties and the females want to be teenagers."

"Just like us. How depressing," Eve said.

In Jane's hands the pearls went back and forth. She kept opening her mouth like she would speak.

"If you two combined your passions we could breed a woolly mammoth using our mom's lab embryos and your elephant," Vera said.

Everyone laughed, even Jane, who looked like someone who had given up caring. Helen said, "My husband's grandmother reassembled the bones of a mammoth in our museum. There are missing pieces and we had to improvise, but it's not bad. We like to picnic under it."

"Your museum?" Jane said. Vera imagined the adult version of the baby she and Eve had cradled across the ice.

Helen said, "Not a museum like this. It's just a room, really."

The story about finding the baby mammoth poured out of Eve. She described the cold body, the cliffside, the camp, the lab. Vera smiled her most trustworthy smile, wanting to show that yes, this was truly how they spent their summer and no, they were not a family of lunatics.

"I'm envious," Helen said. "Extremely. What an amazing young life you're leading."

Eve said, "That's one way to think of it."

To Vera, amazing was a regular family with an alive dad and enough money to buy a house.

Jane passed the pearls from her right to her left hand and in the middle, they slipped. "Shit," she said, and the four women watched the necklace fall and land on a branch, slither off. Three stories of slither and slink. There was the music of leaves being hit and the quick, splashless descent into the pool below.

"Oh, dear," said Helen. "Shall we go get someone to help fish them out?"

"I hate those things," Jane said. The pearls sat on the glass bottom, settled into a ball of white. "If I thought I could take this dress off and walk out of here draped in vines without being arrested, I'd do it."

Eve beamed.

"Ah, it's a night like that? I know those nights," Helen said.

Jane asked, "How have your survived it? Do you ever feel like you'll explode out of your own body with rage?"

"All the time. Truly."

Good ideas seemed scarce, the darkness deeper all the time.

They stood in silence. An electric blue butterfly landed on Jane's hand and she stayed still to make a safe place for it until it flew again. "Blue morpho," Helen said. "My advice? It's true that no one cares about us, most of the time. Women, I mean. Perhaps that's all right, though, and the trouble is just that we care too much to make up for it."

"So, just care less?" Vera asked.

"It sounds small, but it changes everything. Care less, do more," Helen said.

Jane turned to her daughters, Eve first, then Vera, and she said, "That's wise. We should remember that."

Vera had a flash of being an adult and coming home to her own apartment, throwing car keys in a ceramic dish and petting an enthusiastic dog. Happiness always occurred to her as independence and quiet.

"Do you, lovely woman in a black dress in a fake rain forest who has just vowed to stop caring so much what the world thinks, actually have woolly mammoth embryos? Jane, did you say your name was?"

"I have embryos. They aren't really mine. They're edited to be mammothlike. They used to be elephant stem cells and they were revised to look like mammoth stem cells and they got zapped into an egg cell and now they're embryos with a lot of mammoth traits. So no. No is the obvious answer."

"You have mammothy embryos? And you're proposing implanting these in my elephant."

"My daughter said something silly. Please erase this from your mind. I'm so sorry. It's been a weird day."

"All days are weird days," Eve said. With this Vera agreed.

In the pool the fish took notice of the necklace. The pearls were big enough that Vera was worried one would eat it and get sick but each fish inspected and swam on.

Jane said, "Let's go home. Girls, take your mother home."

The four women walked on together to the top of the spiral, rode the elevator down, checking themselves in the mirror for stowaway butterflies. Vera inspected her mother and Helen in the mirror. They looked so much alike. Or the same woman in another possible life. She thought about how interchangeable everyone was, little plastic figures that could snap in and out of lives, families. The professor was alive and her dad was dead for no fair or justifiable reason. One woman was a rich zookeeper and another a poor graduate student with two daughters she had to care for alone. They walked beneath the pool, beneath the carp and trout. The pearls looked huge and distorted from below, green through the water.

"I'm off to bed. Jet lag, and all. But if we're going to raise an extinct species together I guess we'll need to exchange contact information," Helen said.

Everyone froze in place. Jane squinted at the woman's face. "It was a stupid thing to say—"

Helen interrupted. "I love an experiment. Even if it's destined to fail. Maybe especially then." She rummaged in her clutch. "We may as well funnel all that female rage into something fun." She found a pen and she took Jane's arm in her hand and wrote, across the soft underside of her wrist, an email address.

THE NEXT DAY Jane went to work early and the girls finally got their day of sleep and television and microwave popcorn and oily hair. That evening they went to the overpriced Jewish deli for dinner, Jane's choice. Waiting for their table, Jane rolled a receipt from her pocket into a tight tube. In front of Vera was a large glass jar of red licorice and through the jar she could see a family of five—mom, toddlers, baby, dad—eating pickles and laughing.

"You're twitching, Mom," Eve said.

"Hungry," Jane said.

"Should we be spending money like this?" Vera asked. Eve shushed. She wanted this. They had not eaten at a restaurant in weeks.

"I need some nostalgia. And pastrami," Jane said. Vera's face must have given away her genuine worry because her mother added, "We're going to be all right. We can have dinner out once in a while."

The girls ordered matzoh ball soup and Jane kept her eyes fixed on them while they sucked the broth from their spoons. "You're watching us like we're not well," Eve said. "It's making me nervous."

"It's good to see you eating so happily," Jane said. "It's beautiful, actually."

Jane described a woman she saw on the bus that morning wearing a yellow latex jumpsuit. Eve complained about a classic, sexist novel she had on her summer reading list. "You can have feelings," Jane said, "but you still should read the book. We can't ignore all the bad ideas of the past. We have to address them through modern eyes."

"I disagree. I think we have to stop assigning things we know are bullshit. Assign a book by a woman or a person of color. Assign anything else. I should use my time on something better."

"I kind of liked *The Old Man and the Sea*," Vera said. "Is that bad?"

"See? We can't scrap it all," Jane said.

"What would Dad have thought?" Eve asked. "I bet he wouldn't have made me read it."

"Your father was a journalist. His job was divergent perspectives and nuance."

Thick silence fell over them, so quiet it was loud.

Jane cleared her throat and said, "I want to take a few embryos and bring them to that Helen lady in Italy and implant them in her elephant."

"Really?" Eve said, her eyes fire-bright.

"Really." Jane smiled wide.

"I'm not coming," Vera said.

Eve said, "It's *Italy*, Vera."

Vera did not want to be the grown-up. She did not want to have to explain that they were not talking about Italy, they were talking about their mother stealing intellectual property from a major university. Vera looked at Jane. "What is *happening*? Are you serious?"

Along came the waitress with sandwiches tall enough that they would have to be excavated to be eaten. "Chow time," the woman said.

No one spoke while she set a plate in front of each person. The smell was fat and salt and flesh. Vera wanted the mustard but her mother did not look available to pass so Vera stood up and reached across the table. "Sorry," she said, and was not scolded.

"We lose embryos all the time," Jane said. "No one has been suspicious of any of those other losses, right?"

"What will you do if it works?" Vera asked.

"It's not going to work. They're busy making an artificial womb because this is not a viable plan. It's not about working or not working. I want to do one thing, to try one thing in my dumb little life. I'm a thirty-eight-year-old graduate-student single-mother widow. You couldn't string together a sadder list of attributes if you tried."

Vera asked, "Do you hate your life that much?" She wanted to cry but was trying nastiness as a way to stay above water. She had seen it work for Eve.

"Vera, it's Lake Como," Eve said, her mouth slippery with grease.

In Vera, the snakebitten poison of Jane's sadness made its way from toes to fingertips. She put her fork down and closed her eyes. She took a long breath. "I'm sorry. Can you explain what's happening?"

Jane told them about the morning, how she had stood over the embryos in their petri dishes. Steady body temperature, humidity, the right light. Each one with a masking tape label and a notation of its birthday and Jane said she understood that she was just a worker, her hands important only for enacting someone else's vision. "My hands are not my own," Jane said.

Jane flipped the ketchup bottle over and watched the contents slop from one end to the other. She said, "I have been working so hard to be fine. Dad died and I have not missed one day of work. I have done all the dishes and made all the meals and trapped mice and washed clothes and packed lunches and I have managed to pay all the bills and I got myself on the Russia trip and the absolute most miraculous thing happened and it almost seemed like I might finally get some credit, and for a few days I let myself imagine that I'd have a real career and everything wouldn't be so hard all the time, but no. I'm the lab girl. The professor probably thinks I'm grateful to be along for the ride."

Eve said, "Fuck him."

Vera was not yet ready to make her mouth form swear words in front of adults, even her own mom. She said, "I agree. But stealing embryos seems maybe bad?"

Jane picked up her water glass and she did not stop drinking until it was drained dry.

"Oh, definitely. It's unethical and illegal and it has no chance in the world of working."

"Then we can skip it?"

Eve said, "But Italy. Please, let's go. We need to get out of here. We need to get out of our sad ghost house. We're better when we're traveling. We're happier. It almost feels like Dad is still with us."

Jane said, "If we go, we can visit the iceman. Which is as close as we get to visiting your dad."

Vera was helpless against this. She looked at her hands, small and pale. She did not know what they would reach for in her life, what they would make or take apart. Now, at thirteen, the only thing she wanted to touch was the only thing she couldn't.

"So, what, you just write an email to this Helen lady?" Eve asked.

"Should we?"

"Now?" Vera asked. "Right now at dinner we're writing to a zoo-keeper to ask if she wants to make a woolly mammoth?"

Jane flagged the waitress. "Cheesecake, two slices, three forks," she said, and took out her phone.

Eve said, "Dear Helen, It's Jane, from San Francisco. Do you still want to make a mammoth?"

Jane laughed. "Dear Helen, Hey! I hope you had a safe flight home. Do you still want me to bring the mammoth embryos to Italy?"

The cheesecakes arrived, red cherry goo dripping off, and they each dove a fork and Vera felt the jag of sugar and irresponsible choices made in good company. She said, "Hi Helen! I was in my lab and wondered if you are still interested in a doomed experiment breeding extinct species together. Embryos are looking strong!"

They laughed and ate and Vera thought that if other diners at other

59

tables saw them they would think what a nice family, what a fun girls' night out.

Jane said, "Let's get serious. Dear Helen, It's Jane, from the gala. Would there be a time that we could chat on the phone to discuss the idea we talked about?"

"That's not bad," Eve said.

"Send," Jane whispered, and without meaning to, Vera held her breath.

THREE DAYS LATER there was a bright yellow envelope on the front porch. Inside: three economy tickets from SFO to Milan.

"Are we?" Vera asked, and she could see that dreamstate and momentum had already taken her mother over. At the end of the day Jane came home with a small cooler packed with dry ice. Inside were A46, A57, C96 and R33. She said, "I guess this is happening."

Vera asked what she had said, how she explained.

Jane told her girls that she'd written an email: Lost some embryos last night. I cleaned the dishes. I won't be in next week. Death in the family.

THREE FLIGHTS LATER there was Helen, in the front of the crowd, wearing camel-colored wool pants and a crisp button-down, her hair smooth, a gold chain necklace that was somehow both large and tasteful. "Jane. Girls." She smiled, all warmth, like they had loved one another forever. "You came. I was sure you would get cold feet."

Jane looked small and crumpled next to this beauty. The last time they had met she had been evening-dressed, they both had.

"What's in the cooler?" Helen asked.

"What do you mean? The embryos. The whole reason we're here."

"You brought them *now*? I thought, I guess I assumed we were exploring the possibilities."

Doubt fizzed the edges of Vera's brain. She wanted to walk right back through the terminal and get on the next plane home. Her boring summer life, something terrible streaming on the laptop.

"Oh," was all Jane said. "I did. I brought them. We're here."

Eve and Vera exchanged a dark look. Helen was the one who sent the plane tickets without asking, Vera thought.

"Well," said Helen. She took out her phone and thumbed at it quickly, her face twisted.

"Is it okay?" Jane asked. "I'm sorry."

"We are not prepared. But George will go shopping if anything is missing. It's fine. It's going to be fine. Lucky for you he's done this before. Not the mammoth bit." She was already walking away.

"He's impregnated elephants, you mean?" Jane asked.

"Loads. It's what he loved best."

"I thought it was supposed to be difficult. Maybe impossible."

"You brought embryos thinking that we did *not* know how to implant them? I'm a bit confused."

Jane said, "That is a feeling we share."

"Right," Helen said as they got into a white van. "Apparently we are inseminating an elephant today." As if Jane had sprung the idea herself. "Will those things be all right for a few more hours?"

"I don't really know," Jane said. "I'm a lab assistant."

In Vera's head: Dad, Dad, Dad, Dad. He would have known what to do. He would have softened everyone with humor and steadied them with confidence. She had sense memories of him, his voice, but the feeling she had when she thought of the world with him in it was a smooth, level floor. A safe place to stand.

THEY CAREENED OUT OF the city, into the mountains and around a huge emerald lake. It felt like circling the gem at the center of a ring, showoffy in its prettiness, but even after the spectacular approach, the property was a surprise.

"You live in a castle," Jane said.

"You live in a *castle* castle," Eve said.

"Castles in Italy are nothing special. It just means I live in a drafty old house."

Eve whispered to Vera, "That's what people with castles are trained to say. The self-deprecation only extreme fanciness can buy."

The castle had sculptured gardens leading to it—giraffe topiaries on either side of the door, magnolia trees, grape arbors, jasmine. "It's nicer from the front. Everything here is supposed to be viewed from the lake." Helen turned the car off and they opened their doors.

"Yeah, it's a real shit box from here," Eve said, but Helen did not smile at the joke.

From behind a stand of cypress trees: a zebra. Not sculpted, alive. "Oh, hi," Vera said out loud. Her body was uneasy.

"Get!" Helen shouted, and the zebra moseyed away. "They can be terribly bossy," she said.

Helen rooted around in the back of the van. Jane stood by the car with her little red cooler like a kid waiting to go to school. Vera rested her back on the warm metal and her eyes felt swimmy and she let them fall closed. Somewhere nearby a lot of birds chirped. They sounded tropical. They sounded not of this land. She heard a breathy grunt and opened her eyes to the zebra approaching her like she needed inspection and dismissal.

"It's okay," Jane said, putting her palms up. "We're friendly. She's a friend. We can be friends." She wished she had food to give.

"Hey! I said Get! Get!" Helen shouted, and she ran at the animal, her head forward like a bull.

The striped beast paused and trotted off.

Jane's hand on Vera's arm, warm and sure. "You all right?"

"More please," Eve said.

THEY WALKED NOT TOWARD the castle but down a path so thick with jasmine that Vera wanted to bury her face and do nothing but inhale. "That smell," she said.

They went past a fountain and a bench surrounded by pink roses. Past a stone building with rakes leaning against its side. Past a tractor.

Helen stopped at a cavelike structure behind a heavy fence. "She's sleeping," Helen said.

"Who is?" Jane asked.

"The black bear. She's old. I doubt she'll make it to next year." By the fence line was a huge basket of apples. Helen reached in and threw three into the pen. "Her favorite. We like to baby her."

Eve gave Vera a gleeful look. From there it was a downhill walk through oaks. The ground was sharp with leaves and it was darker and cooler. It was here, tucked away from everything else, no lake view, no sunbright day, that an elephant stood swishing the ground with her trunk.

"Hello, Mama," Helen said. She opened a gate and let them all in.

"She's big," said Vera.

"Observation of the century," Eve told her.

Vera imagined this animal in the forest in Thailand where it belonged, where the jungle and trees were yet bigger. Here, she was not to scale.

The elephant looked at them, big soupy eyes, trunk still drawing a rainbow in the dirt.

"So," Helen said, turning to Jane, "here we are!"

The idea that they were here to make an attempt to reintroduce a species that had been extinct for ten thousand years seemed not only silly but embarrassing. Vera felt it, and judging from her mother's face, Jane did, too. They had this elephant, a real creature, alive now, and a cooler with a few slime squiggles frozen in salt solution plus four women and a fairy tale. Jane said, "We should skip this?"

"That's no fun," Helen said. A man with a worn leather briefcase came trotting down the hill. He had a neat beard and wore slacks and a safari jacket. "Georgie," Helen said. "Georgie with the tranquilizers."

"So you're the ladies with the mammoth embryos," he said.

"Embryos modified for a cold-adapted elephant," Jane corrected.

"How fun." He looked Jane over, shoes to hair, then the two daughters. "I don't know what I expected." Whatever it was, Vera thought they had let him down.

"It's nice to meet you," Jane said, "George with the tranquilizer."

George was older than Vera had expected. Older than Helen or less well taken care of.

It occurred to Vera how far away from home they were. On a spit of land down a long driveway at the edge of a huge lake. Mountains on all sides. She saw Jane take her phone out of her back pocket and squeeze it tight.

"Can I see what's in there?" George said to Jane.

Jane opened the cooler. There was no dramatic dry-ice cloud. She removed the blocks and there, in the bottom, were four little plastic dishes full of solution.

"Cute," he said. "Shall I put her to sleep right now?"

"How long will it take her to fall asleep?" Jane asked.

"A few minutes," George said.

"I guess. Actually, do you think we should let them warm up?" Jane addressed this question to her daughters. "Definitely," Vera said, pretending to know. Jane took the three dishes out and set them on a stump. They could have been anything or nothing. If there was magic it was invisible.

George said, "They need to be defrosted, of course. They'd never work frozen."

"I'm sorry. Can you tell me how this is all going to work?" Jane asked.

"Of course," George began. "This is all very routine, except for the mammoth part. We're going to put this female elephant to sleep and then I will put a long, long tube inside her vagina and into her cervix and open a balloon catheter to create space while I place the embryos as gently as possible. Does that make sense?" He sounded pleased, sure of himself.

Helen asked, "How many animals would you say you've inseminated, Georgie?"

"Dozens," he said.

"I feel like deranged Girl Scouts," Eve said. "What patch will we earn today?"

"The Extinct Animal Resuscitation Patch?" Vera suggested.

"The Artificial Insemination Patch?"

"The Illegal Fish and Game Society Patch?"

Helen laughed. "I hope the adults can earn them, too. I'm working toward the Impulsive Amateur Zookeeper Patch."

George knelt and opened his case. In it, a large syringe. He unwrapped, stabbed the needle into a bottle and pulled the liquid back. "Fortunately we keep the shed stocked." Any buoyancy gained from the jokes quickly dispersed.

"I'll do it," Helen said.

"She likes to be the boss," George told Jane.

Helen walked slowly toward the elephant, the needle behind her back. "Come here, girl," Helen said. "It's going to hurt for a second. We're trying to get you a baby. Wouldn't you like that?"

Eve put a palm over her eyes.

"Oh god," Jane whispered.

The animal jerked when Helen pressed the needle into her back haunch. But Helen kept speaking softly, kept shushing, kept smiling, and she depressed the liquid into that big body. Vera felt her chest tighten. Poor thing. Poor, huge thing.

Eve clenched and unclenched her hands.

Within a few minutes, the elephant had knelt. She looked at Helen like she wanted help.

"Once upon a time," Helen said to the elephant, petting her, voice velvet and low, "there was a great king and he lived in a palace in India. He was very, very rich, but the only thing he truly loved were his elephants. They lived in a palace of their own and they were washed with Himalayan snowmelt and fed fresh green bamboo shoots. The elephants were happy, but the king was sad. He didn't like being king." The elephant's body softened and she lay down with a swoosh of dust. She closed her eyes. Helen continued. "One night, he went and slept next to the animals and in the morning the queen came looking and discovered a new elephant. And the king's golden pajamas on the floor, torn open. The queen understood that her husband had turned into an animal. She wept, but every day for the rest of her life she went to the elephant palace and kissed her husband and told him about the kingdom, which was now hers. She lived until she was one hundred and twenty years old and never remarried."

"Are you through?" George asked.

Helen pressed her hand on the elephant's cheek, her trunk. "She's asleep."

Jane picked up a dish and rotated it carefully. It was thawing but not yet thawed. "We should give them a little bit longer. Maybe I should take them to the sun. How long do we have?" Jane asked.

"Forty minutes or so. But once we're ready it will take but a moment."

"Do you need help?" Helen asked.

"We'll go," Jane said, and the girls came to her side. Jane stacked the dishes and let herself out the gate. She led them up the hill, through the oaks and past the bear den where the bear was still hidden away, past the stone tool shed and the tractor. "I hadn't realized how cold I was," Jane said. "Freezing," Vera said.

Here was the sun, bright, and their skin already waking up. They stood over the squiggles of embryos and moved when their heads cast a shadow. "Well, your education continues, huh?" Jane said.

"I am working toward my PhD in weird shit," Eve said.

"And what a star student you are."

Vera went to the jasmine tunnel and did what she had wanted: pressed her body to the bushes and put her face inside and took the perfume into her lungs. The sweet-sharp smell filled her head. The bushes pricked her but it was worth it. She breathed and breathed and

breathed. Be a journalist, she said to herself. Her father had said it to
her once when she was in fifth grade and shy and did not want to go
to school. He stood outside the building with her and said, "Pretend
you're an observer rather than a student." It had worked. It was a method
that would serve her all her life.

THE ELEPHANT SEEMED EVEN bigger now that she was lying
down. Reclined against her great belly were Helen and George, she
with her eyes closed and he reading a magazine about cricket and eating a panino.

"Lunchtime?" Jane asked.

"Georgie," Helen said, "always prepared. At least he uses all those
stupid pockets."

"I don't like to be hungry," he said.

Jane said, "I think they're ready?"

"And you agree?" George said to Eve and Vera.

"Us?" they both answered.

"You're part of the team. I believe in consulting all stakeholders,"
he said.

Eve gave a sturdy nod and said, "Signing off on thawed embryos."

Helen stood up and set out tools on a piece of heavy canvas.

George sent the catheter in. He looked up at the sky, as if it were a
screen on which he could see the tube's journey.

"How many embryos are we implanting?" Jane asked.

George said, "All of them. To increase our odds, which are just over
nil. We didn't use to be able to do this at all."

"I thought you said you'd made lots of baby elephants?" Eve asked.

"I have. And for every success, there were hundreds of failures."

A drugged female, choiceless, someone else's life shot into her. Vera closed her eyes and apologized to the animal. Jane held the ankle while George took the thigh and Helen pressed, and said, "That's that," with cheer. "We'll either be rich and famous, or fail in beautiful anonymity."

Jane's face darkened. "We can't tell anyone about this ever, never, never."

Syringe away, catheter out, cooler empty, elephant drowsing, five people with a shared secret.

"We don't want to get in trouble any more than you do," Helen said. "Nothing to worry about, love."

She should have been victorious but instead Jane looked scraped and sorry and scared. "I need to lie down," she said.

"Hard yes on that," Eve said.

Helen went to the gate. "I'll take you."

The two girls walked behind. Eve said, "I feel older already."

"Older?"

"As in, grown-up. Better."

It sounded nice, but Vera did not feel this. She felt progressively smaller, something being peeled away rather than built up. Everything familiar and steady had been removed—whole family, an adult with an established career, sufficient money. Now, life was only a question—is this enough?

THROUGH THE OAKS, past the bear cave where the bear was now, pawing at the ground, her fur both dirty and shining, past the shed, through the jasmine tunnel and between the giraffe topiaries to a wooden door that might have hung on those hinges for hundreds of years.

"This is the north wing. Normally we enter on the south but your room is there," Helen said, her arm pointing to the top of a tight spiral staircase.

"The turret?" Jane asked.

Every footstep echoed. The rail was palm-polished and when Vera reached her hand out to touch the wall her fingers came back slightly moist with stone sweat.

At the top: a round room with tall, thin windows through which to shoot an arrow at an approaching enemy. The bed was big and there was a white duvet folded neatly at the foot.

"There's a bathroom there," Helen said. "The water comes out hot so be careful. You rest and we'll have a little party later to celebrate."

Helen's heels clicked down the spiral stairs until there was no sound.

Eve and Vera lay flat on the bed while Jane washed her hands for a long time. Eve said, "An entire castle and we get to share a bed."

Jane told them, "I'll change our tickets. We'll get the first flight home."

"Or we could take the train to Rome," Eve said.

"I thought—" Vera said, and did not finish because her wish was too sad to speak out loud.

"We'll come back and do it right. The iceman and the lab and Bolzano and Rome and Tuscany and the coast. All of it."

Jane came out of the bathroom and Vera caught herself trying to reel her mother to her side of the bed, to spoon with her, warm mom-arm over Vera's waist. Jane said, "I have to check my email," and sat by the window, opening her laptop.

Eve was already asleep. Vera said, "Come soon?" but Jane was lost to her, wading through the mud of work she had left behind. Vera listened to a sound that she thought was both probably and improbably the shouts of a troupe of monkeys. Vera was too warm, dizzy. She did not notice herself going to sleep.

VERA TRIED TO WAKE UP but her entire body fought. She wanted to sleep for a hundred days. A hundred years. She had a dreamish thought of staying in this tower for a century until no one knew who she was and everyone was dead and the doors were vined shut and she would have to Rapunzel her hair through the window and hope to be rescued.

"Wake *up*," she said to herself out loud. She forced herself vertical and looked at her mother and sister, both still underneath the wool of sleep. "We should get up," Vera said. "We must."

"Leave me alone," Jane said.

"I hate you," Eve said.

"I am the baby," Vera told them. "Do not force me to be responsible."

She went to stand in the shower but it did not make this day feel more real. Neither did dressing or spiraling down the stairs, or walking into the evening where the jasmine made the air dizzy. Neither did it feel real when Helen found them in the garden and walked them, with a wicker picnic basket, to another building, stained-glass lit, within which was the promised skeleton of a full-sized woolly mammoth. Tusks long as cars, bones darkened by air and time.

"This," Helen said, "is Flora. George's grandmother loved everything prehistoric. Who knows how much she spent to have this brought here."

"This is better than the ones I've seen in museums," Jane said.

"She's a dear." Helen opened the basket and spread a checked table-cloth on the tile floor beneath the mammoth's head.

"Where is George?" Eve asked.

"He went out for a sail. Sit," Helen said. She unpacked wine and glasses, a plate of cheeses and prosciutto, bread, a dish of tiny fishes in oil. "*Buon appetito*," she said. She offered Jane a glass and filled it. Vera looked around. Dead things surrounded them. Taxidermied orangutans, lions, small rodents Vera could not immediately identify. Glass jars of preserved frogs that caught the window light.

Helen tapped their glasses together and the sound rang through the room.

"I've changed our tickets. We'll fly home tomorrow," Jane said.

"You just got here," Helen said. "It should be a crime to come to Italy for one day."

"This seemed like a good idea from a distance," Jane said. "I need to go back to my real job. I have children to support."

Eve said, "Vera and I could stay. She wants to see Dad."

Jane said, "Now there's a sound plan."

"You said," Vera told her mother.

"He's not here, Ver. Any more than he's anywhere."

"The iceman is here. We agreed."

Helen said, "Your dad was a writer. You'll always have his words."

"We'd prefer an alive dad to a dad in books," Eve said. "Right, Vera?" Vera wanted to tuck her face into Eve's lap.

Helen said, "We shouldn't turn away the things that have been left to us. Right now you are children so you want a father but you'll appreciate his legacy when you are older."

Eve's ears turned red and she said, "Don't tell us our future."

"Fine," Helen said. "But I speak from experience. George's great-grandfather was a colonel in India and later helped build the railroad in Kenya and on each trip he collected exotic creatures and had them

sent back to England. He had macaques, mandrills, white-faced capu-
chin monkeys and gibbons. He had giraffes and zebras. His favorite
was a pair of what he called 'nesting warthogs,' which ran around his
Scottish estate with their tails lofted like antennas and their tusks ready
to root out small, edible creatures. Everything I am and have is inher-
ited. I am one chapter of a much longer story."

Eve said, "Colonialism, gross."

"To be sure. Everything here is a trinket of colonialism," Helen said,
looking around. "This whole property was built to house them. He built
the glass aviary, a vivarium and a monkey house. He built this room to
look like a museum in India. All of it because he wanted to and could.
Desire is powerful. It's your story, too, even if you don't have as much
evidence of that." She pointed to a taxidermied lion stalking a taxidermied rabbit. "He raised that lion from a cub. Apparently it slept in
bed with him every night of its life." Vera studied a wall of birds in
colors that seemed unlikely even in flowers. On a wall by the window
were shelves full of jarred curiosities—conjoined twin raccoon babies,
a hairless kitten, the brain of what Helen said was the last known carrier pigeon.

"So, if all these are trinkets of colonialism, then what's what you just
did to that elephant?" Eve asked.

"Smart girl. More of the same, I suppose," Helen told her.

"Colonize the womb," Eve said.

Jane moved away from Eve, squinted at her. "Baby's first PhD dis-
sertation," she said with barbs in her voice.

"No, she's absolutely right," Helen said. "How old are you?"

"Fifteen," Eve said, proud.

"How long is an elephant pregnancy?" Vera asked.

"Two years, give or take," Helen said.

"But the elephant won't get pregnant," Jane added. "So we have already arrived at our non-destination."

Vera looked at three baboons on a high shelf: baby clinging to mother's back, father upright on his haunches, scanning the horizon for danger. A family alive because they each had a role. She thought of the three-walled structure that was her family, one side blown open. They were always going to be exposed to the elements. Eve had turned her body slightly toward Helen. Jane, away.

Jane said, "My father was a Jewish podiatrist and my mother was his receptionist. They left me nothing."

"Everyone in our family is dead now," Eve said. "Except us."

Eve was a ringing alarm clock, going off at random times, deafening everyone.

Jane did not reach a warm hand out. She looked like someone who was being asked to carry one more thing when her arms were already full.

Helen said, "Inheritance is complicated. I'm lucky to live here. But it's not without a cost."

"Colonialism?" Vera asked.

"That's part of it. George proposed to me on the night we met, when I was nineteen years old and he was almost thirty. We were at a fund-raiser for the London Zoological Society. I recall clearly that he had beads of caviar on his mustache. He said, 'I have a small menagerie of my own at my estate in northern Italy,' and I said, 'When will you ask me to marry you?' I was joking, of course, but he put down his toast, took a sip of his champagne and knelt in the middle of the party, all of London there in formal attire. I said yes because I wanted the animals."

"Was it worth it?" Jane said.

"The marriage has not been terrific, but the property has made me happy. And unsurprisingly, it's nice to have everything one wants. That's the thing about power. But you have to be careful what you ask for. After our sudden engagement, we came here to meet his parents. George's father said, 'We're selling Italy.' As if they owned all of it. As if to have a crumbling castle on Lake Como meant that the Colosseum was theirs, too, the aqueducts, canals, ports, lakes, the Alps, cathedrals. I asked about the animals even though I knew I had no place asking a question in this family yet and probably never would. I did not say that I would call the wedding off if the animals were not part of the deal. George's mother said that they would all go to nice zoos and not to worry and I looked out at the lake and the sunset and I imagined George's parents sinking their sailboat and drowning. Which," Helen said, "is exactly what happened the next day."

"Wait, what?" Vera asked.

"Good work," Eve said.

"*Eve,*" Jane snapped.

"I didn't do it, is the thing. I did not sabotage the boat. George and I went to a museum and had a nice lunch and when we got home we had sex in the twin bed in his room and the twin bed in my room." Eve was rapt, glued to Helen. Vera's cheeks must have given her away because Helen said, "Should I not mention sex? My apologies. I forget the whole American puritan thing."

"We're not puritans," Eve said.

Jane raised her eyebrows. "Do you even know who they were?"

"School, Mom," Eve said. "We do learn history."

"We're Californians," Vera said, which seemed to make clear that they stood at the whatever point was opposite from purity.

"That's probably why I like you so much," Helen said. "Anyway,

George called the police that night when it was obvious that something was wrong. But the bodies were never found, the ship never dredged, the mystery was never solved."

Vera had read enough mysteries to know that the killer always said they did not do the killing. Above her the stuffed lion was ready to pounce, the baboons on alert. Her eyes moved fast around the room, a person scanning for clues or exits.

The sun had stopped brightening the stained-glass windows and Helen stood up on a wooden chair and lit the candelabra with a long match.

Eve said, "So, you imagined killing people and that's how they died the very next day but you did not do it?"

"I swear on every animal on this land that I did absolutely nothing except have a thought. My dream life and my nightmare mind."

Jane laughed nervously.

"What I'm trying to say is that it matters what we wish for. What is your heart's desire, Jane?" Helen asked.

The question seemed to take Jane's breath. Her eyes skated to Eve, Vera. "I'm sorry?"

"What is the thing you feel you must do or be or you'll begin to disappear?" Vera hoped to hear her own name in her mother's mouth. To hear Jane's dreams for her daughters, her limitless love for them.

"I want to make something that matters." Jane said.

Am I that? Vera asked in the silence of her head. Are we?

"To whom?" Helen asked. "There's recognition, and then there's the difference a person can make."

"Both," Jane said, "if I'm being honest."

"Good. I would not have trusted you if you'd admitted only the altruistic part."

"But," Jane said, "maybe it's time to revise my goals. Some of us can be helpers rather than figureheads. What if a decent life is enough?"

"Are you telling us to give up?" Eve asked. "To be mediocre?"

"You can still do something great. I might be ready to just be a person."

Helen looked suspicious. "If you want to *be*, there's no better place than Italy. You don't have to rush home. Stay a few days and eat."

Eve said, "On today's episode of *The Disappointment Show*: forty-eight hours in Europe."

Vera looked around at the room, the centuries of collection and breeding and care. "You're lucky. You have the perfect life."

"Is it luck? Maybe I'm magic," Helen said. She turned to Jane, eyes sharp. "Maybe I imagine something and it comes true."

Three

They flew home, too much TV for the girls, Jane answering emails. That was Jane's actual job, it seemed to Vera. That was what science was, what all work was. Thousands of years of evolution and humans had landed here, each person in front of a blue screen trying to reduce the number in her in-box. Salutations and politeness while the earth fizzled underneath. Vera looked out the window at the sunset they were chasing across the globe. The bright edge. California burned worse each summer. There were floods along the southern border. Ice melted on the poles. Vera's biology teacher had had them read a paper that gave humanity another thirty years before the planet stopped being habitable. Vera and Eve would be in their forties. Vera pictured them floating on the endless sea on a yellow life raft. The last generation. The ones who would be there to see the end.

Home again, the three tried to find routines that would hold them up. Jane dove into her regular job with the conviction of a zealot. She wore a blazer under her lab coat. She kept her in-box at zero. She graded her students' tests the day she collected them. To Vera her mother looked like she was in a staged performance of *Lab Girl: The Musical* in a velvet-curtained auditorium under hot lights, trying to make the workaday look like it meant more.

Vera watched free "You Can Learn Italian!" videos and did not, as she had quietly hoped, feel as if she were speaking with her father.

Eve texted a girl from school who was named for an exuberant flower and started going for walks with her. She did not invite Vera, who watched the two girls round the corner beneath the neighbor's lemon tree, hands in pockets, voices woven in laughter.

Jane went to school while her summer-vacation girls draped themselves over various chairs and couches and watched YouTube videos of raccoons dancing and women doing eye shadow and complicated updos. Vera tried fishtail braids on herself in the hall mirror and they came out lumpy. She said, "Nothing is fair. Nothing will ever be fair." She made lemonade with backyard lemons. She put a mint sprig in each glass.

"Thank you," Eve said. "But it's still not real summer. I hate this place. It's August and it's freezing. I deserve to wear shorts. I deserve to wear a too-short skirt with heat as my excuse. I am being robbed."

The terrible summer weather in the Bay was something they agreed on. Vera wanted a morning walk, the sun already pressing down. She wanted iced tea and cold showers and her neck always salty with sweat. Instead it was sweaters and slippers until evening. Instead they celebrated Vera's thirteenth birthday at the park by the bay with hot chocolate and hats while the water foamed on the rocks.

There was news of a hurricane in Texas, predicted to be bad, proving to be worse. Vera couldn't stop clicking the links on the laptop. Cell phone videos of people standing on their roofs, the water up to the second story, waiting for rescue. Cars floating away. A cat in a basket, its fur matted and wet, drifting down the street.

"I guess this is that climate change thing they've been talking about," an onscreen woman in a lifeboat said. "We've had storms but never storms like this." Her accent was heavy. She was wearing a trash bag as a rain jacket.

Vera watched this place where she had never been become subsumed. She watched the rain claim the land for the kingdom of water. She thought of the story children were told of a vast ocean, continents not risen up, the spirals of fossils that would later be found in deserts. She thought of the biblical flood. Water owned everything—land was on loan. Sea levels were rising. Ice caps were melting. It was not a good time to be terrestrial.

Vera went to the kitchen and took out flour, salt. She poured dry yeast into a bowl of warm water and watched the bubbles form. "Good morning, little yeasties," she said. "Time to wake up and eat so I can cook you." She always felt a pinprick of guilt at this stage of breadmaking. These tiny creatures alive for a few hours before going into the oven. But they were invisible and the dough itself was the life Vera cared about. The way it smelled in the oven and the medicine of a warm slice with butter.

That night, the hurricane on the radio in the background and Jane's hands in the dishwater, Eve said, "Any news from Madame Helen?"

"Nothing. Let's put that behind us."

"How was work?"

Jane said, "I organized the pipette cabinet and I worked on a grant for the professor to study human genetics in Iceland. I helped Todd get his tusk project within budget. At least I packed a decent lunch."

Vera took out the broom and swept under the stove. Her mother's day made her sad and then sadder for feeling sorry. She worried about having too-high expectations, for a normal life to be not enough. Jane kept dipping dishes in tubs, one sudsy, one clear. Vera remembered that her dad thought it was ridiculous that Jane did dishes by hand when there was a perfectly good dishwasher. Jane said she liked to have her hands in the warm water, liked the work of taking something dirty and making it clean, the satisfaction of a simple job completed.

THAT NIGHT, Vera laid out a camping pad in the attic, a big space next to their bedrooms with a small window at the far end. The room smelled like warm wood and mothballs. She could stand up only in the midline, where the peak was highest. On either side were piles of belongings—a basket of stuffed animals, the backpacks the four of them had traveled with. They had crossed cities and mountain ranges and deserts together. They had crossed inland seas and lakes and floated down rivers. Movement had been their home. They had been a tiny, migrating herd.

Eve knocked on the door. "What are you doing in here?"

"Escaping."

"Can I escape, too?"

Please please please, Vera said in her head. She did not know how to say the things that were swirling in her head. How afraid she was of Eve leaving her. How she couldn't shake the image of her mother chained to beakers and logbooks and classes full of eighteen-year-old first years who failed every other test and men's hands in and on everything Jane tried to make, every manipulation in the always-closer-but-never-there of science. Vera thought of herself and Eve, their lives on this planet. She had been raised to imagine greatness, difficult and brave work, but she mostly wanted something steady. She said, "What I actually want is to unescape. I want home base."

Eve lay on the attic floor. They were quiet for a long time in the smell of hot wood, surrounded by objects that were unnecessary but hard to give up. Eve asked out loud, "What will be the next thing to go?" They both understood that losing was in the music of being. Sometimes melody, sometimes chorus. "It was Dad, then it was Mom's career goals. What now?"

"Not you, please," Vera whispered, too quiet to be heard.

Another knock on the door and Jane's shadow-shape appeared. "Hi," she said.

"Come in, we're unescaping," said Eve.

Jane sat on a pillow and crossed her legs. She said, "I'm failing at being both parents." A pause. "I'm done with him being dead. I'm ready for him to not be dead anymore."

"I'm mad at him for dying," Eve said.

"Me too," Jane told her.

They had done the hard, immediate work of shock and grief so deep they drowned and the awful, unfair work of insurance paperwork and canceling mail and credit cards and magazine subscriptions. Then they had done the work of grief as tide, receding until the ground seemed almost dry, then rushing back in, foamy and cold. Now they were in the forever part, the endless low-level blue that had become a presence more than an absence. It was the ocean they swam in or the ocean that sloshed in them.

"Why are we mad at him?" Vera asked so quietly it almost wasn't language.

"Because he left us," Eve and Jane said in unison.

"And," Jane added, "because it was always easy for him. Life was easy and death was easy."

Vera asked, "And how do we know that?"

Jane nodded and turned her face to the sky. She said, "We don't. I can't really let myself think how terrified he might have been. Or if he knew what was happening. Or what he thought. Being angry is the easy way."

Vera tried to correct. "You're doing fine. You're a good mom."

Eve said, "I reserve the right to be mad at him."

"Co-signed," Jane said. "I won't try to steal your rage."

Vera reserved the right to be sad, but no one had ever called that into question.

"I already don't remember him all the way," Vera said. "I try to but he goes out of focus."

"Do you want to?" Jane asked. "It's also fair if you want to let him go. You shouldn't spend your life trying and failing to keep him here."

Vera said, "I want to remember." Eve was silent, looked at her sister with an apology in her eyes. Jane told her, "You're like him, Eve. Charismatic and magnetic. Except that he was happy with a book and a coffee in a generic café."

Vera had his plainest parts, Eve the most interesting ones.

"Sal and I went to a city hall in Ohio to get married because I knew I would never meet anyone else like him and I didn't want to wait. I didn't care that he had been my professor or about the age difference or that people would judge me. I was twenty-two and he was thirty-four. I called my parents only afterward and they sent a check for five hundred dollars and a card that said, 'Cheers!' We hardly spoke after that because everyone was hurt and no one was brave enough to fix it. Sal went back to teaching at my old school. I got pregnant immediately." Jane reached to Eve, hand on her knee. "With you."

Vera had a momentary tinge of jealousy that Eve had had two extra years in their family.

"I was a college student there one year before and now I was a faculty wife. I was years younger than all the youngest professors and too old to be friends with students. There was no one left for me to be except a woman with a baby who belonged nowhere. Dad taught and worked on his book at the library and came home while I vacuumed and Eve sucked on a stale bagel. I had fallen in love with him because he made the world seem huge but now my life felt extremely small."

"I'm sorry I ruined everything," Eve said.

"It wasn't you. It was everyone else. One time I went to the grocery store when you were maybe six months old. You grabbed a package of hot dogs and gnawed on them until juice dribbled over your flowered dress and when I handed the package to the checker the man looked at me with the deepest, purest disdain. I said, 'I am on a team of scientists that works on the oldest-ever ice mummy, you fucker.'"

Eve and Vera both laughed.

"When I got home I went up to Dad's office and told him I was ready to go back into the field."

"He wanted to stay in Ohio?" Vera asked. She was pretty sure she would have, too, or at least that was her theory. She and Sal were satisfied more easily than Jane and Eve were. Now, Vera was alone in this way of being and her wandering mother and sister would not stay still merely on her behalf.

"He made all the usual arguments about kids and stability and money but I didn't care about any of that. I had it figured out. He would go on research leave. I would apply for fellowships and grants under his name because he had a name and I was just a kid. We agreed that if we got a grant, we'd go. And of course, we did. His field was human evolution so we went where the discoveries were being made and he interviewed the scientists and went on digs and spent time in museums with collectors—all meetings I set up—and he wrote about our ancestors and the people learning about them. Instead of writing for the academy he wrote for the general population. We made it sexy. I did the background research and edited his drafts. He told it like a love story and a mystery and a thriller. Cave dwellers in France, homi-nids in Kenya, all felt immediate and alive in his hands. The iceman book made him a tiny bit famous and he kept looking for ways to keep that project going. Do you know that he died on a trip where they were running tests on the iceman's testicular matter to see if there was any sperm? He had pitched a kind of sci-fi article about the vanishingly small possibility of the iceman having a baby with a modern woman. He had a big magazine interested and he planned to use the catchy question to think about genetic inheritance and the differences between ancient and modern humans."

"I always think of him as practical, but that is a deeply weird en-deavor," Eve said.

"He got better at using a weird hook to get money or assignments. Maybe I taught him that." Jane smiled at her daughters. She said, "I'm skipping ahead. Vera was born and Eve got big. You girls learned to read, swim, ride bikes and play cards. I was proud because we had achieved the necessary skills even without the cocoon of America."

The memories belonged to Vera, too, now. Memories of her and Eve going to local schools where they had to work out the maze of social expectations and vocabulary and whether it was all right for girls to speak in class and whether it was all right for girls to make eye contact with teachers or students or administrators and whether it was all right for girls to wear pants or all right to wear skirts and which route was safest to walk to and from school and after a while they decided that they had each other and they would rather teach themselves.

Eve and Vera could do a semester's worth of home school in two weeks. They would stock up on snacks—coconut biscuits, rose soda, dried shrimp-flavored potato chips—and work for eight hours a day, quizzing, memorizing, reading, questioning, complaining—until they had finished everything. After that they would have months to do nothing but wander and read and lie on the bed listening to music that made them feel like they were still part of the current moment instead of floating like loose particles in space.

Jane said, "Sal eventually admitted that he was not going back to teach at the college and resigned. He had become an author who used to teach. My own career was always on the distant horizon, and never worth settling down somewhere. I was working, but my name existed only in the acknowledgments. For years, the arrangement made sense anyway."

Vera asked, "When did it stop making sense?"

Jane smiled and winked at her oldest child, her wildest child. "When we were in Paris I watched a YouTube video on my laptop on the tiny balcony of our hotel room. It was the professor, who I didn't know yet, talking about the future like it was an estate that belonged to him and him alone. 'We save ourselves,'" Jane said, imitating his deep voice, "'the same way we almost ruined ourselves—by inventing. Everything we need is here.' And he pointed to his head. Maybe he meant the human brain in general and maybe he meant his own magnificent mind and maybe he saw no distinction between the two. 'Imagine,' he said, 'if we brought them all back.' On his slides were all the missing creatures of the world: the passenger pigeon, the dodo, the Tasmanian tiger, Pyrenean ibex, West African black rhino. And, of course, with tangled hair and sweeping tusks, a woolly mammoth. For a split second I pictured myself sitting on the mammoth's tusk like a circus performer. Before I knew what I was doing, I had clicked to the professor's school page, found an email address and introduced myself."

"Was Dad upset?" Eve asked.

"He didn't know yet. It happened fast. I went inside and took a bottle of mediocre champagne from the minibar, for which we would be charged some ungodly number of euros. Sal's face was lit blue from his screen. He was typing paragraphs that people would eventually read. I hated him a tiny bit. He had a voice and I still had to earn one. I went outside and drank a lot of champagne in not a lot of time. Sal opened the door and peeked his head out. I said, 'The world is possibly ending. We've killed off most of what lived and the rest will follow. People are trying to bring things back.' He asked if I meant those de-extinction wackos and I said yes and he told me that it was the definition of hubris and we could never predict the unintended consequences and I told him that the entire world is unintended consequences. Two people having a baby is a completely unpredictable situation. The combustion engine. The *internet*."

"And look at you, the first person to attempt to implant woolly mammoth embryos," Eve said. "Baby's all grown-up."

"He still thought it was crazy, right up until he died. It was our biggest fight."

"It seems not all the way crazy to me," Eve said. "Humans are the worst. We have moved into every habitable corner and demolished everything. We want elephant tusks and tiger pelts and mountain lion heads.

We're really, really good at wanting. What if we want to add things for once? The worst part is that every hedge fund dude is more destructive than any crazy science experiment but we celebrate them because we love money."

Jane took Eve's hand and kissed the pad of her pinky finger. "My little Marxist."

"Is this colonialism again?" Vera asked.

"Capitalism, bro," Eve said. "But same difference. We colonized because we wanted stuff and land and slaves because we wanted money."

"So, Team Science?"

"Life is experiments," Jane said. "Plus, motherhood forced me to care what happened on this crumbling earth beyond my own years. I didn't say that to Dad because being a woman and being a mother always soften an argument. Instead I wooed him with a home address and a utility bill and a coffee shop he could walk to and a promise to know the names of all the dogs in the neighborhood."

"He should have just been the wife," Eve said.

Vera thought with dismay, I should be the wife.

"He loved teaching and he loved you and he loved a regular old Sunday and he loved doing fieldwork in the summer. He didn't have to choose. That was his magic trick."

Vera was afraid that she loved steadiness and she loved Eve and her mother and that those things were not compatible. She had no magic trick, only her two arms trying to hold together pieces the universe had sent flying.

Jane said, "Someone around here needs to make dinner and someone around here needs to answer three more emails and someone around here needs to take a shower. When was the last time I took a shower?"

"We'll have toast and eggs for dinner," Eve said. "My treat."

"And cookies," Vera added.

Jane took out her phone. Eve said, "Take your shower first. You have to prioritize self-care."

Their mother laughed. "I don't, though. That is clearly the lowest item on my list." Her face turned pale in the phone's light. "I'll just do this quickly." She thumbed. Then Jane said, "Oh god," and upside-downed the phone on her leg.

"What?" the sisters said in one voice. Their mother threw the phone to them and they saw in her in-box the name Helen MacDaniel. Subject: !!!, and one sentence: *The elephant is pregnant.* A mammoth emoji. Vera felt the air leave her body.

LATER, VERA WOULD THINK of this in-between as the most normal eighteen months of her life.

SUMMER FOG SETTLED OVER EVERYTHING, tamping, quieting. Jane worked more and longer hours. Lab hours, teaching hours, hours overseeing the undergraduate interns. On weekends she gathered her portfolio for the job market the following year. Vera sat on the couch beside her mother, screen open to a six-page document called Vitae v12, and watched as Jane translated her lived life experience to one-line notations.

That August they celebrated the elephant's impossibly unlikely full year of being pregnant and Vera's very predictable fourteenth birthday with a tall Italian meringue cake. Jane said, "We're halfway or so to a baby mammoth. Can you believe this?"

Vera asked if Helen had sent any more information. "She wrote to say that she rescued a flock of lorikeets from a South Pacific island infested with rats."

"That's nice?"

Jane showed Vera the lorikeet pictures—so blue, so bright—and Vera saw the thumbed reply: *Fun!* Jane had written. *How pretty!*

"I guess an uneventful pregnancy is good news?" Eve said.

A week later, the three women marked the second anniversary of Sal's death with shortbread cookies and a walk through the midafternoon cool.

School started once again. Vera bought Converse sneakers and drew vines and a peace sign on the white plastic of the toe. Eve studied makeup videos and got angry when her pencil skipped and dragged on her eyelid. The regular world stormed onward in its plainness. It didn't care that there was a maybe-mammoth growing in the belly of an elephant. There was dish duty and classes and homework and meals and street sweeping and garbage day and empty milk jugs and cool kids and nerdy kids and insufficient appreciation from teachers and bosses. Jane complained about her students who couldn't stay off their phones for more than fifteen minutes. The girls took all the classes that someone thought would make them whole—biology, chemistry, British literature, world history, government, ceramics, Spanish, French, dance, band, communications, coding, drama. They played badminton, volleyball, basketball and soccer in PE and ran laps on the track. Adults grew more and more narrow and specialized while their children were supposed to know something about everything. Vera thought of Jane at her computer transforming herself into a CV, flattened down to information, skill set, honors earned and missed.

. . .

THAT WINTER THE ELEPHANT had been pregnant for fifteen months: she was a clock that kept ticking even as they expected her to wind down any day. At the table, Eve drew a tattoo on her ankle with a fine-tipped Sharpie—a ginkgo leaf. Beside her Jane populated the cells of a spreadsheet and Vera mixed the batter for a chocolate cake with rose icing. Vera asked what her mom was working on and Jane said, "D Cas repression data set," and Vera said, "How exciting," and turned on the kitchen radio, always tuned to the public radio station. They all three looked up.

The velvet-voiced host said, "Some call gene editing a Pandora's box with vast and unknowable consequences to the genetic map of plants, animals and especially humans." Vera felt her ears go hot.

"Team Science!" Eve said.

The story was about a researcher in China who had edited the genes of a human embryo. The host introduced his guest, a professor at Princeton, who said, "The possibilities are endless and exciting, but we must not turn a blind eye toward the dangers of gene editing. What's to stop prospective parents from deciding they want children with dark blue eyes and straight blond hair? Families with means could create uniform, perfect, disease-resistant children. And meanwhile teams are trying to reintroduce passenger pigeons and dodos and woolly mammoths into wild populations of similar birds and animals, thus forever altering every generation to come. How can we possibly anticipate the consequences of such projects? This could turn from a novelty into an emergency in a matter of moments."

Jane said, "No one knows what we've done and the pregnancy will end any day. Or the baby will die at birth. Or the baby will be an ordinary elephant. Or or or . . ." She added, "This has a zero percent chance of happening."

Eve said, "What you did is incredibly, unbelievably cool. We need megafauna to stomp around and knock over trees to protect permafrost, remember? They belong. This is your professor's wet dream and you made it happen in secret with no support. You're the queen of the world."

The university in China, the reporter explained, had shut down the researcher's lab after discovering what he had done and he was under house arrest with armed guards surrounding the perimeter. The scientist, Vera thought, was also a person; five-feet-something, thin, hands on hips and looking out at the horizon. Family inside, hidden. Jane said, "He knew it was illegal to edit human genes."

Vera said, "What you did was not illegal?"

"The editing was fine. The stealing was not."

It wasn't true that no one knew what they had done, Vera thought. She knew and George knew and Helen knew and Jane and Eve knew. Five people, at least. Five minds, five mouths.

The next story was about the early season wildfires in wine country. The images in the news had been first of the mansions in the hills burning, then fire running down the canyons, then charred neighborhoods, the shells of cars. In places the fire made it all the way to sea like a red river, smoke and steam and ash turning the air dark. Even in Berkeley, hours away, the cars had been covered in ash every morning.

Vera felt her heart go slant. Everything that could burn.

Jane stared at her screen. "Should I tell Helen that I no longer want to be associated with the situation? Maybe while I'm at it I should let her know that I was married to my professor, that I am *that* kind of girl."

Eve straightened up. "Whoa, Mom. We didn't say anything about you quitting."

"Or maybe me pulling out would make Helen suspicious and give her reason to report me? Or," Jane continued, "is that a handy excuse for a person who wants to see a baby mammoth and is willing to risk her family's safety for it?"

Vera reached for steadiness, though she felt none. "It's just an experiment. Experiments fail most of the time." She set her rubber spatula down, walked quickly across the kitchen and sat on her mother's lap, face pressed into neck. She wanted to say, *Look at us building a perfectly great regular old life. Did you even notice?*

Eve looked at the two others and did not come close. Jane pulled Vera in. "I will never do anything that matters the way this could matter."

Eve said it out loud: "Ouch, Mom."

"It's a woolly mammoth. We implanted a *mammoth*. And no one is ever going to know."

"We know," Vera said. "We could go back there? Like you promised? Just for fun?" A Dad-spark glinted, a pilgrimage to some part of him.

Jane said, "You selfish child." She was smiling but her voice was sharp. "When we're rich, we can go back. Castles, wine, mammoths. We'll see it all." What she meant was: we will never find your father. What she meant was: your heart will always be half empty.

STRESS-WALKING THE NEIGHBORHOOD, Vera found an armchair on the street and dragged it up to the attic and set up a card table and a thousand-piece puzzle of a wildebeest migration. She liked that it was not a real room, that it was not designed to be inhabited. She liked that it was a claim staked. Not wilderness exactly, but one step away from civilized and a place where she could practice survival skills.

Eve climbed up the stairs looking for her sister. She said, "I should have known you'd be in your man cave." She pulled a milk crate over and said, "I know I'm supposed to hate high school but I *hate* high school. This girl told me that Mom seems too old to still be in school and I punched her in the boob and now you're back to being my only friend. Why do we do this? Wouldn't it be better to send us all out for four years of manual labor and then we could go to college?"

"I'm sure there's a strong argument for that." Vera fit an edge piece into her puzzle. A square of blue sky.

"Teenagers are the species least suited to the classroom. Worse than baboons. Worse than goats. Girls are mean and boys are stupid and everyone is miserable."

"At your manual labor work camp, what's the plan for birth control?"

"Gross, Vera. You're too young to talk about that."

"Sorry. But it's something to consider. At the Olympic village they provide tens of thousands of condoms for the athletes."

"How do you know these things?"

"I read the magazines in the checkout line."

"They are all hot. The athletes, I mean."

"Maybe we divide by gender and have zero contact," Vera said. "If it was up to the adults we wouldn't get internet or cell phones."

"I'd like it to be tropical."

"Motion approved."

Vera risked a question. "Are you worried that someone will find out about the mammoth?"

"There's no mammoth. This isn't going anywhere. I'm just happy that Mom got to try something."

Vera hunted for a water piece for the watering hole. "I'll try to feel that way, too. It's weird that failure is the best possible outcome."

"The best possible outcome is a fuzzy-ass mammoth that makes us all rich but that's a fantasy, not real." Eve was working on a baby wildebeest face. "Ah," she said, making a match. "That's so satisfying. Hey, buddy." The animal looked back at her, black eyes and a gray beard. "Maybe we could have animals on our island," she said.

"Maybe we could raise mammoths," Vera said.

Eve said, "Life finds a way." And they both laughed, and laughing felt so good, felt like opening a bottle of fizzy and letting the bubbles rise up and pop.

DURING THE LAST WEEK of eighth grade as the fires flared and settled, as the world grew more tenuous by the day, or seemed to, Vera found herself thirsty to do something real, something good even if it was microscopic and meaningless, so she joined a lunchtime meeting of the Climate Sunshine Group, whose flyers she had seen around school. She figured they would talk about recycling and replacing lightbulbs and compost and she knew none of those would make a future for their generation but she didn't care. She was ready to accept the idiocy of small individual action against a vast, insurmountable problem if it made her feel better. In the room it was mostly boys with patchy facial hair and copies of books that explained in exact detail how the ecosystems would collapse. The girls, meanwhile, were making posters for a march in San Francisco.

Vera was in yoga pants and a big sweatshirt and all the other girls had tight bodysuits and vintage jeans. They used words like rights-of-nature and ecofeminist. One girl was making a sign with a fist on it that said BLUE PLANET, BLACK FUTURE. She said, "You want to make one, new girl?" and Vera said, "Sure, yeah, okay." It felt like she had to prove her value and her knowledge. She started to sketch a globe and that seemed stupid so she erased it and drew the outline of a woolly mammoth. Square head, rounded body, soaring tusks. She remembered the feeling of the baby mammoth in her arms, of carrying it down the beach, cold and soaked. Now it was in an expensive freezer somewhere.

Above the animal Vera wrote "Extinction Sucks" in Sharpie, then she went back to fill the creature in.

"That's cool," a girl with a forearm of friendship bracelets said.

"People are bringing them back," Vera said. "Or trying."

"Dinosaurs?"

"Woolly mammoths. They were way more recent than dinosaurs. People make that mistake all the time."

"Why?"

"It's something about permafrost and grass cover and insulation. It's kind of cool." Vera understood the science and the reasoning perfectly, had been to that permafrost, carried that animal, watched the code of its near descendant injected into a living surrogate, but she felt suddenly self-conscious about knowing too much about a very specific topic.

"Seems creepy," the girl said. "I don't get that."

Vera drew hair on her mammoth and felt her whole body heat up.

The Blue Planet, Black Future girl said, "I think it's awesome. I'd go see one. I'd want to ride it."

Vera was not part of this group yet but she felt like she might get to be. It was the first time she could remember a spark of light in her future, a good thing yet to come. The bell rang. The friendship bracelet girl gave her a side hug. It was a short hug but Vera squeezed her eyes tight and smiled. Her sister had been her only steady friend but it always seemed like Vera stayed still while Eve flew on ahead. Pretty soon they would be miles apart.

"I'm Valentine," the girl said, and the name rose like a song. At that moment, surrounded by half-painted signs and potential but not actual friends, the earth, the actual earth, started to shake.

It was not shaking in Vera's mind. "Earthquake," she said out loud, and even though she knew they lived on two tectonic plates it seemed more nightmare than geology. Vera looked up at the other kids who rattled like marbles across the room. She watched her not-yet-friends put their arms out looking for a wall but there was no wall. Many screamed. They all looked at one another to say, *This can't happen,* though they had practiced for it, knew that it very much could happen. Some kids remembered more quickly to go under their desks. Vera was one. She did not think of this, but knew it; was there before her brain understood what she had done. Her eyes fixed on a boy's fancy basketball shoes. She had seen him Q-tip cleaning them in algebra and now he was weeping into his cupped hands and his shoes were bright plastic. Red and black against the public school brown linoleum.

For a thousand seconds, forever and ever it seemed, what had been solid became a jagged sea. Invisible waves. Vera held her desk and she watched a window crack, heard a crash outside, alarms awaken. At the front of the room a teacher had found her way to the doorframe, her body an X, eyes wide, mouth frozen open.

.   .   .

AFTER, IT WAS REPORTED that the quake had been six seconds long, a 6.3. A car had been crushed by a eucalyptus tree and power had been knocked out in several neighborhoods. No one had died. The bridges still hung across the water.

Parents from all over streamed toward their children. The offices were jammed, school secretaries fighting to keep parents from running through the halls screaming the names of their grown babies. Jane flew into Vera's classroom and they jumped on their bikes and rode to Eve, who stood outside the high school in a long line of teenagers awaiting retrieval. Eve reported that she had been in PE doing jumping jacks on the field and suddenly the world was not under her and it had seemed like she was floating. Where was the ground? she had thought. She fell onto it and it kept moving. Oh, she thought. And Eve had lain down and turned onto her back and floated on the turning earth. Her classmates screamed and some ran and the teacher shouted something about getting out from under trees but Eve did not want to move. Or, she wanted not to move more than she was being made to by the shifting plates beneath her. Above: the sky was flat calm, a smear of steady blue.

Vera turned her head upward, where huge trees loomed and the buildings all seemed old and ready to fall. "Will there be aftershocks?" she asked. "Was that just the preface?"

"This is unacceptable," Jane said. She told her daughters how the lab had been covered in loose glass, stools on wheels had run all over and computers slid off their benches and cracked. "I was so scared," she said. "I kept thinking about the train underneath the Bay in a tube and the people sitting there and the water pressing on the walls. What if I had been on the other side of the Bay? What if I couldn't get to you?"

Vera felt betrayed. She was angry at the earth, at this place that was so clearly not a suitable home and would get worse as time went on.

"I feel weirdly refreshed," Eve said. She was appreciative for how steady the ground normally was, she told them, how much she could count on gravity.

"What?" Jane asked. "Who are you?"

Eve gestured to the asphalt, the sidewalk, the city standing around them. "It's almost always not shaking," she said.

THAT NIGHT THEY ATE cereal for dinner. Jane said, "I want plains and flat grasslands where nothing will ever move." She poured another bowl. "What kind of parents were we for moving here?"

Eve said, "It was kind of fun. Didn't you think it was a little bit fun?"

"I watched my classmates prepare to *die*," Vera said.

"Maybe that was the key—I couldn't see anyone. Only the sky."

"Is this a good time to tell you that I'm being sent to Iceland for the summer?" Jane said.

Home was not a place to stay.

Vera asked, "Were you planning this? Why are we only hearing about it now?"

Jane said, "It just happened. I'm a baby researcher and I have to do what I'm told."

Eve said, "Please. Isn't there a project you could join in Paris or Tahiti? Iceland sounds cold. Why does it have to be there?"

"Most Icelanders are descended from Vikings, with very little other genetic influence. It's an unusually pure pool, and it will allow us to see differences in the genetic code that are otherwise difficult to distinguish," Jane explained.

Eve said, "They have volcanoes there."

"I don't like the idea of volcanos," Vera told her.

Jane said, "Would you prefer to spend another foggy summer in Berkeley?" She reached into her pocket and pulled out an envelope. She said, "Plus, there's this."

"Which is?" Eve asked.

"Which is the final life insurance payout. After this, we're on our own."

"How long will it last?"

"With my funding and this check to supplement, we're all right for nine months, maybe a year if we're careful. And then I graduate and this is gone. Human genetics is a burgeoning field with lots of resources. This is a good move for me."

Vera said, "I could open a bakery."

"Dear girl, do not try to rescue your mother. You're not even legally allowed to work. No, my job is to figure out how turn this year into a catapult that launches us."

Vera whispered, "Or a trampoline."

"Nah," Eve said. "We should launch."

Vera felt her back on the chair, imagined someone behind her drawing her backward and sending her flying.

That night they all slept in the same room, Vera and Eve on the attic mats, dragged now into their mother's room. They did not want walls between them. Walls that could be shaken down, doorways that could be blocked. Maybe they would be crushed but at least they would be crushed together. Vera constructed an imaginary violet bubble over them, impermeable protection against everything that could possibly be.

Four

Summer in Iceland was even less summery than it was in Berkeley. Vera bought an expensive heavy wool sweater to wear under her down coat because she was always cold, always cold and always trailing behind Eve who had met a boy. Eve was the first to fall in love as Eve was the first to do everything. The boy was tall and thin and it looked like his body was still partly unformed. His name was Lars and he could trace his lineage directly to a Viking ship that arrived in Iceland in the year 1200 from Norway. He was blond but there were red hairs in his beard.

Over the course of that summer, while Jane studied the genetic signature of this pure-blooded population, Eve's every molecule was Lars-facing. Vera felt like a negative magnet with no positive pull but Eve let her come along most of the time. Vera was pitied but at least she was invited. As she trailed behind she thought about her mother in this new lab performing the machinations of a new project that might or might not lead to a new job, a new life. Her mother, unspooling and altering the genetic code for people and animals. Vera was bewildered by the bigness of these projects, how much good they could do and how much uncertainty they brought. The work could lead them anywhere, or sometimes it seemed, nowhere. At night Vera scrolled through images of people she had just started to become friends with as they protested fossil fuels and she could almost see herself in the photos, a ghost in a life she might have stepped into if stepping out was not her family's occupation. Meanwhile on the lip of a blue lake in the warm sun, an elephant was pregnant, still pregnant. Vera carried all these truths like luggage she had nowhere to unpack.

LARS LIVED IN A hand-built cottage on the edge of the fjord. It was tiny, with sanded plywood floors and a nook for the bed and big windows looking out at the cold, blue world. He had a huge fluffy white down comforter and a heated towel rack in the bathroom. There was a card table with two chairs and a futon made of Icelandic wool. Lars told Eve and Vera that he had built the shack with his mother over the course of a summer when he was fifteen. When Lars had turned into a teenager, he told them, he had knocked things over, hit his head, outgrown the furniture in his parents' house. In the kitchen there were two jelly jars, two heavy ceramic bowls, two coffee cups and two forks. He had one pan and one spatula and an electric teapot. No decorations, no breakables. All the lights were fixed to the wall. There was a fire extinguisher displayed prominently.

He listened to music so thin and high pitched it was hard to even hear. "Is this music made for dogs?" Eve asked. Vera could not tell if it was a man or a woman singing and the beat always seemed to interrupt itself. "It's arrhythmic, like Iceland," Lars told them. "Here we accept that things are not plannable. Any day of the year the highways can be closed for weather. We belong to nature."

Vera knew her sister was having sex. Vera knew everything about her sister first and it used to be that she would be the only one to ever know so she kept this secret, loyal sister, lonely and loyal sister. Each weekend Lars, Eve and Vera went out to the coffee shop and played cards and dominoes, and each weekend they walked in the door to their rented flat together, a plain apartment on a quiet street, all the other houses cottagelike with flowers and only their building a businesslike block. Vera and Eve peeked into their mother's dark bedroom and whispered hello together and Jane heard two girls' voices, and each weekend Eve went quietly back out the front door where Lars was standing in the night, smoking and petting the neighbor's cat. Vera lay down in one twin bed, no one to talk to before sleep, and Eve went back to Lars's tiny house where Vera imagined him picking her sister up to place her on the wooden counter and kiss her. It had gone this way all of June, July. Sunlit nights with the cold sea outside. Water, wind.

The three hiked an impossible trail to the top of the fjord to a field overlooking everything. It was afternoon but cold and they shivered in their thick coats with fur collars and ate ham and dark rye bread with fat gloved fingers. Even in summer it was wintry here but in winter, Lars told the sisters, it was another planet, so dark that it seemed no longer part of the rotation. Forgotten. No light but the juts of green and purple. Eve and Lars each put a hand in the other's pocket. Vera used her own. She chewed a piece of the dark bread and wished for a body she could lean into. Eve looked at her and said, "Come," and scooted her little sister close, a guest to that warmth.

WHAT EVE TRIED TO explain to Vera was how desperate falling in love made her feel. Lars, the existence of him, the narrow chance that they would ever have met and the fact that they had. She had grown up in jungles and deserts and cities while he had been a fixed mark on the map on an island in the far north on one bank on one of the hundreds of fingers of water reaching inward. He had never left the island while Eve had zigzagged the planet, the line of her life wrapping like a string around the earth. What did the line of his life look like? He had been awake and alive all the same days she had plus more. Vera imagined his line going downward, inward, absorbing like water back into the dirt and moss. He had watched the whales come and go every year, the terns come and go, watched the snow and the freeze, the melt. It was impossible to imagine, that kind of belonging. The first night they had gone over to his little house he had made tea and while Vera and Eve lay on the couch made from wool from nearby sheep and Vera had looked out at the gray-to-blue of sky and sea and the rickrack of foam at the water's edge and she had wanted to bar the door and never be found or taken.

Eve was smitten with Lars but it was his house that Vera fell for. How simple it was and how clean. The view out to the water, the shorebirds, the steep rise of cliffs on the opposite side and waterfalls striping them. She had had two dozen houses but never a home. They had migrated with their parents' projects, each one like fresh grass they had to follow. Vera imagined being a grown-up here, staying still, inhabiting this cottage without plans to leave. The trampoline gone solid.

Lars asked about Africa, about southern Europe, about America, about heat and warm oceans. He wanted to know about being temperate; he could not imagine tropical. Eve told him about a sea urchin sting in the Indian Ocean in Kenya and the green papaya someone had picked and sliced and placed, cool and slippery, on her pulsing foot. Vera told him about a taxi boat overfull of people and covered by torn tarps and the way she and her sister had held hands, expecting to capsize and die. Eve told him about buttery flatbreads and freshly squeezed juice from green oranges and lions and zebras and he looked at her like she was his storybook. Like she had walked herself all that way, filling up with wonder to bring north.

Vera said, "I remember the exciting moments but the things that pop into my head are usually regular intersections in regular places. This spot in Nairobi where we once switched minibuses. I remember the man selling New York Yankees hats from a pole he carried on his shoulder and the loud music from a store. I would never be able to find that place again but I think of it a few times a year. Maybe it's my brain scrolling for a place where I belong."

"You belong with your family," Lars said.

"I belong to my sister."

Eve said, "Awww, Vera. I belong to you, too," but the hand she held was Lars's.

Lars brushed his long blond hair out of his eyes. He felt part animal to Vera. The way you could instantly care about a dog that had put its head in your lap. "You made it to me," he said to Eve, "which is all that matters."

When they went outside for Lars to smoke a cigarette there were arctic terns on the beach. Little white things, flying, landing, flying. "They make the longest journey of any creature on the planet," Lars said. "They go from the Arctic to the Antarctic in one flight. They fly seventy thousand kilometers a year."

They were tiny. Too tiny, it would seem. Vera had not found a landing place, another body on which to rest. She was older but felt smaller than ever. When they were young the girls had fantasized about running away and building a grass hut and living there forever and ever and ever. Once they had made a midnight promise to marry brothers. Lars was an only child. This was a match without a match. Someone was always going to be lonely.

HERE WAS VERA: rocking on a rocking chair alone because at night only Eve was invited to the seaside cottage. Jane was asleep in her room and Vera scrolled through a photo-sharing site where the kids in the climate group at home were posting about a piece of legislation that reduced emissions but not by enough. There was a little red badge that told her that someone had tried to video call her in the middle of the night. Someone who still didn't remember that Vera was on the other side of the world. Who still didn't understand that Vera belonged in the kind of family where the time was always changing, where the map was so zoomed out that the girl on it was a tiny, unfindable dot. She watched a singing competition on television, called and texted for her favorite, a German brother/sister duo with a song that made her cry every time they sang it. Her own sister was two years older, doting and tender, never far away. It had been the gift—Vera had never lived without her sister. The story their mother told was of Eve, bedside after the birth of her sister, in the big armchair waiting to hold the baby, yelling until their father took the swaddled bundle out of their mother's arms and placed it in her own. Eve was Vera's place. They both knew this.

Vera went to the kitchen of their small flat and boiled water, cut a slice of heavy bread and spread Nutella thick. She thought about painting her nails or baking a cake or emailing someone or taking out the hat she was knitting but none of it had a purpose. It was not only missing that she felt but a small and bright fury. Eve was being discovered, every part mapped and prized. Vera was no one's treasure.

At two in the morning Jane got up, sleepless, and found Vera still awake in her chair, scrolling. "What are you doing up? Is Eve asleep?" Vera should have lied, had agreed to lie. But tonight she did not lie. "She's with Lars," she said.

"Lars?" Jane asked. She found pants, boots, jacket. "Show me where," she told Vera, and they drove slowly, the steep rise of the hillside dark beside them. "Let me," Vera said when they pulled into the driveway, but Jane was the one to get out first. She turned the knob quietly and they found Eve and Lars naked under a wool blanket with a sheepskin draped over. They were asleep. Arctic summer sun blacked out by heavy curtains. The couple did not wake up. They looked so warm.

Vera turned to her mother and whispered, "You have to wait in the car. I'll bring her." Jane seemed relieved not to be the one to have to hand a bath towel to her daughter to cover herself, not to be the one to watch her eyes fill. Vera climbed into the bed and tucked herself in beside her sister. "Evie," she said, and Eve smiled.

"Hi, love. What are you doing here?" Eve was so unembarrassed. She did not try to cover her skin or excuse herself. They had shared everything and now they shared this, or nearly did.

"Mom is in the car. She knows. I need you to get up and get dressed and come home."

Eve opened her eyes and got up on her elbows. "You told her."

"She asked." Lars was awake, too, confused by the second girl in his bed.

Eve's body lit like a flame in the bathroom light. She found her clothes and washed her face in the sink. "Hi, Vera," Lars said.

"Hi, Lars," she returned, but what she wanted to say was that he made her sister happier than she did and for this she would never forgive him.

"Is it cold out?" he asked.

"Yes," she said, "quite."

"Okay."

"I'm sorry I woke you up," she told him.

"I shouldn't have kept her. I didn't want to say goodbye. I was selfish."

Eve returned to them and put on her socks and boots. She put on her thick wool sweater, an exact match to the one Vera wore, and her coat.

"Bye, baby," she said to Lars, who sat up and kissed her forehead. To Vera, "You betrayed me. You gave me away."

The air outside shocked their breath away with its cold.

IN THE MORNING their mother was waiting with coffee for Eve to wake up. "Good morning. I got cinnamon rolls."

Eve stood in the doorframe, hair half loose. Jane said, "It's my job to protect you."

"Is that what this is? This situation of us being perpetually homeless and desperate?"

"You have never been homeless in your life. You are extremely lucky but you're also a teenager so I don't expect you to understand that."

"What happens now? You lecture me about responsible choices, embryo lady?"

"You can see him during the day, with Vera. No more nights. And you can't be alone."

Vera was a chaperone, an insurance policy, a witness. She would now sit on the other side of the wall and listen to make-out sounds, her only job to keep it from going all the way.

Eve went into the bathroom and slammed the door. As if her mother were trying to remove her skin, damage her beyond repair. She shouted, "You and Dad must not have ever really loved each other if you can do this to me. If you loved him, you would know how I feel. And Vera isn't invited. She is a traitor."

Vera felt like a piece of trash caught in a wave, smashed, pulled back out and smashed again. She had wanted Eve back and now she had lost her forever. It was the only punishment she was not sure she could survive.

"You spoiled stupid girl. What did I do wrong that you don't appreciate your life?"

"It's your life I'm living, Mother, it's *your* life."

Eve opened the door, squeezing a towel in her hand which she bit and then threw. "I'm seventeen! I'm supposed to be walking the halls of some dingy mall with my three best friends. I'm supposed to be ignorant and young and happy. Instead my dad is dead and I am in the middle of the ocean and when I find something good here I get in trouble for it." Vera thought back to when they had still been a foursome with their parents. She wanted to explain to Jane that Eve loving

Lars was an evolutionary adaptation, the strategy of a girl who had learned to survive in a semihostile environment.

"You made this happen," was what Eve yelled. "And it's not my fault that your job is a mess."

Jane stood with the cool white sun behind her, lighting her like some kind of ghost. She took a series of controlled breaths. "I'm sorry you're upset," she said. "I know you have feelings about this boy."

"He loves me one thousand times more than you do and he's only known me for two months."

"You can't possibly know how much I love you." Every word was an electrical charge in the air. "My person died out of nowhere and what I would have liked to do was buy a one-way ticket to Micronesia and disappear forever but I couldn't do that because I have children and the children needed food and a house and comfort. No one was there to comfort me but I was there to comfort you."

"That is not proof of love," Eve said.

"Love is more than gooey appreciation. Love is devotion and duty even when it's hard. Especially when it's hard." Jane turned her back. "Go get your suits, girls, we're going swimming," she said.

"Swimming?" Vera asked.

"I'm too angry to work and once again you can't be left alone."

THEY DROVE TWO HOURS through a landscape made entirely of black sand and rock. Lunar, Martian. There were no plants, no trees, no animals. Lava had spilled out of the volcano and spread, thick and dark, over whatever had been alive here before. Smothered and hardened. Cracked.

"This place is a wasteland," Eve said from the front seat.

"I think it's kind of beautiful," Vera said. She felt silence radiate from Eve.

Jane told them, "It's the youngest place on earth, geologically speaking."

"Whatever you say," Eve told her.

They passed a turnoff for a Viking landmark but did not stop. The clouds were low and it felt to Vera like they were passing through a thin inhabitable belt between the cold sky and the cold earth. They were lucky to be alive at all.

"I called Helen and told her that I needed to not be involved anymore. We have to focus on reality and on me building a career that will support us, not some pipe dream. The amount that I love you is so great I can't even say it. It's not in the realm of language."

"How will you know what's happening there?" Vera asked.

"I won't."

"I thought trying to resurrect a mammoth was cool. It was the one cool thing," Eve said.

Vera wished she had not been afraid, wished she was not now relieved. She wondered if her mom knew how she had felt.

It was quiet in the car for a mile. Road noise, wind.

Eve said, "It would be so incredible if it happened. Can you imagine getting to touch something that roamed the earth ten thousand years ago? To be the person who got to do that?"

It started to rain. A hush of water on the windshield. Vera pictured mammoths walking across this island. They would look good here. She said so.

Jane smiled. "They would. They'd starve but they'd look good."

Vera could tell that Eve was annoyed that she and her mother weren't still fighting. She had planned to ruin this day like she had been ruined. "I'm still mad at both of you. I still love him," Eve said.

"I believe you."

"That's the worst thing you could say."

"Because?"

"Because then you can't be the enemy and I need an enemy."

"Don't have Vera be the enemy, whatever you do. Choose me."

"She told on me. She was supposed to be on my team."

"She misses you," Jane said, as if Vera were not there.

"I'm sorry," Vera whispered, but no one reacted. She touched her own arm to see that she was really there and not an imaginary girl.

In the locker room of the hot springs they undressed and showered and emerged into the cold, drizzly day wearing plastic sandals. There were three huge pools set in the vast lava lands—opaque blue, pale and nearly glowing—and mother and daughters waded in and submerged themselves in that hot water, their bodies hidden in blue milk.

They paddled to the edge and leaned their chins on the rocks, looked at the desolate world.

Jane said, "You don't have to have sex with people who want to have sex with you. You can say no. I need you both to know that."

Vera felt her stomach flip over. Sex was a distant land she could not imagine actually visiting. She knew, too, that Jane had no need to say this to Vera, that she was only hearing it because Eve needed to.

"I really like him. I really like liking him," Eve said. She wiped rainwater from her face.

"When I was in high school I dated this boy who was kind of awkward but funny and he made me laugh all the time and he made everyone laugh all the time and I thought I loved him," Jane said. "I felt a real thing and since it was the first time I thought that thing was love. We slept together when his parents were out of town. It was fine. It was kind of fun and kind of not. He got a crush on someone else and in a few weeks we didn't talk anymore. Everyone had told me that having sex with someone was such a big deal, but it sort of wasn't, for me. I hadn't lost myself to him." Jane looked at Eve. Her almost-adult girl. "I don't know what I'm trying to tell you."

"Are you trying to tell me that I can keep seeing Lars, by chance? Because that would be great."

"It's love that scares me. We give up everything in a second."

Gray seeped from Vera's chest. She wanted someone to argue love's case.

"I don't want you to get sucked into the orbits of boys and men but to be the center of your own universe," Jane said.

"Are you the center of your own universe?" Eve asked. "The professor? Todd? Dad?"

"Touché. But I'm your mother. Priorities change when you become a parent."

Vera was glad at that moment that she had not been the first child, the one to transform her mother's life. She was just an add-on, a plus mark.

"Did they change when you became a wife?" Eve asked.

"I'm sure they did."

"Is that bad? Would you be more your own self if you had stayed single?"

Four old men swam across the pool beside them, their heads covered in matching yellow bathing caps. They were doing laps and chatting. They looked absolutely content.

"Maybe? I would have gotten so much work done. I would have read

all the books. But we are social animals and we learn from being together. My life was rich because I fell in love with someone who taught
me new things."

"Did you teach him things, too?" Vera asked so quietly she almost
wasn't sure it had left her mouth.

Jane said, "The worst part about the story is how easily everyone
assumes I was the recipient of all the wisdom. We were partners. It was
a really good marriage until he abandoned me with his half of our life
and mine."

Vera wanted Jane to say how lucky she was to have the girls, to be
together in the loss. Instead she said, "Raising you on my own is the
hardest thing I have ever done, exponentially."

Eve shook her head. "I'm not done hating you." She turned to Vera.
"You either."

Vera could have said that Jane was a good mother. She could have
said that she was grateful to be alive and cared for. She could have been
the kind daughter to Eve's blistered one. But Vera did not speak those
truths out loud. Not today. It would have been so easy to win just then,
to be the good girl, but Vera would not set herself against Eve, no matter how hard her sister tried to make enemies. For Eve, Vera let the
silence stand. She was a sister first, a daughter second, and she allowed
this day to keep a little of its pain.

WHEN THEY RETURNED FROM their swim, Vera was determined to
win her sister back. "Want to go for a walk?" she said.

"I don't want to go anywhere with you."

"Mom left a pile of kroners on the table and I think we should
spend it."

"You told on me."

"I was lonely. I said I was sorry. I *am* sorry."

"How many kroners?"

"A lot."

"I trusted you."

"I missed you so much."

"I missed you, too. I did."

It was almost warm out. People were gardening in shorts. Vera made a joke about the paleness of everyone's arms and Eve shook it off. She was walking two feet ahead of her little sister. Her own smallness nipped at Vera as she trotted after. Eve and Vera wore their jackets but left them unzipped and this felt significant. Eve said, "I'm not ready to be okay."

Vera told her, "You don't have to be. Let's eat our feelings and spend all Mom's money."

The girls ordered fish and chips in one place, walked an hour and ordered fish soup, later a hot dog. They had a meager salad and coffee and Cokes. They ate cinnamon rolls and cones of vanilla soft serve. The roll of bills grew thinner but the girls had decided that on this day they would use everything they had.

In the late afternoon they sat on the steps beneath the spire of a cathedral. Pigeons worried the cobblestones on the plaza, rustled, cooed. A tour group stood awkwardly close, looking cold and underdressed, the guide holding a green umbrella high. She spoke loudly in German and the group nodded enthusiastically before following her away like a dozen baby ducks.

"I am incredibly full," Eve said.

"So full." The sun came out from behind the clouds for a minute and they closed their eyes and felt the warm on their faces.

Vera said, "I want to go home."

"We don't have a home. We are like those invasive sponges that get into the bilge water of big ships and wind up ruining everything on the other side of the ocean."

"Except we're the ones that get ruined." Vera looked at the church. The outside was stone with big windows. "Do you want to go inside the church?" she asked.

"Don't turn religious on me."

"I don't want to go in in a Jesus way."

They climbed the steps and walked through heavy doors. Everything echoed and everything was silent at the same time. The stained glass was warm with light, each station of the cross on the south side of the building blinding and each station on the north side dim. Jesus began his walk in softness and ended it in shards of color.

Vera walked to the front of the room slowly, mindfully. She liked the way it felt to be in this room. The air was thicker and Vera was swimming through it. A woman cried in one pew and a man and his children sat in another, saying nothing. At the front of the room Vera dropped a coin into a box and took a candle, tipped it to meet another's flame. The prayer was unspecific—she did not know how to ask for what she needed because she did not know how to name it. "Take care of us," was what she said. "Whoever you are." She watched the candle for a few minutes, a black burn line, the wax pooling until it dropped.

THE GIRLS DIDN'T WANT to go back to the house. They didn't want to see their mom. Eve went into a liquor store and came out with a bottle of white wine, victorious. Even here she was underage, though apparently no one noticed or cared.

The cobblestones were slick-smooth and reflected moons of light and it struck Vera how old everything looked, and how lovely. She stooped down and put her hand against the stone and it came away dusty. Every once in a great while it felt exactly right to live at large in the world— distant, but distant together, seeking, moving, their own tiny species.

"Maybe we're lucky we grew up the way we did," Vera said.

"She doesn't care that I love him."

Even Vera knew that love at seventeen didn't count. "It sucks," she said, because she had to say something nice.

"What if I stayed here forever."

"You have no money. And you're a child."

"I could fly him to California when we go back."

"We still don't have any money."

"I could come here for college."

"You could." And Vera would still be wherever her mother was. She was not old enough to do anything but follow along.

Eve told Vera that she wanted to explode. She wanted to scream and disturb. Being a kid meant being a non-person, voiceless. In a year she could run away. Soon she could ruin or save her own life over and over.

Two old women walked across the square and sat down on a bench on the opposite side. They had long skirts and gray topknots and canes. A matched set of humans, Vera thought. It was almost like looking at themselves seventy years from now.

The old women rocked back and forth, held on to each other. From a distance it looked like they were in pain. Vera said, "Are they okay?" She did not know any lifesaving maneuvers nor did she speak the language but she was young enough to be allowed to not know. Adulthood was knowing what to do even when you did not.

"Should we help?" Eve asked. As they got closer it was clear: the old women were laughing. Hard, red-faced laughter. They held their sides, held each other's knees. They could barely catch a breath. It made the girls laugh, too, these women collapsing under a joke. Vera assumed it was something stupid a man did, because what else? She pictured a useless husband slipping in dog shit.

Vera took Eve's hand. It had been a long time since they had done this—when did they get too old?—yet it was so familiar, that grasp.

VERA AND EVE WERE drunk and half elated, half furious. They could not eat any more foods. They had finished enough wine to turn their mouths sour and dry. They leaned back on the church steps and closed their eyes. They spun. Vera fell asleep for a moment and woke to a policeman standing above them speaking fast in Icelandic.

"Yes, yes, sorry," Eve said, because the only choice to was agree.

"Americans," Vera said. The excuse of their country. Everywhere in the world, people expected the Americans to be dumber.

The policeman waved his hands as though the girls were pigeons. Go, he was saying, shoo.

"I have to pee."

"I think I might need to go to bed," Vera said when she stood up.

The door to their flat did not open with the key. It was bolted shut. "Did she leave us?" Vera asked, and she meant it. This had always been her fear—that their mother would reach her maximum effort and leave the girls to fend for themselves.

Vera knocked. "Hello? Hello?"

A rustle, footsteps, and their mother said, "Just a second," and when she opened the door she was wrapped in a towel and her eyes were sleep-squinted. The curtains were drawn and the room was dark. "Oh, it's you," she said.

"Who else?" Vera asked.

"You might remember us from such families as your own," said Eve. She slammed the bathroom door and Vera heard water in the pipes and the shower spray.

Jane called, "Don't touch the cooler in the bathroom. It's got iceman samples in it."

Vera sat on the couch and tried to steady herself with her feet on the floor. "Can we turn a light on?" she asked.

Jane flicked and the room came awake.

They listened to the water run, to Eve crash the shampoo bottles around.

"What were you two up to today?" Jane asked.

"Drinking wine eating food," Vera said.

"Oh. A lot of wine?" Jane asked.

"A European amount."

Jane said nothing. The girls deserved to get in trouble. Vera expected Jane to narrow the travel lanes for them. "Are we grounded?" Vera asked. Vera wanted to be told what to do. She wanted someone to love her enough to give her a curfew and a firm talking-to. She wanted a wall to press against. "Please," she said.

"You're going to have a headache tomorrow" was what Jane finally said. She rubbed her eyes and looked at the ceiling. That was all. "I'm starving," Jane added.

"I never need to eat ever again," Vera told her.

Vera reached for the remote and turned on the television and there was a show that seemed to be about a German goose breeder and his incredibly hot wife. The man waded into a pond, birds like a fog around him. His wife bent to pick up a gosling, cupped it in her perfect hands.

Vera said, "You aren't alone, you know. Sorry, what did you say was in there?"

"Iceman samples. I wrote to the team in Bolzano and said I would compare ancient humanoid and pure Viking DNA. I thought there was a chance someone from the lab would send a sample to me because of what had happened to Dad. I had the grieving widow story on my side." Vera felt swoony. She stood and knocked on the door. "Can I please come in?" she asked Eve. "I really need to pee." Eve unlocked the door.

On the bathroom counter Vera saw a small cooler. It looked like something in which a construction worker would carry his lunch.

Vera peed while Eve, steam-warm and wrapped in a towel, picked up the cooler. They had not seen this item before and in a life of movement, of packing and unpacking, Vera was used to being familiar with all the objects owned by her family members.

"Don't touch it," Vera whispered.

Eve touched it. She opened it. She took out ice packs and then a small vial. She read, Iceman Scrotal Sample. "Oh, Jesus," she said out loud.

Vera zipped her jeans and came to stand beside her toweled sister.

Eve removed a needleless syringe.

"Ancient junk," Eve said. "This day just gets better and better. Our father died while writing about a caveman and the caveman's sperm is in the bathroom where we now stand."

"Put it away." Vera's nerve endings were shot. She thought about pulling Eve out of Lars's bed at night. She thought about the three of them floating in the warm milky blue pool in a field of black lava. The center of your own universe, she said to herself.

Eve spread towels out on the floor and carefully drew the gray matter up into the syringe. "Are you going to do this or am I?" she asked.

"Put it down," Vera said.

"Fine, I will." Eve lay down on the towel bed, opened her legs slightly and before Vera could take in the scene before her, Eve pressed the plunger. "That's cold," she said. She rewrapped her towel, business-like.

Vera stared at her sister lying on the bathroom floor. Eve was smiling. "Oh god oh god oh god," Vera said.

"Doesn't Mom always say that life is experiments? Well, here we are."

"Are you going to have a caveman's baby?"

"It's five thousand years old, dude. It'll just scare her."

"Or ruin something extremely valuable," Vera said.

"Or remind her that that this life is not freaking normal. That I am a real person. That I am valuable and a little bit dangerous." She paused and Vera could hear the water in the sink drip. "I can't get pregnant from that stuff." Eve sounded like someone trying to steady herself against logic. Vera could not tell if it held her up. "Right?" Eve asked, sounding less sure.

Vera whispered, "Having a teen pregnancy with a Neanderthal is pretty not normal." Vera's brain was thrashing and she saw fear bloom in Eve's eyes. "I'm sure you're right," she said. "Nothing will happen." This was a toothless act of rebellion, no peril, only a temper tantrum. A moth banged at Vera's brain. Her dad felt close. Closer than he had in a long time.

Eve stood and dressed. She set the vial and syringe on a clean wash-cloth. A little stage set. A scene, ready to be discovered.

ON THE TV the goose breeder waded through a muck lake to catch an injured gander. The camera kept panning back to the wife, her con-cerned and luminescent face.

Eve and Vera sat on the couch and waited. The room shifted around them. The world was soup. Vera's stomach rolled. "I don't like this feel-ing," she said.

"I told you," said Jane. She stood up and walked toward the bath-room.

From her, a deep growl. "What did you do?" Jane screamed. She came out, her hands full of the evidence and her face all vein and blood. "What the fuck did you do?"

She stood over Eve like she was a puppy who had shit on the floor. Like she would be picked up by the scruff of her neck and tossed out-side. Jane pulled her hand back and she slapped Eve across the face, hard enough that the sound stayed in the air.

"Where is it?" Jane asked, red.

"Toilet," Eve lied. She was dead still. "It could have been Vera," she said.

"It was not Vera."

As if on cue, Vera, sweet Vera, Vera who would never have done something so selfish or strange, threw up on the floor and on her own feet and on her mother's feet.

The whole room turned sour.

Eve stared at her mother, the burn of hand on cheek. They had not believed Jane capable.

"That was the last of Dad's work," Jane said, every syllable overpro-nounced like pebbles thrown against glass. "I was trying to bring his words back, if not him. And now you've literally put it in the toilet. Do you realize what kind of metaphor that is? I was going to finish the story he was writing when he *died*."

The room was broken. Vera took a series of breaths because that was effort enough. Shame swept over her like a cold wave. She wanted Eve to say sorry, to be sorry, she wanted to be able to say this herself but when she opened her mouth she felt like she would throw up again and would never stop, that she would turn inside out.

Jane went to the bathroom and brought back a towel, knelt to clean Vera's feet and the floor and her own shoes. Vera could hear the halted breaths of a woman trying not to fall into the hole in her own chest.

Vera nodded and tried to find Jane's eyes but her mother would not look back. "Can we help finish Dad's story?" she asked.

"Unfortunately, no."

Eve said, "Fuck."

Now it was Vera at risk of disappearing into the black hole in her own heart.

Eve looked sorrier than sorry and Vera waited for her to say so, to admit the whole of what she had done. Their father's last work, the last thing he had thought about and held, was inside of Eve's body. Vera pressed the point on her wrist that was supposed to keep her from feel-ing seasick.

The ping of a text message from Jane's phone, faceup beside her on the couch. She turned her head to look.

"Oh," she said. "Oh, oh." And there, clicked to enlarge, was a large, slippery, upright, big-eyed animal. A baby elephant. Only this elephant had fur.

Pearl

. . . .

Five

The family skirted the lake's bright edge. Jane drove fast, the curves sending them all to one side of the car, then the other. She gripped the wheel and she barely seemed to breathe. Eve, in the front seat, spun the radio dial. Coves appeared, blue and shimmering, then the road curved away and everything was green. For a moment the lanes ran alongside railroad tracks and they drove beside a clattering passenger train. In the windows Vera watched people read the newspaper, sleep with the white wires of headphones down their necks like new veins. The light in the train was pale green and made everyone look as if they were in an old-fashioned photograph, visiting from another time. At the next curve the train went into a tunnel and the cars went around. Vera watched for the blue of water.

Vera said, "It feels like we're traveling at a hundred kilometers per hour across Italy and a mammoth is traveling at a thousand years a second through all of earth's time." They would crash into one another, or planned to. Jane found Vera's eyes in the mirror and they smiled at each other and Vera felt the drug of approval jag through. Vera, wanting more, said, "The mammoth started her journey in the Pleistocene with glaciers advancing and retreating and the planet dry because most of the water was locked up in massive sheets of ice." She waited for another smile, for appreciation that she carried this earth history with her always. Jane was quiet for a moment, took a turn a little fast and corrected. Vera dug for facts in her brain. "She would have traveled through a landscape of beeches and oaks, conifers and lilies, orchids, grasses. Roses."

"Do you know what other animals there were?" Jane asked. She sounded like a teacher, which Vera remembered she was.

"I think there were bear dogs, vesper rats, hares, Smilodon, dire wolf, mole rats, whales, giant ground sloths, elephants, vipers and tortoises? In the sky there would have been bees, mosquitoes, dragonflies, parrots, gulls, flycatchers. In the water, stingrays, dolphins, newts, coelacanths and nautilus. Nautili. Whatever."

The car hummed over pavement. Jane said, "Good, Vera. Do you know what happened next? Eve?"

Eve squinched her face, "Holocene?" she asked.

"Yes! Good girl. Lots of ice and melt. The glaciers retreated and the world warmed and humankind spread and moved out of caves and planted seeds and cut the forest and built boats and houses and gathered and hunted and milled wheat and made fiber and wove clothes. Everywhere, life spread across the warm, wet earth. There were salamanders, cheetahs, mouse lemurs, white rhinoceros, lemon sharks, millipedes, sea horses, scorpions, spinner dolphins, angelfish, giant clams, blue wave butterflies, howler monkeys, giant squid." Vera was warm. Her mother had joined the story.

"Iceman times," Eve said.

Vera pictured their mammoth flying through each epoch, through the cold and hot, the steam of melting ice, the leaves fattening, the earth loamy and rich.

The family rolled on across the present day, passed a village called Fior di Latte because of a river that ran out of the mountains so steep and so fast that the water was white as milk, a foamy tongue lapping the lake. Over the bridge they went and the water below them was creamy and so loud that for a minute they could not hear anything else. Vera rolled her window down and closed her eyes. Everything was thunder.

When it was again quiet, Eve said, "The mammoth has to pass into the Anthropocene."

"Which is us," Vera said.

"When we ruin everything," Eve said.

Jane said, "There were great extinctions before, but this time we were—are—the cause. It's the end of Tasmanian tiger, passenger pigeon, great auk, dodo, saber-toothed cat, black rhino, Chinese river dolphin, imperial woodpecker."

"And the woolly mammoth," Vera said.

"Plus all the other great work we've done, like deforestation and ocean plastic," Eve added.

"Devastation," Jane said. "Everywhere."

The sound of their combustion engine burning fossil fuels while transporting them across a road paved alongside a deep green lake. "Humans," Vera whispered. To be part of such a cruel and stupid species.

"And yet," Jane said, attempted sunshine in her voice, "along came the possibility of return. In Australia, an extinct frog swam out into a salt solution. A few months later, a mate, and then a cloud of eggs was fertilized and a hundred tadpoles troubled the water. A pigeon with passenger genes, a heath hen. And," she said, but stopped. "I don't want to jinx it. I don't want to say it out loud."

Eve said, mimicking the tone, "The very hands that tweezed or nozzled or whatever they did are now driving a Fiat faster than the driver is comfortable with but not as fast as the Italians behind her wish and she has two teenage girls and despite the peril, this woman has done something no one thought could be done."

"Thanks, sweetheart," Jane said.

Soon they would walk the last steps of the journey to touch the animal that had traveled across millennia to meet them, that body, their bodies, on the earth, on the very same day.

Vera said, "We're coming, little mammoth."

JANE MADE A left-hand turn onto the dirt road that led toward the water, toward the castle, toward Helen, toward the animal. The roadside was green with cypress and blooming with lavender and red flowers. Vera remembered the way by the flowers.

They heard it before they saw: an ambulance. Lights and sirens, in its own dust storm, coming toward them, passing them, and in the mirror after, in the backglass, there was a woman, waving.

"Was that *Helen*?" Jane asked, her head craning.

"Should we stop?" Eve asked.

But Jane pressed harder on the pedal and upshifted.

In another minute, another truck, this one military, huge, with a wooden container on the back out of which there peeked a full-grown elephant.

Seconds later, a text from Helen: There's been an accident. The elephant isn't well and she needs to be taken to the zoo for care and she accidentally stepped on George's leg and broke it. Go take care of the baby.

JANE RAN, FULL SPRINT from the place where she parked the car, pulled barely to the side of the driveway, daughters lagging behind. They ran past the antique farm equipment and a mulberry tree heavy with purple-black fruit, past three geese browsing in the grass, past the bear cave—Hello, mister bear, Vera thought—and through an oak forest. They could hear twenty different bird calls, all tropical and out of place, and the holler of a monkey. In the distance, lakeward, was the small herd of zebras. But these were not their miracles. They had come for only one creature, one living thing, and that animal was in a pen they had stood inside exactly once, a pen that had been built for horses beneath a stand of oak trees so dense the light was mottled and the temperature ten degrees cooler. These three humans ran the path, and the path twisted them along until Jane reached the gate, slipped a pin and let them inside. In the tree-light: a baby animal. They slowed down to approach, breathing hard. Jane licked the sweat from her lip, held her hands out, palms up, pale and shaking. "That's a woolly mammoth?" Eve said. Like a fantasy, as impossible as if they had walked into the pen of a dragon.

It was three feet tall and gray with a halo of red hair. If an animal can look surprised, this one did.

Vera watched her mother. The way her chest expanded as she tried to slow her breathing, the way she stilled her body into something safe. This was her offspring, something she had made come true. Their sister, in a way.

The baby shook its head no. It backed slowly away, swept its trunk on the ground, making a wide rainbow.

Jane knelt on the dirt. "Hi," she said, and this creature in front of her was real, pooling black eyes, yarn-thick lashes, twisted trunk, rounded back and brush tail. The animal was covered in disorganized patches of red hair. Its head was more square than its mother's. It looked like an elephant but not like an elephant.

"It does look like our other mammoth. Our Veve," Eve said.

"Who would have thought that little us would find a very, very old mammoth and also a very, very new one?"

Jane did not wipe the tears off her cheeks but let them drip from her chin.

"Hi, pretty girl," Jane said. She reached out again, waiting to be approached. The baby did not know how to use her trunk yet and it curled and straightened in a confused way. She wobbled on her big feet, looked around for something familiar and could not find it. Her breath whooshed the dirt in a cloud and her eyes were deep and gentle. "Your mama will be back," Jane said, and Vera pictured the mother elephant strapped to the flatbed, headed who knows where. "I can take care of you in the meantime. We can."

Vera and Eve watched from outside the fence line. Vera felt nauseated witnessing her mother in this state, as if it were something she should not see. It reminded her of the feeling she had when she had once stumbled onto birth videos on the internet. To see the bluish baby slip out, to see the mother begin to weep, that first cry, stretched Vera's chest in a way she did not like. It was too intimate, too center-of-the-soul.

FOR THIRTY MINUTES, Jane sat in the dirt while the baby considered her. She texted Helen again: I don't understand what happened. Is everything OK? No answer.

Vera was prepared for nothing. She was a bystander, rubbernecker, to this miracle.

When the animal came close finally, trunk on Jane's hands, the top of her head, her neck, her face, Jane put her hands in the animal's fur. "Do you have a tusk?" she asked.

Eve had backed away from the fence, seemed ready to make an escape, and Vera did not know if it was from the animal or from their mother.

"I was really hoping for tusks," Jane said. Vera thought of those little scissors editing the DNA, snipping out the elephant instructions and sending in the long swoop of mammoth tusks.

"Are we being a little greedy?" Eve asked.

"There!" Jane said, victorious. Her hand was buried deep. "It's in the fold of skin. It's tiny but it's there." She checked the other side but found nothing. This was how the baby was named: Pearl.

"Will it survive having been born early?" Vera asked.

"And coming from a genetically modified transatlantic cooler embryo?"

"She was only a couple months early. We're not in the land of probability," Jane said.

"What land are we in?"

"I don't know. Magic maybe."

"Or tragedy." Eve gave Jane a hard look.

THE MAMMOTH WAS AN ANIMAL on a planet covered with animals. Vera watched a stream of fat ants spiral up a tree trunk. No one was crying at the miracle of this ant colony, though it was likely that the ground below their feet was honeycombed with tunnels and caverns. The ants were the real owners of this place. She was a human girl on a planet overcovered with humans. Too many, dangerous, not only unmiraculous but a disease. Eve and Vera stood under the canopy of oaks and watched their mother melt away. Jane was not well, was what it looked like to Vera. Delirious with fever. Vera understood how unlikely this project was and she knew it was a miracle of science and she wanted to feel pride in her mother's work, did feel pride, but she also saw that this was the moment when Jane's human daughters receded into the far distance. When they were left to fend for themselves.

"Unfortunately," Vera said, "that was the day when the mother fell in love with her new child and forgot all about the first two."

Jane went on parting the animal's fur, examining its skin, its follicles. She put her face close and breathed deeply.

"Fortunately, the girls were grown up enough to be able to care for themselves."

"Unfortunately, they were in Italy on an estate full of zebras owned by a madwoman."

"Unfortunately or *fortunately?"* Eve asked. "Did we just hit some sort of bizarre jackpot?"

Vera said, "It looks like an elephant with mange." Eve and Vera made eye contact and they started, without understanding why, to laugh. Eve's eyes watered. "Stop," she said. "God, look at her." Jane was working her way down the baby's body, inch by inch, like she was a monkey who would live off the lice she found there. There was something almost obscene about watching their mother in this state of reverie and concentration.

"I feel like I shouldn't watch," Vera said.

"Congrats, Mommy!" Eve called out. "Ace work!" To her sister: "I have to pee." Vera understood that this thing in front of her was a miracle, or a breakthrough or a conquest or whatever other words reporters would use if they were standing here, in front of an animal that had roamed the earth thousands of years before. She knew this. She had watched her mother work on the project for years. She had been here for the insemination and the mania of the two weeks since the texted birth announcement. Now that it was here it seemed instantly normal, instantly not miraculous. That's it? It was cute because baby everythings are cute but suddenly Vera was overwhelmingly sad. For the mammoth that woke up on a planet to which it did not belong, for her mother collapsing in joy over a modified elephant, for all of searching, hoping humanity, for the million failures ahead and the small wells of joy and for the question of what she could ever care about enough to fall this in love this quickly. Nothing, was her first response. There was nothing Vera cared about so much. Her heart was just a muscle, not propulsive, not hungry. A boy? A house with a driveway and a basement and central AC? A job in which she made modest contributions to good causes and dinner to cook after? She wanted a life with a shallow swing to it, a life that did not peak and decline, peak and decline.

Jane suddenly stood up, looked at the girls. "What happens to a baby elephant if the mother isn't there to take care of it? What can it eat?"

Eve asked, "What happens to a human child if the mother isn't there?"

"Formula," Jane said.

"Is there that for elephants?"

"How am I supposed to know?"

"You are the scientist? We are *teenagers*."

Jane said, "Look it up. Use your fast teenage technology thumbs and figure this out immediately." She tossed her phone because Eve's was in her backpack in the car.

Eve said, "You have a missed call from the Toddster."

Vera knew that her mom was worried by the way she moved her fingers over her own neck, like she was trying to encourage the breath to travel into her lungs.

Eve said, "Never mind that," and worked on the tiny screen. "Well, this isn't great either. Mortality rates for orphaned elephants are worse than fifty-fifty," she said.

"Yikes," Vera said.

"That is not helpful information," Jane told them. "The odds of this baby are zero, it's never happened. Don't tell me math. Figure out food or leave."

Vera said, "It's good to manage expectations."

Eve thumbed. "Here's something about a place in Africa that rescues orphaned elephants. It says two parts baby formula, one part coconut milk. For enough fat, it says."

Jane searched her pocket and threw the whole wallet over to Vera. "Hopefully we can order cases but get as much as you can right now."

"How much is enough?" Vera asked.

"Drive to every market on the lake. Buy it all."

IN THE CAR, the girls resnaked the drive, rethreaded the cypress passage, the lake on the other side of the car this time.

"We could get arrested for this," Eve said. She sounded high.

"For driving?"

"That, too. Unlicensed driving and illegal animal breeding." All manner of bad things could happen. Instead of worried, she seemed to ring with strange excitement. Eve's hand on the gearshift was tight. She took the turns fast enough that Vera had to hold on to keep from tipping.

"Maybe no one knows."

"Helen knows and has suddenly disappeared with an injured man in an ambulance followed by an elephant-catching truck. We have no real idea what she wants." Eve pulled a piece of her hair out and held it to the light. "This is crazy, Vera."

The road was half overgrown with rhododendron. The flowers looked almost human to Vera, like they had gathered to witness the comings and goings.

Eve said, "Mom could be gone by the time we get there. You hear stories about people in foreign jails."

"Those jails are in Burma, not Italy."

"It's called Myanmar now."

Vera let the idea settle over her. "Then we'd be the orphans."

Even Eve's energy went low and murky.

Science was supposed to be a safe profession. Mom in a lab with liquids, solids and gases calibrated to the tiniest measurement, every single fact noted, backed up, double-checked. Progress made at the pace of a tree, gaining inches a year. The projects could be made to sound interesting and there was the gloss of travel but the actual work seemed to Vera to be deeply, absolutely boring. Her classmates had surgeons for parents, Marines, trial attorneys, one girl who claimed her mother was a prostitute.

Vera said, "Realistically, she'll get her heart broken. The mammoth will die and Mom will be sad just like she was sad when Dad died and then she'll be okay enough to go on. You said half of orphaned babies die, and that's for actual, normal elephants, not science-experiment elephants."

"If she's gone when we get back, you must pinky-swear that we will not turn ourselves in and end up foster children. We will run away. Promise me." Eve turned quickly to Vera and put her little finger up and Vera hooked it hard.

Vera rolled her window down and it felt good to have her hair thrown against her chest and neck. Eve followed and the car was a wind tunnel and it was too loud to talk and they drove in the opposite direction from their mom and the animal that might die and might live and might change the world and might mean nothing and might destroy all their lives.

"I miss Lars," Eve said. It had been two weeks since she was caught with him, two weeks of Vera as chaperone, two weeks of Jane preparing the Iceland project for her departure for "family reasons." She had blamed her daughters and their father-grief, told the professor that they needed time with her. A vacation. In an alternate world the three of them were sitting on lounge chairs with fancy drinks reading magazines about European celebrities, consuming the sugar of gossip until they had erased themselves.

. . .

IN THE FIRST SHOP Vera found only a few dusty bottles of formula and no coconut milk and Eve bought bread to eat while they drove on. In the next shop there was a whole case of formula but still no coconut milk and they got a piece of Parmesan cheese, rough and crumbly. They bought up all the formula everyone had. All the shopkeepers smiled new-baby smiles and Vera said, "For our sister," which was almost true, and the shopkeepers said, "*Bella bambina*," and took the money.

After two hours they found a large market, fluorescent-lit aisles of cheese, a hundred kinds of jarred tomatoes, pasta in the shape of a tied knot, a boat and a shelf full of coconut milk. Eve put all the jars in their cart and had no explanation for the old women who eyed them, found a worker and said, "*Molto?*" pointing at the cans and it took some more gestures but eventually the man went to the back and returned with a cardboard box with Thai writing on the outside.

"*Allora*," he said, and carried it to the register.

"*Tuti?*" Eve asked, and he brought out three more boxes. Eve picked out a chocolate bar with hazelnut cream in its center and Vera chose a bag of soft gummy fruit candies coated with crystal sugar. "Big Frut," she said, rolling the *r*. Vera complimented her sister's effective use of single-word Italian sentences. "We got it done, right? I feel good. We are VIPs in this fucked-up mission." Eve said, "I'll meet you in the car. I need to do one quick thing."

"Okay?"

Leaning against the car, Vera closed her eyes. All the movement of the last two days still hummed in her body and she felt spun around, as if she had been blindfolded and twisted for pin-the-tail. On the plane Jane had looked out her window and said, "I think that's Brussels.

Your dad would have known. You could put him over the nighttime lights of any city and he would recognize it." Vera had wondered whether she would still have been familiar to her dad this same way, or if she had changed enough in the last three years that Sal would have found her strange or hard to see.

Vera imagined the world from above. A body with its veins lit, carrying life to the dark edge.

"Are you asleep?" Eve asked, appearing beside the car.

"What did you get?"

"Girl stuff."

"I have lots," Vera said. "You should have asked."

They wound and twisted the lake road onward, the castle once again in front of them instead of behind, the car full of the milks that might save the baby. Their mother texted, wondering if they had found anything yet, when they would be home. Are you close? she kept asking. They had the car and the milk. No one was more powerful than they were.

"For our sister," Eve joked, and they laughed hard, their hands coated in sugar, their mouths sticky.

THE GIRLS FOUND THEIR MOTHER statue-still and staring at the animal. It was a moment of sudden and extreme quiet. The noise of their drive, of finding milks and laughing and eating candy and having the keys faded into a buzzing emptiness.

"Mom?" Vera said. "We're here."

Jane turned to them and her eyes were sheets, wiped of recognition. "I don't know what I'm doing," she said.

Vera went closer, put a hand on Jane's shoulder blade. "We found the milks." Jane let her head fall toward her chest with relief. She said, "In the history of daughters . . ."

Instead of finishing the compliment, Jane took out her phone and whispered a text to Helen as she wrote it, Do you have a bottle to feed her?

She waited for the little dots of progressive typing to appear.

Vera told her family, "We need to be strategic. Mom can stay with the mammoth. Me and Eve will go look for a bottle. This is a zoo, they have to have bottle-fed some animal at some point."

"Hey, Jane?" Eve said, as they walked away.

"Why are you not calling me 'Mom'?"

"Congratulations. You did it," Eve said. She sounded truly proud, in spite of herself.

Jane looked newborn herself. Wonder and terror, everything to come. "I'm scared," she said, "and I'm glad you're back." The statement was a raft they might be able to float on.

Eve and Vera passed the sleeping bear. Life, the ever twistier road. Their mom had suggested the shed where George had stored the insemination supplies but they did not know where that was.

They made a running loop around the property. Took the path toward the lake, jogged through a rose garden. The girls stood in the sun and looked around. "Okay, Zebra," Vera said, pointing at an animal browsing in a patch of grass.

"Just another African animal next to a castle," Eve said. "The usual."

But when the neck of a giraffe peeked out through a pair of cypress trees, Vera's head went fizzy.

"Oh, wow. Hi. Hello," Eve said.

Do not be afraid of a herbivore, Vera thought to herself. But she no longer wanted to go forward, only in reverse, only away from this impossibly tall animal that was staring at her, its mouth full of leaves and a question in its eyes. Vera ran, taking a turn toward the castle.

"Where are you going?" Eve called, and ran after when Vera did not answer or stop.

Through a tunnel of olive trees, wildflowers, Vera ran until she was looking at a small stone building, then inside. She left the door open a crack until Eve ran through and then slammed it behind them. "Top of the food chain, ha," Vera said to the cold room.

"What just happened to you?" Eve asked.

"Giraffe," Vera said. She could not explain. They had been to Africa, seen the savannahs full of grazers, seen lions and buffalo and crocodiles. It was the mismatch of European castle or the high-wire moment or both.

"I thought you'd seen a body," Eve said.

"I freaked. I'm sorry."

"That's okay. I think you might have freaked right into the storage shed." Eve put her up hand and Vera gave it a low-gusto high five.

It was dark but for the cracks in between planks in the wood door, cracks that spit light like tiny darts filed with dust. Vera took deliberate, slowing breaths. There was what looked like old-fashioned farm equipment on one side—rusted shovels, a scythe, a wooden cart and a giant barrel. On the other side was a stainless-steel shelf with plastic bins, carefully labeled. Suture Kit, Animal Mover, Birth Kit, Fecalizer, Syringes, Floor Scale, Head Cones, Plaster, Scissors and Tape, Funnel IV, Surgical Instruments, Antiparasitic Shampoo, Warming Blanket, Otoscope, Dental Care, Hypodermic Needles. On the top right, Bottles and Nipples. They were joyous to see this thing neither of them had ever thought about until today. The box was dusty, out of use, but it had been carefully packed and when Eve popped the lid off the space filled with the smell of heated plastic. There were many bottles and many nipples and many lids, all of different sizes, and the four hands set to work matching.

As they popped nipples into lids and screwed lids on bottles, Vera imagined the shed ringed with wild beasts, closing in.

THE GIRLS JOGGED BACK past the bear den, into the oak grove and toward the mammoth pen. "Hey, dude," Eve said. "We have milks and we have bottles. Let's feed this baby."

Jane fell on the bottles like a starving dog. "What took you so long?"

"Was it that long?" Vera asked.

"I was worried," Jane said.

"We're heartless teenagers, Mom," Eve said. "We can't help it."

Vera asked if feeding help was needed and Jane said, "I've fed milk to babies. That is the single thing in this entire scenario with which I have years of experience."

Eve said, "But you aren't going to breast-feed the mammoth calf."

"I didn't breast-feed you either."

"What? How did I not know this? Is that why we always get every cold?"

Jane pulled the tab on a coconut milk can and opened it. The cream inside was thick and bright white. She poured the can into a bottle. "Did the thing say half and half?" she asked.

"Two to one, baby formula," Eve said.

Vera wanted to suggest that someone consult another source, that maybe the one website Eve had stumbled onto might not be enough information for the precious animal they were now responsible for feeding, but Jane spoke up first. "I hated being a milk machine. You wanted me constantly and then when you weren't nursing I was supposed to pump to build up supply to buy myself time and the pump was loud and pinchy and I couldn't get the milk to let down and after a few days I drowned it in the bathtub and told your father it had been an accident and he was sort of scared of me so I quit breast feeding and that was that." She looked first at Vera, then Eve, and poured. "I am a heartless mother. I can't help it." She held the bottle to the sun to see if it was mixed.

"I respect that," Eve said. "I do."

Vera had always pictured herself as a baby slung across her mother's lap, ear to chest, a stream of milk connecting them. She thought she had seen a photo of this scene, even.

Jane screwed the top of the bottle, shook hard and then knelt beside the baby and said, "Mama's here, milkie is here." And milk dribbled out of the bottle and the mammoth turned away.

They all watched in silence. Jane petted the baby's cheek. "Good girl," she said. "Good, good girl. This is your food for now." There was the faint smell of a tropical drink. Jane held the bottle at just the right angle to allow for easy transfer, but the baby was not fooled. "We're going to make it. We're going to be all right."

"Uh-oh?" Eve said.

"There are too many people. You need to go away," Jane told them. "Go find us a place to sleep tonight."

"In the castle?" Eve asked.

Vera did not like this idea. "What if there's a monster chained in the basement? There is always a monster at the abandoned castle."

Jane did not answer. She held the bottle at an angle, a bead of milk on the tip, and she started to sing a lullaby about a train.

"It'll be a dragon," Eve corrected.

. . .

VERA AND EVE WALKED the stone path between topiaries. Vera said, "Will the baby starve?"

"Mom will figure it out. Apparently she's highly experienced with bottle feeding."

At the big door, Vera knocked softly. "Hello?" she said. "Hello?" Eve took the giant brass ring in her hand and banged it loudly.

They could hear the clap echo in the stones.

Eve put her hand on the knob and tried to turn it. "Locked," she said.

Back down the path and around the castle. A fish pond, a stone alcove with a crumbling Madonna inside, a fountain and flowers pouring over every surface. It was loveliness cultivated over hundreds of years for the express pleasure of human eyes. Around each corner was new beauty.

They came around to the front of the castle, and everything opened up to a huge expanse of grass and water, cypress trees trimmed into spires as a frame and two zebras grazing. The lake was deep green and the sky electric. Vera felt her eyes drink.

There was a courtyard and a door so huge it seemed more like a wall and this, too, was locked. "We could try windows," Eve said.

"I'm not breaking into someone's castle."

"We could try that museum thing with the mammoth skeleton?"

"We're not sleeping in there," Vera said. "It's full of dead stuff."

"I wonder if the baby is eating."

"I want to go to sleep," Vera said. They had flown from the North Sea. She wanted a flat surface and a pillow.

On the next stretch of path, Eve and Vera saw a small structure they hadn't noticed before. It was on the other side of the castle, tucked into the trees like a fairy tale cottage. It was stone with a stone walkway overgrown with daylilies. It had a patio with a grape arbor for shade.

Eve said, "And the two girls saw a cottage in the wood and they were so tired that it seemed like a fine place for a rest, only they did not realize that the house belonged to a witch who was, at this moment, watching them from her perch behind a sycamore tree."

"Ha." But Eve did not stop walking or turn away. Down the path she went and when she got to the door she called, "Mrs. Witch? Are you within?" but the house was quiet. The door opened before she had even turned the knob all the way. As if the house had been waiting.

"What can you see?" Vera yelled from the path.

"It's cute. There's a little kitchen. It looks like no one has been here for a while. No witches in sight."

Vera walked slowly forward, waiting to be snatched.

Inside was a small kitchen with a table and four chairs. There were copper pans hanging on a rack, an espresso pot on the stove and an old refrigerator. There were two bedrooms and a bathroom.

"What if someone lives here?" Vera asked.

"Then we'll leave when that someone comes home."

The bureau drawers were empty but the cupboards were stocked, everything in glass jars. Eve said, "I claim this witch hut in the name of us."

Eve texted Jane a photo of the room and a sleeping yellow head emoji.

And with that Vera and Eve each climbed into one of the small beds and pulled the white blankets up and let their eyes close. Vera did not dream about being eaten or being captured or being stirred in a cauldron. She did not dream about anything at all. It was bright white sleep, the kind so pure that the sleeper awakens as if reborn.

"WHAT ARE WE even doing here?" Eve said.

"I need cake."

"I want coffee."

They found coffee in the cupboard along with flour, sugar, salt, and in the fridge, butter and eggs, as if someone had known that baking settled Vera, that some days she made two cakes the way another person took two pills.

"Are there ingredients? That seems highly suspicious."

"Thank you, Madame Witch, for stocking the pantry," Vera said to the room. A poisoned apple would have been too predictable. But Vera needed the batter, the stir, the chemistry. It was worth the risk. She dragged the ingredients outside because the house was dark and made her sleepy. The flour on her hands was soft and clouded the air. She mashed butter, sugar. She did not need to look up a recipe. This was the one thing she knew by heart and even though it was not an especially amazing cake she liked it because it always came out exactly the same way. Vera understood how the batter should look at each stage and did not need to set a timer. The smell would tell her when it was done.

Eve said, "I miss Iceland. I miss Lars." Here, the sound was wind and water, monkeys, parrots. This was an exact kind of loneliness, Vera thought, beauty and miracle all around and her sister a silent gray dot in the center.

"Call him," Vera said. "I don't mind."

Lars picked up on the first ring and Eve put it on speaker. They could hear the teapot still whistling where Lars was. "Vera's here, too,"

Eve said. "Hi, little sister," Lars said, and Vera waved to the phone. Lars described the fjord, how ragged it was out his window. He took a photo of the rain pelting his window and texted it. He took a photo of the fat neighbor in his scrapyard, standing high on a pile of old car parts, his hand over his eyes like he was some kind of explorer, overseeing a vast landscape. Lars ate dark bread with smoked salmon and butter and chewed into the phone. Vera imagined him watching the water for whales.

He said, "Tell me what it's like to be warm."

Eve had to admit that it was good to be warm. The sisters walked outside. The lake registered not as water but as sunlight reflected back. There were succulents everywhere, like mouths around them. They were green, purple, pink. Eve tried to describe the color of the lake to Lars. "It makes your eyes hurt," she said. "It makes you want to throw yourself in no matter how high up you are."

Lars grunted on the other end of the line. "Oh? I'm used to water you stay out of no matter what."

Vera pictured herself running across the estate to a cliff, then mid-swan-dive, arms out, soon to break the shimmering green surface. She could feel her feet vibrating with the jump, willing.

Vera's timer dinged. Eve told Lars she wished he was with her. Lars said, "Soak in the sun for me." Vera went inside where the room was filled with butter-scent, lemon-scent, then a wash of heat from the open oven.

VERA HEARD JANE CALLING, searching for them. She ran outside and down the path until she saw her mother. "Mom. Hi. We're here. Will you please come and see our witch hut? How's the baby?"

Jane looked high, almost. Her eyes darted, her hands did not stay still. "Incredible," she said. "Magical. But she's still not eating."

"You don't even like animals," Vera said. "Maybe you should have let us get a cat."

"I don't like her because she's an animal. She's a time traveler. Technically, she doesn't exist, can't exist. She's a myth, and here she is."

They went inside and the cool of the stone house slowed them down. Vera got her mother a glass of water and Jane took it, grateful.

"But she's not eating?" Vera asked.

Eve said, "I don't understand why a hungry animal wouldn't eat."

Jane was manic. "She's in shock. I want to examine her skin cells under a microscope," she said.

"Do we have such a thing?" Vera asked.

"I didn't see one in the shed. I've ordered it."

Vera imagined the list of things requiring examination: individual pieces of fur, the water from the mammoth's eyes, the fibers of her teeth, the jewel of tusk, her toenails. "Do you know what you're looking for?" Vera asked.

"I took biology and sat in on a zoonotic-disease course. I am the scientist here the way a podiatrist on an airplane would have to be the one to help the man having a heart attack. My plan is to cover every base, observe every detail and make perfect notes."

"To show to . . . ?"

"To save forever in secret in a vault."

Jane ate directly from the piece of Parmesan the girls had bought earlier. She drank two more glasses of water without breathing.

"What do you think of the house? Is it a good idea to stay here?" Vera asked.

The cake was cooling on a plate and Vera swatted flies off.

"Oh, Ver, did you make her a birthday cake?"

"Who?"

"You are adorable. That's a good idea, to have a party for Pearl to officially welcome her to the family. Thank you for always knowing what to do, kiddo."

Jane snicked Vera on the chin, a little flick. No kiss, and she was gone down the path to her miracle baby.

"Stupid cake," Vera said to the cake. She let the flies land. Who cared if they laid eggs.

THINGS WERE ADDED TO Jane's camp in the mammoth pen. She rooted in her suitcase and the shed and brought calipers and nail trimmers and headphones and a stethoscope and three pillows, extra batteries, a bigger rubber ball for Pearl to play with, the good camera. The family gathered blankets and pillows and hauled them to the pen for Jane to make a nest. Vera spread a sheet out on the ground, then pillows for a mattress, then a blanket. She tucked and folded to make it look like a real bed.

Jane offered a bottle and the baby turned away. Pearl swished flies off with her brush of a tail. She tried to trunk something into her mouth but missed. She took a step and there was the soft sound of her weight on the earth. When it got dark she grunted and wailed. It was the sound of being lost and it echoed off the stone castle. "Hush," Jane said. With bottle in hand, she sang a song about a hobo, a song about a star, a song about heaven. These were known songs, the ones sung to human children in corners of the world that felt very distant and in a voice that felt yet more so. A dad voice. Vera had not heard these songs in years, would not have known their names, and yet the words and melodies rose from inside her very center. Using a stick to draw in the dirt, Eve made a picture of a house. The baby was quieter until Jane stopped singing. "Those are Dad's songs," Eve said.

Jane said, "Dad was the one with the songs."

The creature started to cry again and she scuffed at the ground.

The sounds the mammoth made were watery, like she was a siren trying to draw them under and drown them. It was the opposite—a land animal on a changed planet. Vera wondered if Pearl's was a body hungry for grassland, for herd. There was no such thing as a house, as a street, as a human, when a body like hers last roamed. Or she simply wanted her actual mother, the body that made her, the body that should have fed her.

Jane said, "She'll eat when she's too hungry not to."

THAT NIGHT VERA DREAMED of being trapped, of being chased, of an elephant mother without her baby. She woke early, waited for Eve. Teenage chemicals made long sleeps possible for Eve, but Vera, still child-wired, was lonely and bored. She read the books she had brought for the third time. She looked at her sister's long hair on the pillow. She thought about wrapping herself in it.

She tried to place herself on the map of her life. We are in Italy with a baby animal. That's all it is. We can do this. The baby did not seem mythical or stolen from another time. She did not seem prehistoric. She was a little elephant, cute, scraggy.

Vera rummaged and found a tray and supplies for breakfast—coffee and a piece of bread, a folded napkin. She found her mother lying in the dirt beneath a standing Pearl, examining the baby's belly. Jane's hair had come loose from her ponytail and she seemed to struggle to get her daughter into focus.

"Come look at this marking," Jane said.

"I have breakfast. Has she eaten? Do you need to sleep? I can stay."

"What? No, I'm not leaving. She almost took the bottle. Almost."

Jane, Vera found, had written ten pages of notes in her notebook about the behaviors of the mammoth during the night (weeping eyes, brittle hair, incomplete molar, six-inch tail, moaning). She had taken urine samples, labeled in small jars. Many cases of coconut milk and formula were on their way but the small supply the girls had gathered was undiminished.

Jane told Vera everything she had discovered—skull measurements, hair composition, tail strength, structure of spine. She walked her through the notes on her pages and more she needed to remember to write down. She could not talk quickly enough. "I can't tell if this is a birthmark or a sore."

"Have you heard from Helen?" Vera asked, trying not to sound too concerned. There were other animals on the property who presumably needed care and maybe George's leg was worse than it had seemed and maybe Helen was at this moment giving a statement to the police who would come with handcuffs. It was easy to let the mind spin downward.

"Radio silence," Jane told her.

"Are *you* worried?"

"I have a baby that needs me. We have no control. We won't leave her and there's nowhere else to go. We'll do our best with what we have." Jane had come down from her high yesterday and fallen into a valley of resolve.

Vera watched Jane move across the animal with her hands, her eyes, her tools, the bottle tipped, as if Pearl were the sea and Jane were a tiny boat, sailing the distance. The baby played with a ball, tried to capture it in her trunk and the two women laughed.

"How can Eve still be sleeping?" Vera whined.

"You'll sleep like that, too," Jane said. "It's hard to be the younger sister."

The mammoth swished her tail. Breeze rustled her hair and her lashes. She took a step and dust whooshed. She turned to look at the people and then snuffed in the dirt.

"Her eyes are cartoon eyes," Vera said.

"She has old-person creases in her forehead," Jane said. "Like she's already been around forever."

Eve, finally, came down the path with a plate in her hand.

"The princess awakens," Jane said.

"I deserved that sleep," Eve told her. "Plus I brought cheese so you can't be mad at me."

The humans put cheese on bread and cheese on cheese. "Salt tastes so good right now," Jane said. She looked like she had been emptied out.

"Any word from your zookeeper?" Eve asked. "Is the mister still laid up with elephant wounds?"

The whole thing reminded Vera of a children's book about idiot adults.

"Nope," Jane said.

"I hope the elephant is going to be all right?"

"I have no idea," Jane said.

This other mother, fresh from birth, far from her baby, milk leaking from her body, made Vera helplessly sad. "Please tell me if you hear anything. I think I dreamed about her last night."

"What was the dream?" Jane asked.

"She was standing in the lake and we were trying to coax her out but she kept going deeper. We were supposed to be at a party and we were all dressed up."

Eve spread a thick wedge of soft cheese on her bread. She watched Pearl watch her. "She does look mammothy," Eve said. "Not a hundred percent but it's pretty crazy that we're lunching with a prehistoric animal. Way to be, Mom."

Jane bright-light-glowed at her daughter. Pride beat hot off her skin.

After they had eaten, Jane said, "I realize this is a little sentimental but I would like it if Vera could go get the cake and we could sing to Pearl."

"Oh?" Eve said.

"And please do it without making me feel stupid," she said. So it was that the three of them stood in a semicircle around the baby mammoth and, following Jane's lead, sang "Happy Birthday" over a day-old yellow cake, the same off-key song they had sung over the same cake for one another at every turn around the sun.

The sky was dark with a coming storm but still blue at the edges and other animals called out from other parts of the property. Pearl looked at the three people, their voices joined. The music stilled her searching trunk and swishing tail. There was no candle but they all made a wish. They ate the cake and it was the same as every other time Vera had baked it this year. It tasted like Vera trying to be okay. Everyone in the family knew this taste.

"She is so *smart*," Jane said, looking at the baby.

"Were we smart?" Vera asked.

"You're smart now. You slept all the time as babies and it's crazy that it takes humans a *year* to learn to walk." In front of them, Pearl scratched an itch on her head with her trunk.

They could hear small trouble in the aviary. The light was brittle. Eve pinched her sister's arm and Vera knew she meant, *Hello strange life.*

"Will you come back up to the house with us? Maybe take a shower?" Eve asked Jane. "Or we can stay with her while you go?"

"Of course not. Bring me a pot of hot water and I'll bathe down here."

THE GIRLS HEADED BACK to their mother with hot water, a washcloth, soap and towel, a small bottle of face cream. Vera said, *"Fortunately,* the two daughters were there to bring a sponge bath to their mother in the mammoth pen," and Eve told her, "That is definitely an *unfortunately."*

As they got closer they saw the mammoth standing and then they saw Jane, lying down beneath her. Vera imagined George's leg. Imagined Jane crushed. Imagined insides spilled. She ran. Eve, too, feet and dust and fear. Water spilled out of the pot.

Jane rolled over and then sat up. She covered her eyes against the sun.

"Mom," Vera said, heart hammering.

"We thought you were dead," Eve yelled.

"I hadn't considered sadness. How it would feel to be the only one," Jane said.

For a moment Vera thought Jane was talking about the three of them. A family of lonelies.

Eve put her face next to her mother's face and seethed. "Did you hear me? We were scared."

Vera set the pot and supplies down and sat in the dirt. She tried to still her breath and body. Quietly, she said, "Because you are a scientist. How things feel is not supposed to be part of your job."

"I'm also a mom and a person. Do you think I don't care about feelings? I need to get a different kind of cream for her skin and something for her eyes. We have to get her to drink. I wish we had a vet."

Eve said, "Are you still our mom? Or just hers?"

"Nothing was wrong with me. A person is allowed to lie down. It's Pearl we need to worry about."

"Well," Eve said, "we can't call a vet. We absolutely cannot call anyone. We have illegally bred a prehistoric animal and are squatting on a giant estate."

Vera zipped her lips. She was all question, no answer.

Pearl threw grass, rubbed her face with her trunk, let out a single wail like a bow across strings.

"She's the most important animal on the planet," Jane said.

The rims of Pearl's eyes were red and she rubbed her back against the fence posts. Jane told Vera to look things up on the internet. *How to feed an orphaned elephant, elephant rubbing on fence, baby elephant sluggish, baby elephant seems sad,* but Vera mostly got pictures of elephants doing circus tricks or safari blogs. Jane used what should have been her own bathwater to press warm washcloths on Pearl's eyes. There was a sound in the animal's throat, a whispering whine—gratitude or helplessness. Jane was on her knees and bent forward and leaned her head on the trunk of this creature before her.

Jane reached down and picked up a handful of dirt, threw it in the air and closed her eyes against the rain.

At this moment, Jane's phone came alive in a singsong ring. She took it out of her back pocket and said, "Again."

"Who?" Vera said, and Jane held the screen out so that they could see the words The Professor.

"What is he calling for?" Eve asked and Jane put her hands in the air in surrender.

It was strange to have a male presence join them, even if he was just a name on the screen.

What if their dad had been here? Maybe he would have sat quietly with a tableful of data and a chapter to write while his wife suffered over the baby. Pearl was watching them. Her big black eyes, the sky reflected in them. She looked weak. Hungry.

Vera wiped her eyes on her sleeve. She tipped her head to the oak leaf and sky above and let it print a shape on her vision.

Eve told Jane, "Here's what we're going to do. You are going to call the professor back because not answering over and over is the absolute most suspicious thing you can do. Chat with him. Tell him how super-much fun we're having at the beach and how you are so looking forward to getting back to work in a couple of weeks. Buy time. That's all you have to do right now." She pointed to the phone. "Do it now," and Jane, shoulders sloped, walked out of the pen and into the oaks to tell a story about heartsick daughters who required rescue from their mother.

The girls watched her talk, watched her roll a green leaf in her fingers. She came back and said, "He's angry. I'm unprofessional." She mimicked his deep voice, "I've given you every opportunity, Jane, but I can see you have different priorities."

"Did you tell him we are little monsters?"

"Basically."

"Good," said Vera and Eve at the same time.

Jane nodded and reached her hands out, leading her two daughters close to the animal. "I really think these are sores. Will you come look?"

RAMONA AUSUBEL

and the three of them sat on the ground and Jane curtained the hair and Vera bent down and she could smell the dirt and animal and the skin was red and prickled and had small cracks. She shined a bright light into the animal's eyes, which were slightly milky. Had they been milky before?

Vera said, "Can I try the bottle?" Jane mixed a fresh batch of milk and Vera brought the nipple close to the animal's pink mouth. Her bottom lip drooped open. Vera said, "Little little little sip. That's all." She touched the spot where milk leaked out and then put her fingers on Pearl's lip, which was warm and wet and the creature turned to Vera and seemed so sorry, so unsure. Pearl did not turn away but neither did she drink.

"Hey, you," Jane said. "Hey, little one." She shushed, she cooed. "You're a sweet thing, a sweet big thing." Pearl whinnied like a pony. She reached her trunk around to Jane's cheek, begging with it. Jane soothed, told Pearl that she was loved. As much as Jane tried to console, Vera thought that the baby wanted the body from which she emerged the way Vera wanted Jane to love her, her plain human self.

After Pearl's eyes had been washed, Jane lay down in the dirt. She said, "I'm so sleepy."

"Take a nap," Vera said.

"We might not save you any salami, though," Eve added.

"I'm just going to close my eyes for a few minutes."

The girls sliced and ate, salt and fat on their tongues. Pearl wandered, whined at the fence line, foot pads on the dirt, trunk snuffing, tail swatting, a meager puddle of pee, called for her mother, for her own geologic era, or maybe she was only hungry and complaining the way any living being would. She shushed the ground with her trunk, swept the dirt back and forth. Want and want and want.

They stayed like that for a long time, the children watching, the mother sleeping, the animal searching. The wind changed. It grew warmer. Pearl breathed and the dust gusted. Pearl walked to a pile of hay, grabbed it in big batches and threw it onto her back as if she were trying to disguise herself. She stared at Vera the whole time as if to say, *There is no miracle here, only a small green hill. Only landscape.*

After a long wait, silent and still, Vera walked slowly toward the animal, palm open, bottle in the other hand behind her back and said, "I know you did not ask to be born, but none of us do."

Pearl looked right at her. Two huge, pooling eyes. She moved her trunk over Vera's face, smelling, searching. Her breath was hot and grassy. Her nostrils wet. Vera let her feel around.

"I'm sure you miss your mom," Vera said.

"We understand that feeling," Eve said. Vera hadn't known that her sister had been listening.

Vera slowly brought the bottle close to that soft lip and Pearl did not shake it away. She closed her mouth over the nipple and let it sit there, dripping slowly. Vera hardly breathed, waiting for the baby mammoth to suck. The mammoth swallowed once and tiny fireworks burst in Vera.

Like an apparition, someone appeared on the path. A woman. Vera gasped out loud. Eve screamed, "Jane! Mom!" Their salvation or their demise. Jane sat up, leaves in her hair, eyes squinting against even the dim oak light.

The woman came closer. She held a picnic basket. Her hair looked done and she had on khaki pants and a trench coat.

Jane jumped up and brushed herself off, tried to look in control.

Helen waved grandly, laughing. "Greetings!" she called, as if this were all part of a lovely summer holiday.

Jane let herself out of the pen, jogged to meet the woman, arms out.

"How is the babe?" Helen called out.

Jane shook her head. "She's not eating."

Vera whispered, "She was maybe about to."

Helen set the basket down in the shade and unlatched the gate. To the girls she said, "Ladies," and gave a nod. Her hair was backlit and full of blow-dried air, like a separate organism.

Vera wanted to clear the pen. She wanted to shut them all up and let the animal try again to eat. She wanted an apology though she was not sure if they deserved one. It was Helen's husband who had been maimed.

"How is George?" Jane asked, pouring concern into her voice.

"He's a big baby. He'll be fine." Helen approached the mammoth, knelt, lifted fur to examine the skin beneath.

"How is the mother? Will she come back?"

"She was very weak after the birth and though she nursed her at first she stopped. She rejected her. Sometimes mothers who reject their babies hurt or kill them. We called a friend from the Milan zoo, who agreed to take the elephant, at least until she recovers. It was in the loading process that she stepped on George."

"Mother elephants hurt their babies?" Vera asked.

"Occasionally in stressful situations, especially in captivity. This happens in many species."

Vera pressed the heels of her hands on her eyes.

Helen said, "I'm sorry we weren't here to give you a proper welcome. What terrible hospitality."

"We didn't know if the other animals needed to be fed," Vera said. "And we set up in the stone cottage up there. Is that all right? We didn't know where to go." They had been here a day and there was already so much to explain.

"That's all fine. In the wild, animals go much longer than a day." Helen parted Pearl's fur and looked at the sores.

"They're getting bigger," Jane said. "Can we get milk from the mother? Is pumping a thing for elephants?"

Jane and Vera found each other's eyes and even if they could have spoken there would have been no good thing to say. They were in this.

"Oh, no," Helen said, laughing.

Helen had been the kind of distant, interesting friend a person talks about at parties but never sees. Now they were bound together. She was less warm than Vera remembered, less like a kind aunt. Helen inched over Pearl's body, pausing at the rashes. When she came to the eyes she pulled the lids down and the mammoth bucked. "It hurts, doesn't it?" Helen said. "We need some antibiotic cream and eyedrops. It would also be good to use a comfrey salve in between to protect against irritation. It should heal up fine. Her pulse is fast, but babies always have higher pulse rates. I'll warm up the milk and see if she likes that better." Helen let herself out the gate. "There's food for you in the basket," she said. "Please take a shower and change your clothes and try to get ahold of yourselves. You three do not look well."

Six

In the house, clean for the first time in days, Vera was Swiss buttercreaming. She hadn't made a cake because she wasn't in the mood for baking, only for whipping. The egg whites turned glossy and thick and Vera stared into the bowl, watching the whisk move, feeling her wrist make it do so. On her laptop screen was an email from the climate group about a day of action later in the summer in which students would show up at San Francisco City Hall to demand emissions caps. To get anyone to actually pay attention, they planned to be shirtless with signs that read PUT A TOP ON GLOBAL EMISSIONS. In the thread, one girl suggested that it be open to women only, so that boys didn't show up just to stare at a bunch of boobs. Another said, *We're using our bodies for the planet. It's fine with me if everyone stares.* Vera admired the willingness to risk something personal yet she was more than a little glad that she had the handy excuse of being on the far side of the globe. She licked the frosting spoon, cold and generous in its sweetness. Other kids were vegan for environmental reasons but Vera was sure that she would take her shirt off in public before she gave up butter.

Her feet were chilly and she went for socks, found her suitcase empty and decided to borrow some from Eve. Vera called out, "Evie! I'm borrowing socks!" They had been raised with the rule that you never took something that wasn't yours without asking. Except, apparently, modified embryos, Vera thought.

In the suitcase Vera found socks and she also found a thin plastic stick. A small window in which there were two blue lines. On the back was the code: one line, not pregnant; two lines, pregnant.

"Holy," Vera whispered.

She dropped it on the floor like it was a condition she could catch.

Instantly, her feet and fingers itched. She felt bitten. She ached. Vera was there the day Eve injected herself with ancient genetic material, picked Eve up at Lars's seaside cottage in the middle of the night, but she was not a partner in this. She stepped on the test and tried to crush it, but it was sturdy.

Eve came to the doorway. Her eyes were rimmed in pink. She said, "Shit, right?"

Vera found bowls and spoons, served them frosting like it was yogurt and they devoured it.

"Take me somewhere," Eve said.

"I can't drive."

"Then be my partner in crime."

Vera shook her head. "No more crimes."

"Fine. Bread, then."

. . .

THE GIRLS DID NOT ASK permission and drove themselves to town. They walked the lake's edge in brittle silence behind a couple holding hands and a child carrying a grasshopper in a jar. Ducks nicked at each other's wings, a swan drifted. Alleys wound up from the lake, steep with stone steps, cats and geraniums and cushions for ice cream lickers to rest upon. Italy seemed made up, an overperfect backdrop for their impossibly strange reality. Vera kept having the thought I could be an aunt, and it never made sense.

Eve said, "I bought the pregnancy test on the baby formula hunt. I thought it was more a private joke than a real possibility." She said that the box had instructed her to use the test the first thing in the morning so she had tried not to think about it as Jane had worked to get the mammoth to eat, as she and Vera had hunted the property for a place to stay. "Last night I started a college application essay in my head. *What being pregnant with a Neanderthal taught me about myself.*"

Vera didn't want to joke. She wanted to be afraid out loud.

"It would be about a girl whose parents were scientists and had dragged her around the world while doing obscure research. In the ultimate twist, the girl became the experiment. I'd describe the iceman, whose leathered face I know well because he is a proxy for my dead father." Eve put her hands out in typing position and fingered a pretend keyboard: "*Now he's my baby-daddy.*"

Vera said, "Can we be serious?"

"It seems like a trick math problem: which is more likely to cause a pregnancy—(a) the frozen sperm of a five-thousand-year-old man, injected while drunk and enraged on the floor of a bathroom, or (b) a properly used barrier method in a loving encounter with a pure Viking descendant?"

Vera said, "C. Neither."

"Neither is very fucking likely, and yet, that does not appear to be the correct answer."

Vera thought of Lars, his fine and sturdy form. She did not know if this counted as love. "Do you picture living in the cottage with Lars forever?"

"I do not," Eve said.

"Then, what?" Vera asked.

"If I were in California I would make an appointment, take the bus, buy myself a burrito and watch television after whatever had taken up residence had been sucked out. I think that's how it works."

"And here?"

"There's no way to accomplish the whole procedure alone."

Vera would do whatever she needed. Vera was dedicated and available, always, for whatever Eve asked. She said, "You're not alone."

"Why did I have to be the idiot whose rebellion resulted in this tragic absurdity." Eve dug her fists into her belly as if she could extract whatever was in there. She looked like something had its teeth around her throat.

Eve and Vera sat on a wall looking out over the lake and Eve pressed Lars's name on her phone. She put it on speaker but this time did not announce to the voice on other end that Vera was listening. "Hey," he said. "I just woke up. Are you good?"

Eve said, "Sorry, I forgot about the time difference. Hold on, I'm texting you something."

It was a picture she had taken earlier of the pregnancy test, two lines instead of one, two lives instead of one in Eve's body.

They listened to the emptiness on the phone. Eve's mouth was closed tight. Vera could see that she would make Lars be the voice of this situation. She did not tell him about the vial in the hotel room. She waited and listened. Vera almost spoke, just to crack the silence.

"Okay," Lars said. "Okay."

Vera watched the lake spread out over the rocky beach below. A ferry cut a white track across, everyone in sun hats on this good day.

"I care about you," he finally said. "What is there to do?"

"Let's see. I'm seventeen. You are twenty-three. You live in a seasick shack on a cold dark island in the middle of the ocean. I am indisposed in Italy and will eventually return to high school in California." Vera noticed that Eve's voice was not warm. Three days and a few thousand miles seemed to have changed the temperature of her feelings toward him. But what was the other choice? She imagined Eve bringing Lars to college, leaving him and the baby with a hundred bottles of milk while she went to a class on poetry. She imagined parties while the baby—her niece or nephew, Vera thought again—slept in a cardboard box beside a twin bed.

That was if they could ever leave this fairy tale with the conjured beast that surely could not travel, a secret they both had to keep.

"I don't want this," Eve said. "This does not belong to me."

They could hear Lars flick the lighter to turn the burner on. Vera could picture the kettle he placed there and the cup he would retrieve for more coffee.

"That's a relief," he said.

"I can't imagine that a Roman Catholic country is the easiest place to end a pregnancy. Fuck." Eve did not cry on the phone, but she cried after. She tucked her face into Vera's neck and soaked her. She threw rocks into the water as hard as she could. "I keep picturing rolling myself down over stones, not to die, but to knock out what is residing in me."

Eve said, "If you were not my sister I might evaporate. I have no friends, the first boy I loved turns out to be a shit. It feels like you are the only thing that keeps me tethered to this dumb earth."

Vera kept herself from grinning. She was Eve's most important person again. It wasn't that she wanted her sister to hurt, but this struggle had clasped them back together. It was almost worth it, she thought with shame.

Vera looked around, feeling watched. An old woman on a balcony had her eyes set on them. As if she could see the mutant twist of cells deep inside, as if she knew that Eve would lead a long, tortured life, caring for a child that had no place in the world. Or else she would end the pregnancy, end a life, and the woman in the window would pray for her even as Eve burned for all of time in the cinders of the underworld. And Vera, the sister who selfishly rejoiced in the tragedy.

The woman in the window watched. She swatted at something. She leaned her head back and spit, hard, off the balcony. The spit was sunlit and spun into a long, twisting shape, landed right at Vera's feet. They looked up to see if the woman was sorry or happy, to see if they were the intended mark, but the woman was gone. All that was left was a spit-star on the polished stones, three pigeons already showing an interest.

LATE AFTERNOON and Jane and Helen were examining the bottom of Pearl's back feet while Eve and Vera sat on a blanket and made piles of small stones. Helen said, "She'll need to toughen up. She's still showing a lot of tenderness when I press."

Jane said, "My lab just published a paper on shorter life expectancy after genetic modification."

"Wait, is that why Todd was calling? To report good news?" Vera asked.

Jane looked at the ground. "No one told me. I saw it online. Todd wanted to tell me that he got a grant for the tusk ring study. The professor wanted to know when I would be done with my mothering or if he needed to send someone to finish the job in Iceland. I told him he should send someone. He's pissed."

Vera's stomach did a tiny spin-flip. Her crush on Todd had faded but there was still a residue. She concentrated on the pattern of shade and sun as warmth and cool on her skin.

"So no one was calling to accuse you of theft?" Eve asked.

Jane said, "Unless this is a cover for that."

Helen unpacked creams and drops and ointments from a woven basket, a picnic of veterinary supplies. "I thought we were about to learn why modified creatures have shorter life expectancies," Vera said.

Jane told her, "In this case they were looking at humans who are homozygous for the $\Delta 32$ allele, which the professor, my professor, estimates has a twenty-one percent increase in all-cause mortality."

"I'm sure you are saying real words," Eve told her mother, "but might you also want to translate them for us?"

Jane said, "Remember the scientist in China? $\Delta 32$ is a co-receptor for HIV. It's the gene believed to be associated with disease progression. The idea is that if we alter it, we can make people resistant to the virus. But meanwhile it turns out that they are more susceptible to other diseases, like the flu."

Eve said, "Breaking news: Scientists shocked to discover that genetic code is very, very complicated."

Helen put her fingers on Pearl's neck and looked at the sky. "Her pulse is still fast," she said.

"Any news from George?" Eve asked. "Maybe he can help us?"

"He'll be back in a day or two. They had to put a pin in his bone and he needs to heal. He's old and eats a lot of meat and is not exactly a light drinker. It'll be costly, but we can sell a giraffe to pay for it all if we have to." Vera wondered what a giraffe was worth on the open market. Money, she had assumed, was endless here.

Helen moved her head closer to the animal's belly. She said, "I've never been a mum. Haven't you got some kind of magical instincts to care for this baby? Or a well of practical experiences to draw upon?"

"God, no." Jane thought. "I remember a night baby Eve had been crying for six hours and the sound felt like sand in my veins and I made Sal call the nurses' line and a woman on the other end asked him a thousand questions—has she eaten has she pooped what color seedy or not seedy has she peed how much what color is the light off is there something in her eye is it hot is it cold—finally she asked Sal to check the baby's feet to see if a hair was wrapped around one of her toes and there was. Can you imagine how many possibilities there are for something to be wrong? We never, ever would have guessed that one."

Eve asked, "Could I have lost a toe? Like if Dad hadn't called the nurse and no one had figured it out, would the toe have died and had to be amputated?"

"The point is that you were all right."

Vera wanted to know if her digits or life might have been saved by their father's diligence.

Helen handed Jane a tube with Italian writing on it and told her to rub it on, to form a protective layer. "If they begin to heal in a few days we're on the right track."

Jane squeezed and gently applied. The mammoth jerked away. "I'm sorry it hurts," she said. "I'll be so, so careful."

"You're a good mum," Helen said. "What shall we call her?"

"Oh, I was calling her Pearl, for her tusk. We can change it. I should have waited. We didn't know when you were coming back."

"Tusk?"

Jane buried her fingers, found the jewel of ivory. "Here," she said, and Helen's fingers joined hers.

"That's a lovely buried treasure," Helen said, and Jane smiled hard. "I feel like a lucky pirate."

"Aaargh," Eve said.

"What's a pirate's favorite letter?" Vera asked her sister, and Eve groaned.

"Pearl it is," Helen said.

"I still like Veve," Eve said. "I'm gunning for a namesake."

Vera thought of the baby mammoth they had found, frozen and prehistoric to this animal's warm, futuristic self.

"Someday you'll have a child and you can name it whatever you want," Jane said.

Vera looked pointedly at Eve but her sister's eyes stayed stubbornly down.

"George wanted children and that never worked. He's grown very concerned with passing on the lineage."

Jane looked sympathetic.

Helen put her hands on her hips and took in the beast in front of her. "We haven't said this enough: we bred a bloody woolly mammoth. I can't believe it. We should not be so focused on imperfection or possible early expiration. We have done the impossible."

Both women buried their hands in the animal's tufty hair. "I've never been this close to a baby elephant so I don't know what's different. Hair, obviously," Jane said. She sounded like someone who had been given an expensive necklace she really wanted to like.

Helen ran a palm down the creature's forehead, which was a pronounced square, and she kissed her trunk, the bristle and leather. "She has a different head shape and the fur, but there's also a feeling that's different. Baby mammoth, *je ne sai quoi*."

"She smells like Brie to me," Eve said.

"But not stinky Brie," Vera said. "Mild and creamy."

Jane laughed and put her head to the baby's chest. "She's so docile and sweet. I hadn't really thought about the possibility that we'd make something cute and charming. I was thinking more science experiment, less overgrown puppy."

Helen cheered up. "Ah! I forgot to say that Constantina is making supper for us all to welcome you." She looked at her watch. "In fact, it's time now. We should head up."

Vera sat up. No changes, no additions. Helen looked less perfect than she had this morning, her hair flatter, her face a little pink. "Constantina?" Vera asked.

"You are a nervous child, aren't you? She lives in the village. Her family has been helping to take care of the place for generations." Vera's ears turned hot and she looked at the ground.

"I'd rather not leave the baby," Jane said. She petted Pearl.

"Then bring her."

Pearl pawed the ground. Her eyes were a puddle. Jane held her hand out and the animal trunked it.

Helen said, "Girls, there should be a leather lead in the barn."

What they found was a long leash veined with cracks, and this was wrapped loosely around Pearl's neck by Helen, hook and eyed. "And now she is domesticated," Jane said, sounding blue. It was possible, Vera thought, that until right now no one in the history of history had ever walked a woolly mammoth on a leash.

"We need to bring food for her," Jane said, already gathering hay and milk bottles in her arms. "To keep trying."

"Speaking of food, a pallet of coconut milk and several crates of baby formula were delivered. It's quite a large supply, if only she'll eat it."

"Is there a chance the mom will come back?" Jane asked.

"A little R&R is good for mums. Wouldn't you say?"

Jane scoffed. "I wouldn't know."

Here was the procession: Helen at the front, moving with a confident lope, mother leading a newborn mammoth on a string, with two girls in sundresses following because this was the family they had been born into and they had no means to leave it. The animal's feet pancaked against the grass. Her trunk was curious and she turned to look in every direction.

They walked a path through a vineyard, new grapes like green gems, an olive grove, and there were pale roses tangled everywhere and in the distance, the glint of light on water. Emerald coves, knots of pine and poplar and the bank rising steep and dark, a village of pink and yellow and a church spire. Two ferries pressed in opposite directions, their foamy paths making a big X on the water.

Helen turned the handle on the huge wooden door and it creaked wide. The girls entered. Inside it was dark as a church, a stained-glass window and no other light. Everywhere were paintings that looked like they had come off the walls of a museum—Madonnas and babes, twelve men around a table with Jesus at the center, a marble bust of a curly-haired man on a huge wooden table, books stacked everywhere.

One side of the room was all fireplace, stone and black from six hundred winters of burning. In the corner, the anomaly: a treadmill. It stood like a joke. Everywhere else was God and here was the place for a small and mortal human body to move without moving.

Pearl fussed, swept the threshold with her trunk, looking for grass or earth. What was indoors to her? There should have been no such place. Ten thousand miles of grassland in every direction, until an ocean cut a line. Jane gentled the animal's neck. "It's all right," she said. "You're all right."

"I could eat outside with her?" Jane said, in the doorway with the mammoth. Pearl would have physically fit, even if she fit in no other way. It was a reasonable suggestion, reasonable except that this was not a dog, reasonable except that the animal was also a specimen, more valuable than any of the expensive works of art in the room and maybe more dangerous.

"You'll eat inside because you are not an animal," Helen said, a smile on her lips but her voice sharp. "She'll be just fine on the porch."

"We could take turns," Vera offered.

"It's suppertime, my husband is injured and won't be home until tomorrow or the next day and I am requesting that the three of you wash your hands and sit down to eat. Jane, the animal will be fine outside. Girls, the washroom is through the hall."

IN THE BATHROOM Eve lost control of her breathing and sat down on the floor. She said, "I feel like I'm going to faint." Vera dropped next to her, faces close, said, "Breathe in, one, two, three, four, and out one, two, three, four." Eve let her eyelids fall and followed the count. Her face was pale. When she looked up again her eyes were glass. She said,

"This woman is going to poison us. Have you seen the way she looks at the mammoth? She sees money. If they can make money selling a giraffe they can make way, way more selling mammoth. We are standing in the way."

"No, what? None of that is true. Her husband was badly hurt. She's afraid. You are having a big moment. We are going to take care of you and figure out what to do. No one is trying to kill us."

Vera wet the corner of a hand towel with cold water and pressed it to her sister's forehead. She said, "We need to go out there. Just focus on the food. Focus on your breathing. Focus on my face."

When the girls walked into the dining room, two people stood at either side of Helen's chair at the head of the table. They were wearing identical outfits—plaid brown pants and white button-down shirt. The man had creases in his face, deep channels Vera had the urge to press a fingernail into. He wore a newsboy cap that matched his pants. The woman had eyes so pale they looked almost missing. *"Dottoressa,"* the man said, "shall we seat the guests?" Eve gave her sister the look for suspicions confirmed. See? But Vera shook her head.

"Please, Pietro," Helen said. The huge chairs were pulled out and each member of the family took a seat. The woman pushed Vera's chair in hard and tight, Vera's ribs touching the table. She smelled like steak fat and her hands were red and cracked.

"Thank you," Vera said, trying to press herself back but the woman held her fast.

"Prego," she said.

The pair of servants disappeared into the kitchen and Helen said, "Don't look so suspicious, they just work here."

"Have they been here while you were away?" Jane asked.

"They live in town and come to work when we request them. George's parents hired them when they were teenagers. They are brother and sister, orphans. They were found on the steps of the Vatican in a basket made of reeds. The papers called them the Moses babies."

Eve said, "That definitely makes everything seem super-normal."

Pietro returned with two green bottles. "From the vineyards of the estate," he said, pouring the purple-red wine into Jane's glass.

"*Grazie,*" Jane said with attempted warmth, while Pietro's face went too close to her neck.

None of them seemed to know how to behave as guests in this house. The girls had wine in their glasses, too, because this was Europe or because this was a day when everyone needed it or because no one noticed or cared that they were too young. Jane's eyes darted over the room and back to her daughters like someone assessing strategy. Helen's glass was empty almost immediately. She called for a refill, though the bottle was within her reach.

"You are all so tense! Relax, have some wine. You're in Italy, you should enjoy it." They all raised their glasses tentatively in a toast. "To Italy," Jane said, and Helen winked at her.

"To women," Helen said. "You know elephants are matriarchal. The mothers are the holders of all the important lessons. How to find the watering hole, how to use the thousands of muscles in the trunk, how to grieve. Most of the sounds they make are inaudible to the human ear."

"How to feed," Jane whispered.

They did not know how to teach the baby what she needed to know. Did not know how to manipulate a trunk to reach the high leaves, drink. They would fail this animal in every important way, were already failing.

Constantina appeared with a platter of pasta, red and glistening, torn basil. The smell changed the whole room. If it was poison, Vera thought, it was lovely poison. The first bite was a sweet slip across her tongue.

"It's a wonder George isn't dead," Helen said, when they were all eating.

"From a broken leg?" Jane said.

"He fell and she ran right over him. She stepped on his leg but it could just as easily have been his chest. And it's not just this time— he's been maimed by all sorts of animals."

"Oh?" Eve asked. Vera put a hand on her sister's knee. Squeezed.

"He was bitten by a macaque and contracted rabies when we were first married. He was scratched by a lion and considered orangutans members of the family. He has no sense. I was always the better zoo-keeper. But we have him to thank for the property." Vera remembered the story Helen had told about George's parents' boat sinking, about how Helen had imagined it first.

Jane said, "We're here to help in any way we can."

Vera was hungrier than she had maybe ever been before and every-thing was rich and the wine was poured each time glasses were half empty and for a long time, everyone's heads were low, and they ate like there might not be food after this, or a world to which they would return.

Vera noticed Helen's breathing first, choppy gusts. She looked to see if the woman was crying, expected her to be, upset at the thought of her husband's accident, and grabbed her napkin so she could offer it as a handkerchief, but no, Helen was laughing. Her head was back, her face red. It was a silent laugh and Helen looked half suffocated by it. Eve and Vera turned to each other and in the look was the wish to run. Jane locked eyes with each daughter, admitted to herself this small emergency where they saw clearly the business partner she had chosen in an endeavor to resurrect a species.

Helen did not breathe for a full minute. Her whole face was hot red.

Constantina arrived to clear the plates but stopped over Helen. "Helena," she said. "You must have some water."

Helen settled herself, wiped her eyes, took a long breath.

"I'm sorry," she said. "It's that he looked so *surprised.*"

"Who did?" Jane asked.

"George, poor George, of course."

Plates were swiped by Constantina and Vera thought she saw a little foam at the edge of the woman's mouth. Her jaw was clenched tight. She rattled all the silverware, stacked the plates precariously, everything ready to crash.

Outside, a song, something off-key, minor. Music from the kitchen? Jane wondered. But no, they understood soon. It was the mammoth, calling out. It sounded like a bow on strings, a cello played by someone who did not know how.

Jane jumped up and ran through the dark rooms, daughters behind her, Jesuses watching, horsemen of the apocalypse watching, flipped the heavy bolt on the door. Pearl stood alone under the grape arbor, having stripped all the low leaves off the old vine. The song was loud and cut through to the gut like a serrated knife.

"Hush, hush," Jane said. Before anyone knew what she was doing, Jane had pulled her shirt down to reveal a breast.

"Mom?" Eve and Vera said at the exact same time and at that second Pietro appeared in the shadow of the doorway. "Maria," he said, and looked at the heavens.

Jane snapped her shirt back up, "Oh, no," she said. "I don't know why I did that."

"You sure did do it, though," Eve said. "You sure did just try to nurse a baby woolly mammoth."

Vera did not say that the animal was the first of Jane's children that she had actually wanted to breast-feed.

"This is not okay. None of this is okay," Eve said. She started to walk away, then picked up the pace and ran. Vera's body could not be divided, though her heart was. She watched Eve disappear behind a grapevine fat from hundreds of years of growth.

Pearl wrapped her trunk around Jane's leg, entangling her. What sounds she made in the secret register of her kind they did not know.

VERA GAVE UP ON sleep that night and got up, late, to look for food. She found her sister sitting at the table with candles lit. She was already used to her mother being in the pen with the mammoth. They both were.

"This is romantic," Vera said. Humor was bait that almost always worked on Eve, but this time she did not respond. Before Eve, spread across the table, was their dad's first book along with photos of his iceman. Feet, hands, the things in his bag photographed on a velvet background with little white number tags. "I found these in Mom's suitcase," Eve said.

"What were you doing in Mom's suitcase?" Vera asked.

"Apparently looking for trouble," Eve said. She was leaning back in her chair and swirled the water in her glass.

Vera tore off a piece of baguette and buttered it. She sat down across from her sister, who looked like an adult in the warm light. Eve looked at the photographs. She was a person missing someone.

"This is what's left of him," she said. He had been the person behind the camera. His notes, his handwriting, the story he had worked to re-construct of a person who had lived millennia before any of them had been born. It felt as if their father had transferred his own aliveness into the ancient hominid.

Vera picked up Sal's book. Iceman on the cover, their father's bearded face on the back. Vera turned to the introduction and began to read.

Almost five thousand years after he died, a frozen man was discovered by German hikers in the Italian Alps in the water-shed of the river Adige. The couple saw a skull in the ice and called police, assuming that it was a climber who had recently gone missing. No one knew that what the hikers had discov-ered was a mummified early human and a link to our collec-tive past.

This ancestor would have weighed 134 pounds and stood five feet five inches tall. He was forty-five years old when he died. By studying dust grains on his body and the composi-tion of his tooth enamel, we know that the iceman's last meal was chamois meat, red deer, berries and herb bread. In his pouch he had einkorn grain and seeds of flax and poppy.

Because of pollen in his belly, we know that he ate this meal in a conifer forest in spring. Imagine the iceman sitting on a fallen log, softened after the thaw. Maybe he thought of a woman while he ate or maybe he thought of his crops or maybe he thought of his father.

His bones revealed that he walked long distances over hilly terrain, perhaps because he was a shepherd, though no sheep were found with him in the ice. His right ribs were cracked by the ice that preserved him. Lines on his fingernails revealed that he was sick three times in the months before he died. His teeth were rotted from grain. He had sixty-one tattoos, lines grouped across his body: lumbar spine, back of the knee, ankle. The bones beneath these tattoos had deteriorated with arthritis. The tattoos were medicine—to ease his pain, someone had made a paste of fire-ash and water and, with a sharp point, pressed it under the iceman's skin.

"I know this introduction by heart," Vera said.

"Don't stop reading," Eve told her. "It's nice to hear it in your voice." Vera would have read the whole book aloud if it helped Eve.

The iceman was wearing the hides of four different animals. His hat was bearskin, his loincloth was sheepskin, his leggings goat leather, his shoelaces were cowhide and his quiver wild roe deer. Beneath the fur he had a cloak of woven grass.

The iceman had a copper axe with a yew handle, dogwood arrows, a knife with a flint blade. He had an antler, which he might have used to sharpen arrowheads or blades. He had two birchbark baskets, medicinal mushrooms and a fire kit: flint, pyrite, tinder mushrooms. He was lactose-intolerant, part Neanderthal, and may have had Lyme disease. There are nineteen modern men alive in northern Italy who are related to the iceman.

For ten years after his discovery the scientists thought he had died of exposure. A storm, a fall on the ice, unrelenting cold, but now we know that the iceman's death may not have been an accident. He suffered a blow to the head, an arrow stab in his shoulder, the arrow itself carefully removed. The iceman's hands were bruised and cut and his thumb had been broken without time to heal. There were traces of the blood of four other people on his things, the blood of two more on his knife. Maybe he died at a lower altitude and was carried higher to a stone burial platform, a sacrifice to an unnamable god. His body would have moved each season as the ice melted and refroze. This singular and specific body surfed the changing mountainsides, crossed ridge after ridge for thousands of years, riding the thaw and freeze.

Vera waited for her father to feel closer but all she could see in her mind was the mummy and his wax replica.

"Are you okay?"

Eve shook her head. "Nope. Not at all."

"Is there anything I can do to make you be okay?"

"This is a depthless chasm of my own making, little sister. I think I'm stuck down here."

They stared at the photos for a long time. Vera wanted to suggest that they talk to their mother, that Jane would understand, would know how to set things right again. It seemed like the only clear path, yet she was afraid of making Eve angry.

"Good old iceman," Eve said. "Hell of a guy." Vera laughed because she knew that making people laugh helped Eve feel that her existence was justified.

Vera said, "He sure is. Look at those eyes. Doesn't he seem like the kind of guy you'd have wanted to be stranded in a blizzard with?"

"He'd have shared his dried meat and fire-starting fungus for sure," Eve said.

"No one wielded a stone ice pick better. Best hand-sewn leather booties this side of the Danube."

"He was a fucker if you ever touched his medicine pouch, though," Eve said.

Sal had poured his life into the iceman and now that ancient hominid was better known to Vera and Eve than their own dad had been.

"Do you think Dad loved the iceman?" Vera asked. Serious Vera, always hauling them back to the dreary real world.

"Are you asking if our dad was gay for a prehistoric hominid?"

"Eve, no. I mean we know that he was fascinated, that he thought about the iceman all the time, but do you think he loved him, too, like a relative?"

The most familiar picture they had of Sal was the book jacket photo. His hair was thin, his eyes set deep. A man's face, living in his own time, like everyone must. He cared about ancient history with his whole being but could never have gotten there.

Eve put her hand on her belly. The spark there. "What would he say about this?" she asked. Love jagged through Vera like an electric storm. Torn between caring for her sister and the desire to bring some part of their dad back into the world.

"A good dad would put his daughter first," Vera said.

"So, then, mazel tov on being an ice auntie?"

"He was a good dad. He didn't want to die."

"He was reckless."

"He made a mistake."

"Do you still not think Helen is going to murder us for our priceless animal?" Eve asked.

"If she wanted the mammoth she wouldn't have told Mom about it. It would have been easy for her to keep it to herself."

"Good point, detective," said Eve.

"I feel like the biggest danger is that Mom's reputation will be ruined. We sound like a fake headline. California Woman Claims Calf Is a Baby Woolly."

Eve said, "You're smart, Vera. May she live long and be written off for her gender."

"That would be great news?"

Eve's lips split in a smile. "The most terrible good news of the day."

Vera stood and kissed her sister on the top of the head.

Eve squinted at her sister. "Stop looking at me like I'm a weirdo."

"You are a weirdo. But you're a lovely weirdo and you're my sister and also my only friend. Good night, Evie. Good night, iceman. Good night, ice-baby," Vera said.

"Try to get some sleep," Eve told her. "Another big day of de-extinction tomorrow."

Seven

A green Fiat rumbled down the drive. It was old and tiny, making a clank like it had one square wheel. Vera watched the car approach with breath held. It parked in front of the castle. She was waiting for someone to discover what was going on here on this property and haul them all off. Maybe someone who had seen the girls buying up every milliliter of baby formula on the lake. Someone one of the creepy caretakers had told. Maybe Helen herself, ready to cart Pearl away to a rare animal dealer who would sell her to a Qatari trillionaire. There was a van parked in the lot with no seats in the back which looked ready for exactly this size animal.

Pietro came out of the driver's-side door of the little car and rushed around to open the passenger door, where George unfolded himself into the day.

He had a cast and crutches, a wool hat like a Swiss shepherd might wear. His cheeks were pink. He stretched and looked around, smiled at his domain.

The smaller man collected a small suitcase and a bouquet of sunflowers from the trunk and the two made their way toward the house. Beyond the vineyard, a giraffe head reached into a tree.

"Man of the house is home!" Vera called.

Jane was inside, napping in a bed for the first time in three days. Eve was eating bread and butter. In a minute, they all stood under the grapevine with Vera and watched George crutch up to the house while Pietro carried his things.

"Average hospital stay for elephant wounds is three days, apparently," Eve said.

"You have to have more than one data point for an average," Jane said.

From Vera, "All's well that ends well?"

"In about an hour I'm going to ask you two to go up there with a batch of biscuits," Jane said.

"Us? No, that's your job," Eve told her.

"He can't be angry at you, you're innocents. You'll gauge the situation. Like spies. Get baking. I have to go back to the baby."

VERA KNOCKED ON THE huge door, unsure if her small fist could make a sound on the thick wood. Eve stood a few feet back, not at all happy to be given this task. Vera had wrapped the biscuits, still warm, in a clean towel and tucked a dish of butter inside. She wanted it to look American. A postcard from a dumb young nation that could not possibly have meant harm. Which she knew was the least believable kind of fiction.

From the other side of the door, the squeak of crutches.

"Mistress Vera," George said, big voiced, smiling. "Mistress Eve."

Eve said, "We prefer miz."

"How's the leg?" Vera asked, jovially as she could.

"Crushed it nicely, but it'll be good as new in a few months."

"We made you some American biscuits. I recommend a lot of butter."

They stood in the old room in the old castle full of old art. A cat crossed and ducked under a dark wood table. Vera was pretty sure it was a house cat, but on this property it might as easily have been anything: jaguar kitten, ocelot, pygmy lynx.

"Where is the lady of the house?" Eve asked.

"Haven't seen her since I got home. She must have taken a boat out or gone walking. I can't very well crutch around to look for her."

"Well, we should let you get back to resting," Eve said.

"Unless there's anything you need help with?" Vera asked. They were supposed to be learning things, gathering information.

"As a matter of fact, I'd love a coffee. Someone put the beans on the top shelf and I can't reach. I thought about climbing on a chair but it seemed unwise."

Eve said, "Vera is glad to help."

Vera said, "What? You're coming." She had never had the urge to punch someone before this.

George said, "Eve can sit outside. Vera and I will bring coffees out. Miz Vera, if you'll be so kind."

Vera, abandoned, followed George through the oaken dining room into the kitchen. It was not a kitchen such as a home would have—countertops, a sunny window over the sink. This was a castle kitchen, the curved brick ceiling black from centuries of smoke, two bare bulbs hanging from a wire, a large table in the center on which there sat an unplucked chicken and a tower of leeks. There was a modern refrigerator, which looked out of place, and beside it a brass espresso machine, mirror polished.

"It's there," George said, motioning to a glass jar of coffee beans on a high shelf. Beside this jar were others—white beans, flour, sugar. Vera was annoyed. Eve could stand up for herself because she had Vera to step on. Vera pushed the wooden chair close and climbed carefully up. The chair shifted beneath her, squeaked as if in displeasure. It would have been easy for George to take his crutch and knock the chair out from underneath. Vera might have hit her head on the way down, her neck twisting. She thought of this as she tiptoed higher, reached for the jar, George in perfect position to bring her to the ground. If he did, at least her sister would feel guilty. Stop it, she said to her brain. Stop imagining that everyone here is after you.

George said, "Got it, sweetie?" and Vera had, but she now wished otherwise. Sweetie was a fuzzy caterpillar on her leg she could not swat off. George said, "Come on down before another of us winds up in hospital." She passed the jar and climbed down. She tried to catch her breath.

"Come on, I'll show you how to make a proper espresso." Feet on the floor, heart falling back into a regular trot, Vera looked around her. The chicken, the leeks, everything like a still life in an old-masters painting. But there, beside the bird, she saw something else, a small specimen tube. It was three inches tall, and in it was a lock of reddish-brown fur. On a sticker affixed to the tube, the handwritten words: *Capelli Mammut*. Mammoth hair. Someone who was not Jane was taking samples.

Vera imagined the tube up her sleeve. A spy could do this. Eve could probably do it. When she moved to walk toward the table, casually as she could, George said, "This is called the portafilter. Which isn't a sexy name. Come help tamp." She made a quick motion, tube into hand, hand into pocket.

George said, "You interested in chickens?" He was smiling, side-eyed.

"I didn't know if it was real," Vera stammered.

"You think we're the sort that have a fake chicken?"

Vera tried to laugh casually.

George ground the beans and Vera tamped them. The coffee hissed out into bone china cups, caramel cream at the top.

"Let's bring them outside," he said, and motioned for Vera to go first. The barely audible hum of peril in her ears.

Eve was sun-slow, her legs stretched out in the warm day. She said, *"Prego."* Vera wanted to tell her what she found and what she did and that she was angry to have been abandoned and she had to pretend like everything was fine so she turned her attention to her tiny cup. The coffee was bright and hot across Vera's tongue, burning a path.

"Careful, there," George told her, "or you'll hurt yourself." His smile was slick, a tool he clearly used well. "How is the little bugger?"

"Pearl?" Eve asked.

"Ah, she has a name. I might have gone with something more ferocious myself."

Vera tried for a neutral laugh. She was in the underbrush of subtext and history and stories she did not know or want to know. "She's not eating and she's got a lot of sores. She seems more okay than she should, considering those things. And the fact that she doesn't have a mom."

"The sores sound troubling," George said. "But not eating is a much bigger problem."

"Are you worried about something in particular?" Vera asked. "Should we go down there right now?"

"I don't work well until I've had coffee."

Eve nodded to George's leg. "Does it hurt?"

"Not since they set it. Before that it hurt more than anything I've felt in all my life."

They sipped in loud silence. Vera wanted a side door. "You've lived here for a long time?" she asked.

"The property has been in my family for four generations. Helen married me for this place. If we ever lost it, she'd be gone."

"Then I guess you'd better not lose it," Eve said. It was the same story Helen had told them; Vera was surprised that George was aware of it, and repeating it to strangers.

"I'm doing my best. It's not always easy," George said. He rubbed the fingertips on his right hand together in the sign for money. "I can't think of having to sell. It's the only place I've ever loved. When I was in uni I convinced my parents to let me come for the summer. The castle was covered in thick dust, dining chairs had fallen over, there was a chandelier hanging by a thin wire.

"I wanted that man-in-the-wild thing but I wasn't brave enough for the wilderness. An abandoned castle with a lot of weird animals and grouchy caretakers seemed like the best bet. I thought it would make a good story to tell the girls."

"All girls love a man with a falling down castle," Eve said. "Known fact."

"Any castle. A boy with a castle is a prince even if he isn't. Plus, girls love animals and we had six zebras, three giraffes, a herd of yak, an aged leopard and a pair of orangutans. They were the best, like the king and queen of the land. They were called Koa and Rumi."

"I don't want the whole princess thing but I do like the idea of apes," Eve said. "Were they smelly?"

Eve, easy Eve. She could talk to anyone, just as Sal had been able to. Vera was chilly and awkward, always searching for the right words.

"Very smelly. But those faces. So wise and sweet. Koa's fur hung twelve inches from his body and he had those flat disc cheeks. When he slept he looked like a mop."

"Worth it," Eve said.

George had shifted his focus to Eve, clearly the sister who had bitten the end of his line. Vera might as well have been invisible. "The orangutans liked to be taken out for walks so they could climb the oaks and pines and sleep through the heat. I took naps underneath them in the grass. When they woke up I held the hand of Koa who held the hand of Rumi and we walked the path to the lake where I took my clothes off and hung them on the gooseberry bushes."

"Great," Vera said, but Eve did not join the scoff. Instead she asked for more. "Did they like to swim?"

"The orangutans were afraid of water. They held hands while I swam out and waved back to them." This was obviously a story that George had told before, well-crafted for reaction and approval, and Eve approved.

Vera pictured this scene. George naked in the lake, the apes watching, anxious for his return, the beach, and beyond that the path up the cliff, the succulent garden, the medicinal herbs, the orchard, the walls of jasmine, the pastures with the zebras and giraffes and castle. It was too much bounty for one person.

"That's so cool," Eve said.

"Leaving at the end of the summer was pure misery. The orangutans died the following spring. I never saw them again. They're stuffed in the museum now."

Vera had found those stuffed animals deeply sad, their glass eyes and dirty hair.

George leaned closer to Eve and said quietly, "I know it sounds strange, but I started to think of them as my parents."

To this, even Eve was silent.

"You came to deliver pastries and I've told you about my taxono-mized ape parents and you must think I'm completely nutty. They were much better than most of the humans I know." George laughed. Eve laughed. Vera felt a scream come awake in her chest. She thought of their father and his life like a short spiral, the circle ever tightening until it wound down to the final dot. How irreplaceable he was. How exactly hers.

Vera had been patient enough. She put her cup on the table and said, "Good chat. We have to go. Our mom is down there alone and we should check on her."

George said, "Is she always so flustered?" he asked Eve.

Eve shrugged. "We'll all go," George said, "I miss that woolly."

HE SPED UP AS they drew closer, crutch landing hard in the dirt and scraping on the pebbles. Jane leapt up to greet him, gushes of well wishes and welcomes. To Vera, Jane looked like a clock chiming, pro-grammed to chirp manically whether she meant it or not.

George said, "You can thank me for teaching your daughter to make a proper Italian espresso."

Jane said, "We're all so happy to see you up and running," and Vera wanted to find the off switch to this version of her mother but she did not need to because George pressed past her to the baby and he began the immediate and silent work of examining her. He made grunts of approval when he touched ears, tail, spine, and grunts of disapproval when he felt her pulse, looked in her eyes with a light he had in his pocket, opened her mouth, rimmed the holes in her trunk with his fingertips.

"Have you been feeding her?" he asked.

"She won't eat," Jane said. "We have been trying."

"Her pulse is racing. She has open sores. This is not pretty."

George mixed coconut and baby formula as if he had been doing it for years. He shook the bottle with one hand while pinching the nipple closed with the other. When he tipped it to Pearl's mouth she looked at him with her doll eyes, lashes reflected in the black, and she did not drink. He said, "Come on, you dummy. You'll die." And Pearl looked at him as if she heard, as if she welcomed this. George tossed the bottle to Jane and said, "This is not what I hoped for. Keep trying."

When he turned his back to go, George was a silhouette, legs and crutches, like something four legged, something creaturely, prowling.

THE GIRLS WERE HOT and angry for no reason or every reason. Vera grouched to the kitchen for toast, for coffee. Eve shut the curtains because it was too beautiful outside. Vera ate a slice of cold butter off a fork. She thought of the mammoth hair now tucked inside a sock in her suitcase, of the possibility—now probability—that Helen or George or the caretakers could have their own intentions with the mammoth. She had not told Eve about the vial because she had nothing else of her own and this secret was a small gem she could clutch in her palm.

"I wish we were sleeping in the castle instead of the witch hut," Eve said.

"Seemed like George would love to have you there."

"Oh, stop it. I liked the orangutan story. I'm not going to sleep with an old man just because he has a lot of animals. Although, maybe I could sleep with him and claim that the baby was his baby and take him to court and this would all belong to us."

"Eve, gross gross gross."

"On that point we agree."

"Also, there's no way it ends up in our favor. You'd be disgraced and his reputation would be untarnished because that is the way the world works. Even I know that. Plus, what happens when you gave birth to a cave-baby?"

"What if we ran away and went to Iceland?" Eve said.

Vera wanted to disappear but she did not want to go where Eve had love and she had nothing but perpetually insufficient clothing for the cold, the wet, the wind. "We can't afford it."

"We could stay with Lars."

"*You* could stay with Lars. I could sleep on an abandoned fishing boat in the fjord until the fairies took me in or I was eaten by a narwhal."

"No narwhal in Iceland. You have to go farther north. Kidnapped by fairies is likely, though."

"Also, this is not our baby. This is yours. You should probably stop being a total asshole to me since I'm the only person who is helping you."

It was hot and Vera lay down on the tile floor. She felt the ridges on her skin, a cold press. Eve said, "Let's at least go for a swim. We'll bring a picnic and pretend we're having a lovely holiday."

"I'm mad at you."

Eve said, "That's fair." She packed a jar of jam and a block of asiago and two bottles of water. She held the bag out like an offering. "Please?" she said. "Let me earn your love."

. . .

THEY SUNSCREENED AND found hats because they were good girls with experience in the tropics. They wore summer dresses, sandals.

The path led them away from the mammoth and they did not take a detour to tell their mother where they had gone or when they would be back. They were the children for whom she was not concerned.

On the right: the twenty-foot-tall iron bars of the monkey enclosure. The cage was decorative, with a family crest in the center. Inside the animals swung from branches of a tree long dead. They stopped, their white faces and big eyes, and watched Eve and Vera cross in front of them. The monkeys had been born here, a generation without a natural habitat.

"Hey, guys," Eve said, saluting.

"Don't insult them. I think they throw poop."

Beyond the monkeys were the birds, more huge cages, these with additional netting and brightly colored slices of fruit on the trees like ornaments.

With heads of royal blue and bellies of orange, their wings bright green, these were the lorikeets Helen had written to Jane about. Vera remembered the story. The birds were collected in Polynesia and Timor by Helen and a group of guides she had paid in cash. She claimed it as a conservation effort, moving the birds from islands where they were being hunted by rats. If she had waited for a permit the birds would all have been dead, she explained, dragged to the ground and eaten, even their bones too small to slow the rats down. Illegal animal capture with an altruistic intention.

The lorikeets sang sharp knives of notes. There were too many at once. This song belonged on a jungle isle dense with fern, palm, vanilla.

"Hush up," Eve said. The birds shrilled on.

The path wound through the succulent garden, all those open hands extended to catch ambient moisture. Eve had not called Lars since she told him the news. They had expected him to call her, to be the consoler, the dear boy concerned for his girl, his voice all tenderness. But no. Two silent phones, two silent mouths, a cluster of cells that might or might not bind them. It was the loudest silence, shouting to Eve that he did not love her, had never loved her. He wanted her and the potential life within her to disappear. For her to call him now would be an act of desperation. And there was nothing he could do to help her.

The girls followed the path down the hillside. It was steep, zig-zagged, paved with stones. The water, as they drew close, smelled like fish and weeds. The cove was deep green, all temptation. Oleanders, dark as blood, overgrew the stones. The path widened to a set of steps and at the end was a boathouse built on pillars. It had a terra-cotta roof and sunset stucco walls, but instead of a floor it was open to the lake which they could see through an arched brick doorway where boats could go in and out. Steps ran alongside to a person-sized door. "Of course they have a fucking *boat garage*," Eve said, and entered the small doorway which led to a landing and steps that descended into lakewa-ter. Floating there: a cigarette boat, mirror-varnished wood with a red racing stripe.

"Shit," Eve said, "that's a fancy boat."

"I wouldn't have expected something so Bond."

Helen seemed like a woman who would have something nice but practical, rust on the wheel, fiberglass seats, made for heavy use. Like what the tourists rented, embarking too fast across the lake and return-ing two hours later red and drunk.

Eve said, "I want to make a great escape."

"It's a lake. We could only escape in circles."

"You need an imagination transplant."

Then: bubbles came up to the surface beside the boat. Smaller, then bigger, the sound of air from below. A shadow appeared under the water like a long fish. Vera backed up and put her arm out in front of Eve like a seatbelt. A sea monster. A flutter and the shadow turned pale and broke the surface. It was a person in a mask, long hair pulled into a bun.

"The fuck," Eve said.

The person put the mask up. "Helen?" Vera asked.

The woman took the breathing apparatus from her mouth. "Ladies," Helen said. She breaststroked to the steps, climbed out. She was wearing a wet suit and scuba tank, but no flippers. Her feet looked too small, delicate beneath so much black. In her hands: a sponge and a rubber-coated flashlight, still lit. "What brings you two down here?" Helen asked politely, as if they had all run into one another at an outdoor café.

"We were fantasizing about stealing your boat," Eve told her.

"We weren't going to do it," Vera said.

"She's pretty, isn't she? The *Ophelia*. She belonged to George's parents."

"Just out for a morning scuba dive?" Eve asked, false sunshine in her voice.

"You have to scrub the hull or it gets covered in algae. I find it meditative."

Helen unzipped her wet suit and peeled herself. To Vera's surprise, she was completely naked underneath, her skin goose-bumped, her stomach soft. Her breasts hung like bells as she bent to pull each leg out, holding the wall to keep from falling. Helen stood up, the black suit at her feet, and shook her hair. Vera tried not to look at the wild tangle between her legs, the breasts rounded out again now that they were upright. Vera thought they looked good to cup. One was visibly bigger than the other. Helen stood still and did not release the girls from their view of her body.

"George is home," Vera said.

"And now you've discovered the other reason I was scraping barnacles. It's hardest to find someone when she's hiding underwater."

Helen spit into the lake and walked to the entrance of the boathouse and reached around the corner where she pulled down a thick white robe from a hook in the bricks. Why had they not noticed that before? "You seem like good girls. Would you consider yourselves good?"

"Vera is definitely good. I'd say I'm medium. Why do you ask?"

Helen smiled. "I guess I'm surprised that I like you. I thought I didn't like children."

Eve was easy with her answers and Vera looked at her in admiration. "We're teenagers. You'd probably have hated us when we were small."

"Good point. Maybe I should have consented to having a few."

Eve said, "I'd skip it. So much fuss and my impression is that it makes everyone very nervous."

"If you are good or medium-good teenagers you should take her out," Helen said. "The boat, I mean. You just have to remember *southwest*." She pointed to a compass rose on the ground and followed the southwest line to the wall where a key was hidden between two bricks.

"Oh, no. I think this boat is a little above our pay grade," Vera said.

"I cleaned it so it would be ready for an excursion," Helen said. "You could all go."

Vera said, "I don't think the mammoth would fit and Jane won't leave her."

Helen flipped her head over and squeezed her hair. Water dripped out. "That's a parenting thing? Not wanting to leave your baby? Or is that just American parenting?"

"I have to imagine the Italians worry less," Eve said.

Helen looked younger when wet. Vera imagined her in the castle, composing herself. She would shower, lotion, blow-dry, dress in linen and leather, draw black at the lash line and darken her lips. At the end she would be a lady, but now she was a clean form.

"Jane will need a break at some point," Helen said. "And when she does . . ." She gestured to a gold compass rose on the top step. "Southwest," she said, and walked toe-to-heel to the wall, reached high up and pulled a key from an invisible ledge. "If you can drive a car you can drive a boat. Start her up, switch to forward or reverse, pull the lever slowly. Steer. Stay between the green buoys that mark shallows. Bring water and sun lotion. My favorite swimming is by the little island and my favorite lunch is in Menaggio."

She replaced the key and winked, her robe falling open as she bent to prop her oxygen tank against the stone wall, gather her sponge, wet suit and flashlight. A row of wet prints marked her ascent. "Good luck!" she called, without turning around.

EVE FOUND THE KEY and took her shoes off, no pause. Down the submerged steps, feet wet, ankles, calves, until she could reach the boat and pull it close. It wobbled but she got in without falling. In the cavey darkness, three champagne corks floated.

"Today, we ride," Eve said.

"I don't think we should do this."

"We won't go far. We'll go to that little island and get a coffee and come back. A skinny-dip is the craziest we'll get."

"We should tell Mom we're going."

"Hike back up if you want to. I'm not."

Vera thought of the walk back, her mother in mammoth-land. She thought of how much Vera was not what Jane was tracking.

"Undo the rope," Eve said. "Send me out to sea."

Vera waded, boarded, tucked the snacks under her seat.

"Good girl. Glad you decided to join. So, we ignite, reverse, throttle, steer," Eve said, turning the key.

The boat hummed alive, soft, like something just born.

Eve backed out better than she should have, this being her first time. The champagne corks spun in a spiral. Daylight was too bright, the water catching sun in darts to the eye. Eve changed direction and took them outward, the water darker, tracks of foam behind the craft.

Vera looked behind them at the path they had traveled. The boathouse, the stone steps, the huge expanse of grass, a neck-bent zebra, the castle turret, the cypress grove. Terraces of flowers up the slope, hundreds of years of loveliness cultivated on this stretch of land. The mammoth was on the other side of the hill. Their mother was hidden. Aside from the extravagance of a private zoo there was nothing out of the ordinary—the lake was dotted with villas, with columned pools, with topiaries carved to look like mermaids. Most properties were not visible from the road because they were meant to be seen from the lake. Everything on display, a sugared ornament of wealth between water, mountains, sky, seen only by those who could afford to travel by water.

Eve pulled the throttle forward, the boat's nose tipped up and they sped. It felt good to go fast, to cut the water, nothing in their way, no obstacles but the jolt of waves. Vera closed her eyes and let her hair whip.

They could live like this, Vera thought. Range across the fingers of the lake, gather thrown-away food in each fancy town, scavenge like strays. They would jump off the bow and be clean and pretty enough to go unnoticed. Vera thought about the secret baby stewing in her sister's body. It was summer, so this would be a spring babe, born in the quiet season. These lake towns would be empty, rooms unfilled, only the ferries plying. The ferries plus Eve and Vera, sisters, and the swaddled bundle they would raise together. Vera pictured them curled in the bottom of the boat with the baby between them. Eve would nurse because her body was the one instructed to do so—Vera's breasts would continue to be milkless darts.

They could live this way for a season, a year, but they would get hungry and tired, would want feet on city pavement, the baby would need room to run, or it would be part-cave, part-ancient, part-iceman and they would need a kind of help not available here.

Eve slowed and the engine shushed quiet. She tossed the anchor over and watched it sink. They were in the shadow of an island in the lake's center. Across on one bank was a village, church-steepled and inviting, on the other side steep mountains. The island was uninhabited, with a dock and a café and walking paths. Eve said, "Swim time," and took her dress off. "What's wrong?" she asked. "Are you crying?"

"I'm fine. Let's keep our underwear on," Vera said. They were in view of the village, passing boats.

"You can," Eve told her, bra unsnapped. Vera looked at her sister, a body she had seen grow up. She knew the freckled constellation on Eve's low back, the scar on her shoulder from a tree branch and a game of chase. The body did not look different, though it housed this new thing.

Eve jumped first, came up laughing. She looked like a pale fog under the water. On the island's bank a pair of paper-white geese nested among the ferns. "Are those real?" Vera asked, standing in blue cotton bra and underwear, keeping her balance. They seemed too perfect. Porcelain or wax. So much of this place was a fantasy.

Eve splashed their direction and they flapped. "Real," she called back. "Now get in."

Vera swan-dived, hit the water hard. It was warm at the surface and colder below. She swam toward her sister and they both hung on to the gunwale and rubbed the water out of their eyes and swished their hair back and kicked. They had swum a thousand swims together. Jumped the waves in Morocco, had their breath stolen by alpine lakes, thrown themselves into the slosh and bubble of California surf, handstanded and flipped in hotel pools on four continents.

They hung there, wet, Eve naked and Vera nearly so, out of earshot of every other soul.

"Eve," Vera said, bravery gathered, a statement practiced in her head, which came out fast and as one word. "I'm scared." Instincts pulling hard, she reached through the cool to her sister's warm body, touched her naked belly. "Can we please be serious and talk about this?"

Eve held her breath and went under, her hair rising around like a forest, like a hiding place.

She stayed down. Vera filled her lungs and went down, too, opened her eyes in the green world. Eve looked back. A column of bubbles escaped Eve's nose. Smaller bubbles gathered on their lashes.

They stared for a moment and Eve reached her hands out and poured an invisible cup of tea with an invisible teapot and another for Vera, held the delicate imagined handle, pinky up. They each stirred sugar in, milk, and faked ladylike sips through tightly closed lips. They held their breath until their lungs were fire and they flapped to the surface, the invisible tea party falling into the bottom muck.

When they caught their breath Vera asked, "What would happen if we told Mom?"

"It's a nightmare-dream. The bad news is your teen is pregnant, the good news is you might meet a living Neanderthal who was your dead husband's imaginary friend! It's like the worst television show ever made."

Vera flipped herself over and floated on her back. The sky was heavy with clouds. She felt the sun and the warm surface water. Eve floated herself up, too.

"Do you *feel* weird?" Vera asked.

"I feel tired and my boobs hurt. I don't know how to tell caveman-pregnant from regular-pregnant."

"Would your decision change if you knew it was from the iceman?"

"Either way the thing is a parasite. And I officially hate Lars."

"He's a coward," Vera said. She did, though, continue to feel grateful because his failure meant Eve was hers again. "At least now we know."

"When I think of him I feel violence. For making me into someone who needs help."

"We all need help," Vera said. "I need help to not worry all the time. I need help with chemistry homework. I will need help getting dressed for high school. I need help missing Dad."

Eve shook her head but Vera knew she was saying yes.

Vera continued. "Mom needs help with her mammoth. She needs

help making dinner and cleaning the house. She needs help remembering doctor's appointments and signing permission slips. She needs help missing Dad."

"We're losing her but she's also losing us. When I think about me going to college I feel like I'm going to drown. There were four of us and now there are three and the numbers will just keep getting smaller until, what? Zero. Extinction."

Vera reached for the boat, wanting a rest. She couldn't touch the gunwale. It seemed to have risen a foot in the air.

"I'm cold," she said.

"Freezing."

They swam around the stern and from there, the problem was clear. The boat was listing, one side deep, the other side high. The ladder was above the waterline.

"Is the boat sinking?" Vera whispered.

Eve said, "Did we crash it into something?"

They had noticed no bump. Eve hung onto the high side and tried to bring it lower. Vera hoisted a leg onto the step.

"Wait, this is bad," Vera said, pulling herself up.

The boat was not going to go under right now but it was sinking. They had been swimming for only a few minutes and it had taken on water.

"How is this happening?" Vera asked. "Are we the unluckiest girls in the world?"

They crossed their arms into an X and Vera hauled Eve up.

"Should we swim for shore?" Eve asked.

"We can't leave *this* boat to sink. Helen was down there cleaning and she would have noticed if there was something wrong. We must have hit a rock."

"We went right through the middle of the lake. There aren't rocks in the middle of the lake."

Eve had been tuned toward certain doom and Vera had tried to get a different signal but sometimes the worst thing really was happening. "Eve," she said, "I found something in the castle when I was there with George. A test tube with mammoth hair in it. Someone is taking samples."

Eve said, "A scuba diver emerges out of the water in the marine garage and, naked, suggests we go for a little pleasure cruise in a boat worth more than our dumb little lives and lo, it promptly begins to sink! She wants to kill us or she wants frame us. She's trying to kill us, V."

"Also, George maybe saw me take it."

Eve threw Vera a towel. "Let's try make it to Mom."

They dried themselves fast, put dresses over their heads. Eve turned the engine on and Vera crossed her fingers, relieved when the boat purred awake. They motored across the mirror-still green. Eve drove and Vera sat on the high side to add weight. They went slowly to avoid splashes. When water came over the side Vera bailed it out with a plastic cup from their picnic bag. In addition to fear and anger, she was hungry, she realized, her head fizzy. She bailed and threw the water overboard and ate a piece of bread from the bag even though it was a little soggy.

All along the bank were white and yellow and pink palazzi with the glisten of swimming pools, statues of angels standing guard, hedges high enough for privacy but low enough to facilitate envy.

A sailing yacht skated past. "*Que cosa?*" a curly-haired man yelled, his dark skin shining like marble.

"*Va bene!*" Eve called back, flashing a pretty-girl smile. "*Grazie!*"

"We are not *va bene*," Vera said to her sister.

The man let the sails out, turned the motor on, pulled up alongside. "No, no, no," he said, motioning to the low side. *"Malo. Multo malo."*

He hauled them on board his boat, radioed for help, gave them dry towels and white wine in plastic cups. "Giorgio," he said, his hand out. His skin glinted, his sunglasses, his watch.

In five minutes there were three police boats skimming. Giorgio and the *carabinieri* shouted at one another, telling a story they did not themselves know. Vera and Eve sat silent, girls in need of rescue—no reason to talk to them.

The cigarette boat was hitched to the back of a police boat, the girls were handed across, their wine passed once they were settled.

"Dove?" the policeman asked.

Eve pointed the way.

"Il castello?" Vera said, motioning north.

"Si, si." And they were aloft, skirting the surface, their craft bumping along behind.

Before they got back and discovered their mother and the mammoth gone, or before Helen showed her disappointment at their ongoingness, or fury for the damage to her boat, or their mother's disappointment for their bad teenage choices, Eve and Vera were being rescued by nice policemen in a nice police boat, skimming a stranger's lake. They were only now starting to feel warm again.

"Every day is the strangest day yet," Eve said.

"What if all we had to do was go to high school and watch the boys play football and cheer and sneak alcohol into our sodas?"

"And try not to get date-raped and humiliated and kill ourselves over dead-dad trauma."

"Right," Vera said.

"There are more fucked-up lives but we're definitely on the map."

Soon the *Ophelia* would be inside its little house, sinking lower and lower into the cool emerald. Shipwreck, rot, sunken treasure.

Eve said, "If Dad hadn't died, do you think we'd be here right now? In this crumbling castle baby mammoth Neanderthal pregnancy horror farce?"

"Probably not. We probably would have been in some other distant land waiting around in a boring hotel while he reported for a chapter. Nairobi or Johannesburg."

"Or right up the road in Bolzano."

Vera said, "The fact that our father is dead has made him this weird mythical force in my head. Like he's a god."

"Meanwhile Mom is the one doing all the actual work and keeping us alive and reviving extinct species so she'll have enough of a career to support us, and yet she's the one I end up mad at."

"You're mad at them both."

"True."

"If Dad wasn't dead, you would almost definitely not be pregnant. We never would have gone to Iceland and the iceman cooler would have been safely in a lab or freezer."

"What a shit deal. For all of us."

"Eve? You can still go to college and maybe we'll both get married someday and have amazing, genius children of our own, but I don't want to grow out of you. I don't want you to grow out of me." It was the scariest, most honest thing she had ever said.

Eve slipped her arm under Vera's, laced their fingers together and squeezed hard enough that it hurt.

The sun fell below a cloud and the lake turned dimmer for a moment. It looked like a photograph of a place rather than the place itself. At the helm, the *carabinieri* laughed loudly at their own joke.

"The baby makes us four," Eve said. "Even though I know it's a terrible idea I can't stop thinking about that number."

"It's not going to bring him back."

"I wish he could tell me that himself."

"Are we really that close to Bolzano? In my head it's farther."

"Italy is small. It's probably a few hours away," Eve said.

"Could we go there?" Vera felt like a fish on a hook, someone or something on the other end, reeling. She didn't know if she should flip to get away or allow herself to be pulled.

"To Bolzano?"

"To where Dad died. To the last place he was alive. To ask him, or something?"

The cloud moved and the lake was glitter-shot and stupidly beautiful.

"We've already survived one doomed mission."

"So, no?"

"Yes. Of course it's a yes."

The engine quieted as they neared shore and the *carabinieri* tied the *Ophelia* up in the boathouse and the girls *grazie*'d and the *carabinieri* did not ask for an explanation for the sinking boat. They just waved, as if this were a common occurrence, routine. "*Ciao, ciao!*" they all shouted.

Vera could have run. She felt the hook in her chest, bitten deep into the muscle and meat. She said the word "yes" in her head. Yes, yes and she was sure that Eve had echoed the same refrain. They had not stopped holding hands and did not stop all the way up the hill.

. . .

JANE HELD A SMALL JAR of mammoth pee to the light. It was dark, almost amber. The mammoth, meanwhile, was leaning against a cut log.

Vera scrolled through the news they had to report: possible drowning attempt, mammoth hair in specimen jar, general sense of doom. Those, though, were not her highest concern. She said, "I want to find the place where Dad died. Can we go there, me and Eve? You don't have to come."

Jane's head rolled toward her chest. When she brought it back up she had her eyes closed.

"I'm sorry," Vera said.

"It's just a road and a mountain. You won't find him."

"We need to stand there."

Eve said, "You should come along! It's sure to be terrible and sad!"

Vera could hear in Eve's voice a chasm she might fall through. Mania was a crust on the surface but it would not hold.

The mammoth tracked a butterfly across the sky, wings blue and shimmering, the animal so plain in comparison. "I can't go anywhere. I also don't like the idea of you being far away." The mammoth clawed at the dirt. She walked a few steps and clawed again, as if she might find a secret passage out.

Jane squeezed a full feeding bottle. She said, "I just want her to eat."

Vera said, "Please."

"I don't know the exact location. It was on a tiny highway in the Alps."

"There must be a record," Vera said.

"It's hours away," Jane said.

Eve said, "You can stay here. We have there-and-back drive time plus a good cry in the middle plus gas and dinner. It's two fifteen now. Vera and I will be home by midnight full of disappointment and anguish."

"And maybe relief or a small sense of completion?" Vera whispered.

"Sure, that too," Eve said. "Keys, please?"

"No. I'm sorry, but I'm still the mom." At this, the mammoth let out a long wail.

Vera wanted to tell Pearl that Jane had been their mother first, though now she would have gladly accepted some motherly negligence if it meant they could complete their sad mission.

Jane said, "I don't want you to look the accident up. Once you have a picture in your head you can't ever get it out again. I did not read the police report. I did not read the newspaper clipping. Sometimes being responsible is about what we choose not to know."

The mammoth was running now, loping along the edge of her small world, and it seemed possible to Vera that she could gather enough speed to launch herself over the fence, maybe even fly. Possibility was malleable, expandable.

Eve said, "Helen tried to drown us."

Jane's attention turned sharp. They told her about the scuba diving and the boat and the *carabinieri*. "It could have been a mistake," Vera said.

"Although someone is taking hair samples from the mammoth. Vera found a specimen jar in the castle," Eve added.

Jane did not fight off the notion of foul play like the girls had expected her to.

"We didn't plan this part so carefully. I didn't," Jane said, gesturing to Pearl. The two-hundred-pound animal bittered the fence, looking for a way out. They all wanted an exit. Needed an exit. She corrected: "Another way to say it is that I didn't plan this at all."

"What now, science genius?"

"Can you not be such an asshole all the time?" Jane asked. "What is wrong with you?"

There was something wrong but Vera kept her teeth tight and shook her head. In her sister's squeezed eyelids, she could see the glisten of tears. "I'm actually serious," Eve said. "What are we going to do?"

Somewhere there was the low roar of an airplane engine. Somewhere there was a car horn. Everywhere, birds, flies. Pearl slowed to a walk, picked up and tossed leaves onto her back.

"She deserves vast wilderness. I understand now why Dmitri's place is part of the professor's vision. You can't only make something, you have to put it where it belongs."

"How far away is Dmitri?" Vera asked.

Dmitri, whose cabin looked out on a thousand miles of Siberian permafrost, thick with mammoth bones. Dmitri, who lived far enough from civilization that no one would know what he was raising on his land. Who was waiting every day for this exact beast.

Eve thumbed at Jane's phone. She read, "Sorry, your search appears to be outside our current coverage area for driving."

"Try Yakutsk," Jane said.

"One hundred and thirty-six *hours*. Yikes."

Jane said, "He's as far away as a person can be without leaving the planet."

"Russia is like half the world. Remember all those flights?" Eve said.

"Could we at least try?" Vera was not usually the first to volunteer for a difficult job.

Jane put the pee jar down on the ground, patted her youngest daughter on the back of her neck, took her earlobe between her fingers and rubbed it the way she had when her girls were young and sad. "Thank you, sweetheart," she said. "Another tiny issue is that Dmitri is good friends with my boss."

"So we're stuck," Vera said.

Dusk settled in and Pearl resumed her wailing. Vera could not stand what the sounds did to her guts. The noise was almost solid, a dust storm Vera expected to be able to see in the air. The crying cut like any blade would.

"Please hush," Jane said, going close, but Pearl shook hard and kept the woman away.

The mammoth found new registers for her anguish.

"She's homeless," Vera said.

"Landless," Jane said.

The idea came and Vera said, "Evie, come with me. We'll be back in a minute."

Vera led them at a run back to their house, where she pulled the white sheet off her bed, found a length of string in a drawer, clothespins from the drying rack in the bathroom. She gathered her laptop and the small projector they carried for watching American television on whatever blank wall in whatever country in the world. She handed the electronics to Eve and took the rest herself.

Eve did not ask questions. She carried what was hers to carry.

In the pen Vera strung the line across the space, from one fence to the other, and she hung the sheet over. "Make a stand for the projector," she said to her mother, and Jane rolled a log into position. "Sit," Vera said. Pearl continued to weep, to hunt for an opening.

Vera searched in the search bar, clicked. "Let's try this one."

In a moment, a cone of light shot out of the projector, yellow and full of dust, and on the sheet appeared a scene: tall grass, forevers of grass, wind shifting as one body.

The sheet shuffled in the breeze and the image panned from a shot of the sea over a tall cliff jagged from thousands of years of pummeling. Pearl stood still. Her voice quieted. She watched. The family sat down in the dirt. The mammoth stood behind them, her eyes on the sheet.

From the computer, a tinny voice with a deep, authoritative English accent said, "The Pleistocene. A period of glaciation sometimes known as the Great Ice Age."

The camera panned over the huge blue tongue of a glacier. Snowy peaks, sunset, dark, the sky a shatter of stars, jagged green and blue lights across the black. Below the lights, coats dusted in white, great tusks curved toward the sky, a pack of mammoths pressed forward. The three humans all looked at the real animal to see if she saw her relatives. They were generated by a computer, but so was she, in a way. The human mind and all its gorgeous, awful possibility. Imagined, then real.

Wide shots of endless grass, a sweeping view of waves crashing on the dark sand. Is this your home? they wanted to know. Do you have a home? "Large grazers roamed the steppe," the voice continued. "Mammoths, woolly rhinoceros, mastodons and giraffids, and they in turn were hunted by saber-toothed cats and dire wolves. It was the end of the Neanderthal and the beginning of *Homo erectus*."

They didn't know if Pearl saw clearly, if she could resolve the image on the sheet at all. Unlikely that it made sense to her as a place in the past from which she had somehow come. It stilled her, though. When Pearl came close enough Vera reached out and pet her, combing her fingers through the long hair. It felt like wire. The creature smelled of mud and minerals and fruit-rot.

Pearl looped her trunk and unfurled it again. Her thick eyelashes made her look half dreamed. In her eyes: the reflection of light on fabric, faint green of grassland.

All through the tundra was the music of bodies, huge bodies, and they were moving, moving, moving, moving. Toward food, toward seasons, toward life, toward light. The narrator faded and a single flute played over the mammoths walking, trunks tearing up food as they went, their reddish hair glowing in an imagined sunset.

Jane said, "I will figure out where Dad died and I promise to take you, us, before we leave Italy."

Pearl approached the sheet, smelled it, twisted a corner around her trunk. In a single whoosh, the whole thing fell over her. The world of grass gone, and Pearl stood still, a huge child in a ghost costume with flutes playing for a herd that had disappeared into a beam of light. Jane jumped to help but Pearl shook and the sheet fell off and she looked around and around for something lost.

The voice, now unattached to image, said, "All the music was huge feet trudging through soft snow, and breath—the sound of air in and out, those huge lungs pulling the cold in and exhaling a fog of warmth. Each breath was a cloud and as they went the low sky was made cumulous."

The three women hushed her and Vera tried to restring the sheet but Pearl had gone to the far corner, where she was shaking a post with her trunk.

Vera paused the video and the night was silent.

Jane took out her notebook, turned to a blank page in the back and wrote a note. She read it aloud.

Dear Helen,

Everything that matters to me is here. I hope we're still on the same side. I need a favor, please. Can you find the police report for the death of my husband, Sal Drake? My Italian isn't good enough. And tell me only the highway number kilometer marker and nothing else?

Jane

"Put this under the front door," she said to the girls, "and then go to sleep. We'll need our strength." Vera clutched the note tight, hoped it would be enough, wished that it had never been needed in the first place.

Eight

I n the morning the girls found a tray outside the door. A sterling carafe of orange juice, three moon-shaped pastries in a waxed bag, a bowl of apricots and an envelope. Inside, on a lavender note card, in looping script: *Looking forward to seeing you tonight for a party in honor of George's birthday. 7 p.m., dress up.*

Vera shook her head and said, "Mrs. White, with the wrench, in the conservatory."

"It's just a matter of time."

"Although if she really wanted to kill us all we'd be dead by now. There's still a chance she's just a weird lady with a weird husband and an animal obsession."

Eve said, "And we're just a family of science nerds with a priceless extinct beast, so everyone is a winner." She flipped the paper in her hand and noticed something on the back. One line.

"Vera," Eve said. "The location." Vera came close and they burned the numbers into their eyes. *The accident was on SP98 2.3 kilometers north of Salonetto.* A tiny, tiny key unlocking the black hole. "Should we look?" Eve took out her phone and typed Salonetto, Italy, and a map opened with a white squiggly line and names of towns in both Italian and German. Meltina/Mölten, Vallesina/Versein, Frassinetto/Verscheid. It was a thin line compared to the thicker, straighter yellow one nearby. Vera wished their father had taken the yellow. If he had, he might be alive.

Vera was afraid of revealing this code to Jane, of the way it might burrow out inside and rebreak her. They could not afford to lose another parent. But Vera needed to go to the place and look for some part of her father with a certainty that was beyond sense. "We should at least bring coffee."

They put on bras, jeans, shoes and carried the tray down, now with a cappuccino added, to the pen where they found their mother sitting against the fence, the mammoth under the sheet from the movie, asleep. Her round belly moved with breath, her trunk was in a perfect spiral on the ground. The once white sheet was scuffed and brown.

"Breakfast in bed, sweetie pies," Eve whispered.

Jane reported that Pearl had cried all night. That the animal's eyes were foggy and yellowed. She had worn off a patch of hair on her side from rubbing on a fence post. "She finally fell asleep at dawn," Jane said. She sipped the coffee, grateful. She closed her eyes. Her face looked like an abandoned building. "You are good girls."

Vera did not ask if the mammoth had eaten because Jane would have been victorious if she had. "We didn't make the tray," Vera said. "And you might like this part less." She handed over the card. "It was all on the doorstep this morning."

Jane opened her eyes for a second and took the card, which Vera had turned to the back side. She looked at the highway number and town name the same way the girls had. Vera said, "It's a mountain highway, like you said. Really twisty. Probably gorgeous."

Jane did not look up. She said, "GPS coordinates for the end of life as we knew it."

The sound of a car on a dirt road, coming closer, then stopping in the drive. A door slam. Everything made Vera's blood jag.

"Turn the card over," Eve said.

Jane read. "A party invitation to a ball? As if we are on a cruise, on holiday? Absolutely not. We decline."

"Whoa, Gloves-Off-Mom, I like it," Eve said.

Vera said, "I thought you trusted her."

"I did."

"You no longer do?"

Eve said, "She knows what we have, she knows who we are, she knows where you work."

"When can we go to Salonetto?"

Jane's eyes were red. She said, "I'm so crushingly tired. Maybe we should let Pearl die and give Helen the body. I don't even care anymore. I just want to sleep for a year." They all looked at the sleeping mammoth, tucked under what was probably an expensive sheet, dreaming something none of them could ever guess at. Jane said, "Our brains are too powerful. We can invent things that are then out of our control. We are massive and minuscule at the same time."

"It all lands at once sometimes, huh?" Eve said.

"You can't not try to fix the problems. Giving up on the planet and the species and all species is also not an answer," Vera added.

"So, what then?" Jane asked.

"Onward," Vera said. "What else?"

"I still think there's an argument for quitting all the good intentions to have fun while the ship sinks," Eve said.

Vera told Jane, "Don't listen to Eve. Go snuggle down with Pearl and take a nap. All of these questions will be easier to answer when you've had some rest." She took off her sweatshirt and balled it up for a pillow.

"Don't listen to me," Eve said. "Sweet dreams."

Vera put a hand on Jane's head. She had never done this before, never felt the heat of her mother's scalp and the slip of her hair. Warmth traveled the length of Vera's body like she had submerged herself in a bath. Defeated, eyes flat and sad, Jane curled close to the animal, wrapped herself up in a corner of the sheet. She had been trampled by attention and care and was out instantly. Her daughters listened to the music of the two bodies at rest—long rattle of the mammoth breaths and short pull of the woman's. They looked like a plate from a leatherbound book of fairy tales. Beauty and beast.

Vera would remember this image all her life. Her mother, brown hair full of leaves, bent around a mass of fur. As if she had been meant to sleep this way, as if this animal were her natural kin.

"She seems weak," Eve said quietly. "What if she's dying?"

Vera thought Eve meant their mother. Of sadness, of exhaustion. Air caught in her throat and made her cough.

Eve continued, "I guess if she dies we'd have lots of choices. Freeze her for study or bury her for dignity or have her stuffed for Helen's museum or sell her body for millions."

Not mother, Vera realized. Of course not. Relief prickled her neck. Vera thought of a girl she had met once whose mother had frozen their dead kitten until the spring thaw when they could bury her in the yard. "I think she won't fit in the freezer?" she said.

"Fair point," Eve said.

"We could bury her right here and pretend none of this ever happened."

"What's wrong with her, anyway?" Eve asked.

"Aside from starvation? And whatever the professor discovered about modified animals dying early? Alleles?"

"Maybe it has nothing to do with the science experiment. She needs her mother's milk. She needs her mother."

There was a thin whine in the leaves, air caught and trying to press through.

This animal had been alive for almost three weeks, a miraculous three weeks. She had not eaten in five days. Vera wished the fact that she had been conceived, gestated, born at all had been enough. They had already far surpassed any dream. Science was a hungry profession. Progress found no resting place. Heat filled Vera's cheeks, her hands. She wanted to harm something. She wanted to scream at the sky for the thing that was alive in Eve's body, for the life that was missing in their family. She wanted to climb out of this day, this skin. No one was happy here. Had they ever been?

"You look like you're about to catch on fire," Eve said.

"What are we going to do? What what what?"

"Let's see," Eve said. "Sinking boat, mammoth-hair specimen tube, stolen embryo, rich people who are used to getting whatever they want. Coordinates for a treasure map only it's not treasure at the other end. And I'm pregnant! This is so fun! The *funnest*. But I feel weirdly calm."

Eve seemed to see in her sister's eyes that the wires were burning. She said, "We are going to be fine. We have already survived the hardest thing." She sounded like a mother. Like a person who knew how to be an anchor, to steady. She would be all right if she had the baby and she would be all right if she didn't, Vera thought. Eve put a hand on her own forehead and tried to cool herself.

Vera said, "I'd feel better if Mom had any plan at all."

"It might be up to us."

Here, the silence was sharp as a sword. The danger was impossible to assess and therefore so was the escape.

"Come on, little sister, let's get ready for the party." Eve led Vera through the gate, latched it behind them quietly so as not to awaken the sleeping pair. Eve made two pots of hot water and the girls soaked their feet, scrubbed them with a piece of sandpaper they found under the sink, lotioned, painted toes. Eve stirred a jar of honey and reached her two first fingers into it and said, "Close your eyes," and she spread a thin layer on Vera's face. "Honey is antiseptic and moisturizing," she said. This was the medicine they had now. Vera tried to believe that it was enough.

"Let's say Helen is trying to kill us. What should we do? If this were a movie, what would we be yelling at the girls on screen?"

Eve thought about it. "Mom won't leave the baby and she doesn't think Helen and George are dangerous, so running away is out. What else? Could we be proactive and try to befriend the devils? Make some kind of deal?"

"Deal?"

"If the baby is going to die anyway, we could at least get in on the profits. We could promise to keep the secret if they pay us a cut?"

They lay on the grass in the sun in bathing suits and pretended that they were rich girls, lazy, time always spacious and plentiful. As if their life were dedicated to the enjoyment of the world's pleasures—the sweet, the salt.

"Mom feels like a ghost. Almost like she's disappearing," Vera said.

"No one else can disappear."

"You sound like a grown-up," Vera said. Eve had always seemed infinitely older, but it was Vera who was used to acting out responsibility. "Did this ice-baby make you into an adult?"

Eve laughed hard. "You know those Mardi Gras cakes with the tiny plastic baby baked in there and whoever gets the baby buys the cake the next year? We should make one of those only put a little Neanderthal in there and bring it to the party and make an announcement about my 'situation' and say that whoever gets the plastic caveman gets the baby. We could really ruin everyone's evening."

"I do feel like baking."

"You always feel like baking."

"If you're going to befriend the devil, bring sugar."

So they baked. They had no replica hominid but they did know where to pick lemons to zest and they had flour and butter and Eve helped Vera instead of watching from the table. "Beat the whites," Vera said, "till they form little mountains." And Eve beat, her arm burning, her face red, and then Vera took a turn and it felt good to work hard, to change the form of a simple ingredient from a liquid into a pale delicate range.

WHILE THE CAKE BAKED they went to check on the rest of their family and found their mother still asleep. The mammoth stood up and stretched. "Hey, little love," Vera said.

Jane's phone, on a stump, was buzzing. Vera looked at it. "The professor," she said. When it stopped she saw that he had called three other times. "Yikes."

The mammoth walked to the gate and looked out at the forest. She wrapped her trunk around the handle and pulled at it.

"You want to go for a walk?" Eve asked.

"We shouldn't?" Vera said.

"We'll be careful," Eve said. "Mom needs to sleep." She unclicked the gate, wrapped the big rope around the animal's neck and took her into the world. Out the gate, through the oaks. They stopped under the mulberry tree covered in tiny black fruits and Vera reached to pick them. She opened her palm for Pearl who eventually turned her head and licked the berries up. "She's eating!" Vera said in a shout-whisper so as not to disturb the mammoth. She searched immediately for more and Eve quickly reached and picked and fed and reached and picked and fed.

The baby looked at them, big eyed and sloppy with juice. She might have been smiling. Vera said, "We were giving you elephant formula but you're not an elephant, are you? You're the kind of animal that eats berries right from the tree."

Pearl licked and swallowed the tiny fruits, her tongue turning dark pink. There were thousands of gems on the tree but most too high for Eve and Vera, even if one boosted the other. Eve said, "You reach," to Pearl and put her arm beside her face like a trunk. Pearl swished and breathed and searched Vera's body for sweets. "They're there, on the tree," she said.

Eve picked a handful and the fruits popped open on her tongue, tiny beads of sugar. "So good," she said.

Vera's mind had normalized the mammoth-in-pen still life. This, though, was a surprise all over again: a baby woolly standing at the berm of a hill beneath a mulberry tree, her long lashes lit by sun. They picked and ate until all the reachable fruit was gone. Pearl turned and began to walk the other way.

"Maybe you're thirsty? Would you drink lake water?" Pearl's trunk swished the ground, marking her presence with arcs in the dirt.

On the path to the shore Vera said, "I've been reading about elephants. Their feet are sensitive enough to be able to feel the footprints of herds that passed years before. And they cover their dead in leaves."

Vera watched Pearl move, wondered what she understood, the story she was detecting with her feet, her trunk, her big eyes.

"I wonder if she can sense that her mother is alive somewhere else," Eve said.

If Vera had let that fact settle in her she would have wept for the rest of her life. An elephant, rare and beautiful, wiser than they were, had suffered for the sake of a project their own mother had conceived. The math was too much.

"It feels like we don't deserve them," Vera said.

"We don't deserve anything," Eve added. "We are a garbage species."

Vera felt rotted desire in her chest, how the professor's want, the university's want, had gotten them to the farthest edge of the earth, where they dug up a frozen animal, which had contributed to the process of making embryos in petri dishes, squiggles full of grand and valid justifications and money and potential acclaim. Her mother's own hands, desirous hands, had taken the embryos and made them come to life and she had all the reasons to do this—the planet, the deletions humans had made, working against the expectations of her gender, of motherhood—but Vera knew that plenty of what had pressed Jane across the planet with the potential miracle in a cooler was a wish to be singular.

Jane had gotten this wish. She was the only one of her kind, just like Pearl was. They were a mother/daughter pair unlike any the world had ever known, except no one knew, and hopefully never would. Jane had made herself so special that she had to disappear.

"She seems better already," Eve said, patting the animal's back. Pearl was combing the ground, almost trotting, her feet flattening with each step, accordions letting out breath.

"Maybe she was just terribly bored. And sad," Eve said. She squinted hard, wiped her eyes on her sleeve.

"Are you okay?" Vera asked.

"I'm hanging in. This"—she held her breath a moment, looked up at the sky—"turns out to be very hard."

Vera said, "We'll take turns."

"Being idiots? Don't follow in my footsteps, please."

"Knowing what to do. Eve, I have money in my savings account. I never spend anything I'm given. We'll take the train to Germany or France or wherever we need to. I'll cover it all." Vera wanted their bodies to match again.

Eve closed her eyes. "You don't have to jump into my sinking ship."

"Your ship is not going to sink. I'm your *carabiniere*. I'm your lonely yachtsmen with chilled white wine."

Eve nodded, pressed her palms into her eyes. "Thank you." She let out a long breath and said, "I am furious at the world and I wish we at least had something good to wear tonight."

"Being furious and having nothing to wear is our teenage job. But we are taking a woolly mammoth on a walk. No one else has ever done this."

The stone path led them through succulents and magnolia trees and oleander to the pebbled beach. Pearl trotted to the shore, dropped her trunk into the green, green lake and sucked, and sprayed the water into her mouth. She shook her head and did an almost-dance. For the first time since they had arrived, there was enough air to breathe. Joy was a bubble, rising. Vera and Eve laughed while before them, a woolly mammoth drank from an alpine lake and sprayed jewels of water into the sky, bright and wild, which made a song as they landed. Vera felt something so pure it was almost painful. Love, helpless and fragile. A baby, discovering water for the first time. What luck to be there to see it.

SEEING THE PARTY PREPARATIONS was seeing how money could blur the border between the lives lived inside one's head and the ability to make those lives real.

A long table was being set up outside with a fabric tent over it and strings of lights hanging in the trees. There was gold thread in the tablecloth and deep-pink rose petals all over the ground. The cake Vera held looked meager and ridiculous. She wanted to be back in the mammoth pen celebrating the mulberry-eating, lake-happy mammoth. The day kept flipping over, manic and then bottoming out.

"Can we skip bringing this in?"

"She's real classy. If Mom recovered from injury, what kind of party would we throw?" Eve asked. "Maybe a Black and White Ball? A Vegas-themed casino party?"

Vera did not pick up the joke like Eve seemed to think she would. This—Jane dying—was too scary to speak of.

The house smelled like olives and lemons. In the arched brick of the kitchen, six women were cooking, Constantina and five others. There were serving dishes stacked, someone standing in front of a counterful of silver with a polishing rag.

A sound from outside: violinists practicing.

From the dark of a long hallway, in a gold robe, Helen appeared. Her hair was twisted up in a turban, also gold, and she had cotton balls between her red toes.

"Queen Helen," Eve said, curtsying.

"Shush," Helen told her. "Don't be jealous. You'll be the honored guests."

"I thought the honored guest was George," said Eve.

"And after him, there's you all."

Vera heard this as a soft threat. As if the path to honor in this house was pain. She thought of Pearl, precious because she had been brought back from the dead. "Shit," she said without meaning to, because Eve was hosting her own resurrection.

Vera remembered when they were kids, stuck close in increasingly foreign lands. They played checkers in France while their father went inside a cave full of Neanderthal bones; they made up dance routines to pop songs in Kenya while he measured the eye socket of a hominid; they painted their toenails in a Cape Town bathroom while in the lab the femur of a long-ago child was carbon dated; they had made a regular-seeming life in California while their mother turned an elephant stem cell into a mammoth embryo. When they still had two parents and moved all the time, Eve and Vera were each other's normal, this home base carried like contraband. Then they had one parent and lived in one place and they were each other's normal, again and still. Normal kept changing. Normal kept being less so, and now Eve had been joined by a force that changed the chemistry of their twosome. They might be a family of four again, dad replaced by baby. Numbers that again seized at Vera.

"You don't have to serve this," Vera said, holding the cake out.

There was probably something architectural for dessert, sugar-work, chocolate flowers.

"How cute," Helen said. "You can leave it there on the side table. Come. You need something to wear. I assume you did not pack for a ball."

The girls looked at each other in the dark room surrounded by oil paintings and stained glass. "We'll be all right in what we have," Vera said.

"I wouldn't mind," Eve said.

Good choices were harder and harder to gauge, Vera's instincts muddled and grabby.

Helen said, "You girls deserve to be gorgeous."

Eve walked toward Helen, drawn by the promise of her own beauty. No more tempting bait could have been offered.

Vera turned back and saw her cake, misplaced, a child's attempt in an adult room. Open doors led to a blue-and-white-tiled patio overlooking the sea, pots full of flowers, and across the water, houses running up the hillsides like vines. Monkeys howled and birds chipped at the air with their song. The person standing here was meant to feel as if everything was theirs. All water, all earth, all life.

HELEN LED THE GIRLS up the twist of stairs to a room with a giant iron bed made up in deep red silks and a woven tapestry of maidens and unicorns in a wood on the wall above.

Vera hovered by the door in case she needed to make a run for it.

Helen studied them. "You don't trust me," she said, and opened an armoire of intricate inlay and deep wood-smell. "But not all old women who do what they want are witches." She took out dress after dress— ivory, indigo, gold, rose, vermilion—and laid them out on the bed. They were a flock of spirits to Vera, lovely emptiness awaiting bodies.

Eve ran a palm over the indigo, firm shantung silk. "All right then, if you are not a witch, why might you try to drown us?"

The little sister, hands twisting together, readied herself to defend, to explain, to escape.

Helen jerked in surprise. "Drown you? Are you talking about the hole you put in my boat? And how I told George I myself hit a rock to protect you?"

"We did *not* hit a rock."

"Evie, maybe it's true," Vera said. "We don't know."

Helen smiled at Vera and Vera searched for truth in the woman's face, good or evil or love or hate. Helen said, "Everyone is crazy, dear girl. We're all capable of goodness and we're all capable of hurt."

"Fine, sure, philosophy blah blah. But we didn't hit a rock and the boat sank right when you sent us out in it. Doesn't that seem like a clue?"

Helen tucked a strand of hair behind Eve's ear. "Life isn't something that just happens to you. Your mum is caring for a woolly mammoth because she didn't wait for someone to give her permission. Maybe it's time to start making your own luck."

A flash of the luck Vera wanted most darted across her mind. It was the most boring kind: Dad at the stove with pasta boiling, Mom feeding some entirely unexotic pet, the girls working on math home- work at the table. California light through the window. Unremarkable, complete.

"What is that supposed to even mean? I'm accusing you of attempted murder and you're giving a TED talk." Eve was angry and Helen was a perfect target, but Helen did not seem to mind. She put her hand over her heart and said, "I solemnly swear that I did not try to kill you. All right? We don't know each other and I won't ask what you want from the world, but you should ask yourselves. You're old enough."

Vera studied this woman, this everything-in-the-palm-of-her-hand adult. Helen reached into the armoire and took out a metal case the size of a shoe box. It was red enamel, and from her bra she drew a tiny key on a golden chain that she fit into the lock. She said, "I should be happy, shouldn't I? I have all the things that people think will make them so." Covering the contents of the case was a piece of black velvet, which Helen rolled up, revealing more black velvet, this dotted with large, glittering jewels.

Eve audibly gasped. "You should definitely be happy."

Helen unpinned a necklace with a diamond at the center the size of her thumbnail and a string of sapphires going all the way around. She picked it up and brought it to Vera's neck, draped. Vera held perfectly still, caught in an expensive trap. The stones were cold and heavy on her skin and she could feel Helen's breath as she did the clasp. Helen said, "You'll have happiness and you'll also have misery and loss. What matters is what you *do*. Create something. Cultivate something. Grow something."

"Like our mom?" Vera asked.

"Exactly. I admire her very much. It's why I invited her here."

Helen stood back and assessed Vera in her T-shirt and jewels. "You look better in that than I ever did." Vera did not know what to say or do. The stones were warming, she was warming them, and they felt good, the weight on her chest. They almost seemed to vibrate.

"It's gorgeous," Eve said, peeking into the case to see what else might be waiting there.

"Anything for me to luck into in there? While we consider our life's great purpose?" Eve asked.

"You need rubies. You need heat." Onto Eve's neck Helen strung a red teardrop.

"Hello, friend," Eve said, tucking her chin to admire.

"They're yours. Keep them. I've had my fun."

Vera no-no-no-no'd but Eve was silent with manic hope-joy and Helen pivoted back to the closet, where she paged through dresses like they were a huge, silken book.

Helen turned to Vera. "That's the second lesson of the day: if someone gives you a gift, accept with gratitude and humility. Don't turn the good parts away."

"Thank you?" Eve said, the words enough for a glass of wine but not crown jewels.

"It's too, too much," Vera said. Her sister had been sure that Helen was an evil queen but she was easily shushed with the candy apple. Someone needed to be the antidote, or at least refuse the poison.

"I won't force you. But I don't have daughters and I don't need so much stuff. You owe me nothing."

"We really, really shouldn't," Vera said, her eyes on Eve, willing her to understand.

"Then we'll borrow them," Eve said. "Just for tonight."

"Fine." Helen seemed annoyed.

"Should we see about that evening wear?" Eve prompted.

Vera cut in. "Eve, no. We don't have to. We can wear what we have."

"Eve is right," Helen said. "Enough dillydallying. Time to make you lovely." Helen put her hands on Vera's shoulders and studied her face and hair, the necklace. She reached for a blue dress. "You'll be beautiful in something cool." She draped it over Vera's arms. "And you," she said to Eve. "You want to be cold but you're not really. All the undertones are warm." She took a white dress and held it under Eve's neck. "Look at that," Helen said. "It sets off your gorgeous eyes." Everyone wants someone to admire their undertones and overtones, Vera thought. Eve smoothed the white dress, falling clearly in love. The blue ghost over Vera's arm pulled her downward.

"You can change in there, if you'd like privacy."

Vera could see a clawfoot tub, patterned tile floor, a window looking out at the vineyards, but Eve said, "It's fine. We've seen you naked."

Vera undressed quickly and, without unfurling her body, slithered into the blue. It was a little loose and it felt like a substance rather than a garment, a pool of water.

"Oh, V. You look amazing," Eve told her sister. "Your little boobies. You're a fox."

In the mirror, Vera saw someone she had not met. A near woman. "Oh," she said, because she couldn't find the language.

"Perfection," Helen said. "I must have known a young maid would one day visit me. It was waiting for you."

Eve stripped to her ratted black bra and pink lace underwear and rubies. Mostly naked, Eve squared herself to Helen. "So, just to be clear, are you saying that you definitely did not put a hole in that boat?" The stones and the silk were motive to trust, to accept Helen's story.

"I look powerful and you feel vulnerable. But I'm just an old woman with a lot of pets. We are not enemies."

Maybe it really was a rock or an old, slow leak. They were here because they shared a woolly mammoth. Probability did not seem to be part of this summer.

"Can we bring the elephant back? Maybe it will be fine now," Vera said.

"We've had the elephant for twenty years. She's like our child. She's already rejected the baby so there's no point in making them both suffer."

Eve stepped into the white dress and pulled it over her shoulders. Helen fastened the tiny pearl button at the neck. She turned, checked out her back and butt and then faced the mirror again. "I look incredible in this. On that we can all agree." She touched the necklace on her collarbone.

Helen said, "You look like a bride, but better because you don't have a groom."

"I am super-excited not to get married today. I can't *wait* to not walk down the aisle."

"That's the spirit," Helen said.

"Thank you for the dresses," Vera told her. "And the jewelry. We'll take good care of them and return them in the morning."

"Now go back to your cottage and do your hair and makeup while I zip this body into something that will make my husband miserable with lust. Time to make some luck." She winked.

THE GIRLS DESCENDED THE PATH, Vera in floor-length blue, her hair in a tight bun. Eve, wearing a white gown, like a woman who was about to make a promise. Neither of them was wearing shoes. Their mother and the mammoth were both covered in hay, the sun patchy, the smell of animal thick in the air. The animal was sleeping.

"Are you jerks ready to party?" Eve asked. She held up the yellow sundress she had brought for their mother, the best thing they could find. It all landed on Vera hard: the jewels and the gowns and the way she looked and felt older than she had in the morning and the baby she might be an aunt to and the precious beast and their mother who was dirty and unprepared for all the care she needed to give and the distance they all were from home and the fading idea of their father and the person he had once been.

Jane took in her girls, light jagging off the gems they wore. "Are those real?" she asked. "Those can't be real."

"You bet they are," Eve told her.

"We're giving them back," Vera told her mother.

"Of course you're giving them back," Jane said.

Jane had not been taken into the magical wardrobe. She held the yellow sundress up to her chest. She looked old and childlike at the same time. Behind her was the small, sad pyramid of mammoth shit that Jane had shoveled and shaped, evidence of starvation.

"How is she?" Vera asked.

"She's alive," Jane said. "At least for now. At least we know she loves mulberries."

"It's almost time. Do you want to change?"

"Not really."

Vera had something she wanted to say. She had practiced in her head. "Hey, Mom? We don't know how long she'll live. Pearl. It's unlikely to be the usual span though, right?" Pearl with the soupy eyes, with the playful trunk, with the tufty hair.

"You sound like a good Berkeley Buddhist."

"I'm just a kid."

"She could start eating and live for a hundred years. She could die today. We have no idea."

"Now who's the Buddhist?" Eve said.

Jane said, "When you were tiny your dad used to walk you around and name everything he saw. He said, 'Oak, poplar, ash, honey locust,' and also 'Cadillac, Toyota, Mercury, Ford,' because he wanted to explain the world to you. Usually he returned cheerful but one time he came in from a walk when Vera was a newborn and Eve was two and he was crying and told me, 'They are going to die someday.' He had made something mortal. He couldn't justify it."

"He should have been worried about his own life span," Eve said.

Jane said, "He was the one who always insisted we pay for the better hotel, the safer train instead of the dangerous minibus."

Eve said, "So, the lesson then is to be less careful and survive longer? Or is the lesson that fate will come for us all? Or is the lesson that there is no such thing as a fair shake?"

"She's the only one," Jane said. "I'm finding it harder to accept whatever comes because that's *it*."

Vera felt like the only one of her kind, too. Alone in her head, trying to match up with another soul along the journey. Her parents' marriage, which was, by definition, a joint effort, now belonged to one person. Eve would go away to college, and the likelihood that the sisters would live in the same apartment in the same mid-sized city was low. Vera would keep losing what now kept her alive. Somehow she was supposed to exist on the fumes of faith that she could choose a new partner and conjure an entire existence with that person, a person she had not yet met, who was floating in the world somewhere, their lives waiting to crash together and entangle. What if she wanted to be spinster sisters, witches in their own witch house, for absolutely ever? Faith was foreign. The idea that someone might genuinely believe, that belief could cut a window into a grieving heart, was unfamiliar to Vera.

"She's the only mammoth," Eve affirmed. "For now. May Pearl live long and prosper. You've proven that it's possible. You've proven that it's not the end of the line. We can keep watch while you go get ready."

"The professor called and I answered," Jane said. Her daughters met her eyes and waited for the rest. For the accusation. "The mummy you found is the most recent mammoth specimen ever discovered. It proves that mammoths were alive under five thousand years ago. We used to think the last ones were gone ten thousand years ago."

"Whoa?" Vera asked. "That sounds important."

Eve said, "High five! Do we get a prize? Veve for the win!"

"It means woolly mammoths aren't prehistoric. That they could belong now. The prize is that he wants me to come back to help author a paper. The mammoth will be displayed in the natural history museum in New York, in a freezer with a window, just like the iceman. He wants to send Todd to finish up in Iceland. The prize is a line on my CV. A good one. If I do it." She did not need to say the reason she was not sure if she would go back. The reason pushed against Jane's leg. Not frozen and ancient, but here and now. "You guys found him. Maybe you two should write the paper and I should stay here and take care of Pearl," Jane said. She sounded part serious.

Eve laughed. "That's ridiculous, Mom. We're scouts. We know nothing about anything."

"I don't want to go to the party," Jane said.

"She'll be fine for a few hours," Vera told her mom. "We'll check on her."

"I'm her mother. That's the part I hadn't anticipated."

"What if we thought of it as being her shepherds," Vera said. "Rather than her family."

Eve said, "Are you the lone yachtsman for Mom, too? How much chilled white wine do you have in that boat of yours?"

Vera did not know how much of anything she had. She was fifteen. Estimating how far she could get on reserves was entirely unproven.

"Look," Eve said, "you've gotten two humans to near adulthood and here stands an almost imaginary creature. You and your amazing daughters are responsible for a major fossil find. That's more than a lot of moms can say, and you did the last two, almost three years without any help."

Jane slipped her T-shirt over her head, unbuttoned her jeans and almost lost her balance taking them off. She stood back up in her underwear, brushed hay off her stomach. Her skin was soft and loose around the middle. Vera handed her the yellow dress. Jane said, "I wasn't quite ready for you to be so beautiful so soon. Does that sound like a terrible thing to say?" Vera and Eve were swishes of white and blue, the scent of perfume. "I feel like an underdone piece of chicken," Jane said, looking down at herself.

Eve tried for good humor. "It's like they always say, you look down for one week to breed a woolly mammoth and when you look up again your little girls have turned into women."

IN THE DRIVEWAY, guests tumbled out of cars in silvers, reds, golds, hair shined, jewels bright. Jane kept looking back over her shoulder toward the pen and Eve and Vera kept pulling leaves out of her hair.

There were twelve people at dinner, all English except a young couple who spoke only Italian and sat together at one end of the table talking as if no one else were present. The guests had questions about a good hotel in Cyprus, and someone suggested a little fish restaurant that alone was worth the plane fare. They compared notes on a luxury train in India and a safari outfitter in South Africa.

In the background, the violinists played all the soft parts of every Italian opera. They were like a sprinkle of salt—enhancing everything without being a distraction. It felt like a stage play of a party. Scripted and neat. Not an impossible and doomed secret experiment. These people were just people, enjoying their sweet, gilded lives.

Helen was an overflowing glass. She wore a red velvet gown and her skin was smooth and shining and in her lap sat a small black monkey with a white face wearing an embroidered collar and leash. The monkey ate walnuts off Helen's plate and reached its long fingers up to feed a bite to its master. Helen took the nut, patted the animal and continued a funny story about warthogs. She topped off everyone's Prosecco while they laughed. She interrupted herself to recommend the olives, cured here, the essence of this place on earth.

Before dinner was cleared, Jane was drunk and the girls watched her list slightly. Everyone was dressed for a ball and Jane looked like an oblivious American on vacation. No one was talking to her.

"I want to hug her," Vera said. "The great scientist."

Constantina appeared with the first plates of a pasta course. "Everyone's favorite creepy caretaker," Eve said under her breath. Next came a meat course, a cheese course. The food was bright beauty, every bite. The monkey ate everything everyone else ate, fingers plucking noodles, bits of steak that Helen had cut small, bread.

Helen climbed up on her chair and clinked her glass. The music stopped. The monkey jumped to her shoulder and perched like an exclamation point for everything Helen wanted to say.

"Friends," Helen said. "Thank you for being here. Georgie claims he doesn't like parties or birthdays, but sometimes you have to celebrate even if you don't want to." People laughed. They cheered. Gelato melted into lemon pools in their bowls and the flies waited to feast.

Helen continued, "George is a difficult man to please. He likes animals better than people. And I know most of you are aware of the women. Some of you maybe *were* the women." Deep quiet from the guests. The monkey wrapped its arm around the back of Helen's neck, its black hand resting on her collarbone. Vera scanned the table and there were downcast eyes. At least the guests would wait to ridicule until they were safely back in their luxury vehicles. George, however, was looking directly at Helen, eyes locked to hers, a smile pasted like a gag. Helen said, "We may not have had the life either of us imagined but we've done things no one else has. To George." Clinks across the table.

George stood. "To my lovely wife, who always gets what she wants." Everyone drained their glasses. George took Helen's hand and waltzed her slowly, his bad leg a constant interruption. They were a couple hauling with them a lifetime of wrongs. The monkey clung to Helen and played with her hair.

The guests danced because there was music and the night was warm and someone had lit a hundred candles in glass cups all over the patio and the trees were full of tiny lights and there were the stars beyond, and the night jasmine opened and made everything sweet.

THINGS GREW BLUER, the air all watersmell. Jane sipped bubbly, moonlight on her face. She looked like a safe resting place. "Would you please dance with me?" Vera asked, and they danced, mother and daughter the same size, hitting the beat the same way, eye to eye.

"When did you get so tall?" Jane asked. "You were supposed to be the baby."

"I have been here all along," Vera said.

"But you were a kid and now you're not a kid."

Vera took her hand from her mother's waist and put it out. "Nice to meet you, Mom."

"It's lovely to meet you, Miss Vera," Jane said, and they shook.

They danced past George and Helen and overheard George say, "Did you ever love me or just the animals?"

"Trouble in paradise," Vera whispered to her mother.

Jane said, "You'd think they'd be the happiest people on earth."

"You doing all right?" Vera asked.

Jane nodded without conviction. "My job is to be all right."

Vera kissed her mother on the cheek. "We could help?"

Eve walked up and said, "Can I join?" and Jane said, "I was admonishing Vera for growing up too fast," and Eve broke. Tears and tears.

"Evie," Jane said, "Hey, hey." She pulled her daughter closer.

Eve had managed to be fine in every moment until this one.

"What is happening?" Jane asked. She pulled her daughter in, this grown body, but one she had held when it was six pounds, twelve pounds, forty.

"So," Eve said. She looked at her mother, eyes still smudged with party makeup. "I am pregnant."

Vera waited for the storm. For the sky to split. Jane stepped back from Eve and held her by the shoulders. Jane's eyes were not fury and fire. She looked almost relieved. She said, "There are moments that mothers are taught to fear and this is one of them."

"And?" Eve said, waiting for a slap or a scream.

"I remember a mother at the park saying, 'They're cute now but in a few years they'll come home pregnant.' As if that was the worst it could get."

"*And?*"

"And here we are."

They were at the cliff's edge and Vera could still feel breath in her lungs, blood in her body. Neither Jane nor Eve looked monstrous or transformed. They looked sad. They looked like people who needed to be held on to.

"Lars," Jane said out loud, and Vera pictured the head of blond hair, the red beard. People were strangers and then they were part of your life forever.

Eve did not offer the other possibility. "Lars," she said, and Vera could hear the cold North Atlantic.

"I'm so sorry," Jane told her, and surprise lit Eve's face like a bare bulb.

"*You're* sorry?" Eve said.

"When did you find out?"

"A few days ago," Eve said.

"I won't tell you what to do, but I will help you in any way you need me to," Jane said. She looked so calm, like she had been built for this. "I got pregnant in college, before I met your dad. It was some dumb boy who didn't have a condom and I was too scared to make him stop. I never even told him."

Eve squinted at her mother. "It's weird to think about you as a stupid kid."

"Really? I feel like I wear my stupidity on my sleeve. I married my professor, which could have turned out way worse than it did, and I'm sure I don't have to point out that our current situation is entirely my making."

"You're the only person I know who's brave enough to do what you want," Eve said.

Jane found Eve's eyes. "Thank you for saying that. My Eve. I think you are an amazing person."

Eve, prepared for every possibility but this one, leaned her head on her mother's shoulder and soaked her through.

Vera stood close, a satellite planet in orbit. This felt like one of the most important moments ever to occur in their family and she was only sort of part of it.

Around them, the party guests danced, because that's what they had come for.

Helen and George dipped and drank, glass for glass, until Helen wobbled away. Vera watched her stumble and, a sudden brave storm in her chest, followed. Helen, it turned out, was headed to the row of rose-bushes at the edge of the castle where she put her hands on the stones and bent her head and threw up into the leaves and blooms. When Helen was finished emptying herself, she stood and there was Vera with a napkin and a glass of water.

"Hi," Vera said. Helen's monkey stared at her with suspicion. "Nice monkey."

Helen took the water. "Thank you. She's my best accessory."

"We're an accessory, too, aren't we? That's why you said yes to my mom's proposal."

Helen smelled of amber and animal skin and vomit. She turned her head away, her earrings glinting like caught stars. "I've never been anything but nice to you all."

"What do you want from us?"

"I got more than I asked for already."

"Are you able to listen, because I have something important to ask."

Helen drank water. "All right," she said. "Go on."

"I need you to tell me if we're safe here."

Helen steadied herself against the wall. "I always knew you were the smartest one in your family," Helen said.

"My sister still thinks you are an evil witch queen even though you gave her jewelry, and . . ."

"You are."

". . . my mom is so sleep deprived she can't think at all and I am not supposed to be in charge. We are?"

"I wasn't finished."

Helen ran her hands through her hair and wiped the mascara from under her eyes. "You are safe, but George wants to sell the mammoth."

Vera did not move. Was this true? There was no evaluating reality here. The place and the things happening in it were sometimes solid, sometimes liquid, sometimes gas. The monkey spit an olive pit on the ground.

"I wanted to raise the thing and let it live its life and then stuff it for the museum. Everyone always suspects the witch, but it's the king you have to worry about."

"Sell it to who?"

"A friend. He stocks the private zoos of people richer and more absurd even than myself."

"Now?"

"Soon. George was hoping Pearl would be healthier first."

Helen bent to kiss Vera on the forehead. Vera was frozen. Warm lips, the lips of the suspect. Helen smelled slightly sour. "The hole in the boat?" Vera asked.

"Not I, sweet girl," Helen breathed. She brought her face close to Vera's ear and whispered, "The keys are in the van."

Vera repeated this to herself. The keys are in the van. "Where would we go?" she asked.

Helen shrugged. "I like you even if you don't like me," she said.

"I thought you were tired of us. I thought we were getting in your way."

"Other things are in my way. Being a jealous wife is in my way. Not having my own money is in my way. And I'm *plenty* tired."

"Is this a trap?"

"You have no choice but to trust me."

Vera reached around to the back of her neck and unclasped the necklace, dropped it into Helen's hand and squeezed the woman's fist shut around the treasure. "You swear this is not a trap?"

Helen gave a single nod.

Vera gripped hard, punctuation for a forced promise. The monkey climbed down, put its black mouth on Vera's wrist and, gently, bit.

VERA MET EVE'S EYES from across the floor. The musicians took a break and the night's sounds returned. Bugs, wind, lake water. South Seas birdsong and the hoot of something large and wild. Some guests left the party but not the property. Vera glimpsed two men in the olive orchard kissing, while two women sat on the hood of a Jaguar and drank limoncello and reapplied lipstick.

Constantina and Pietro carried debris into the kitchen so that in the morning everything would be ready for a clean start.

The family gathered at the drinks table and Eve poured a half glass of Prosecco.

Jane said, "Come with me," and reached for her daughters' hands and led them through the rose garden, past a marble fountain worn smooth by water, beneath an arch of jasmine, to the property's little museum. She pulled the great door, which itself felt like something extinct, heavy as a dinosaur, and lit the kerosene lanterns with matches that sat in a tiny glass jar.

Vera's eyes adjusted and she saw the huge skeleton of the full-grown mammoth. "Hello again," she said. Jane knelt in front of it like this was a holy site, and she touched the foot bones and brought her fingers to her mouth and tasted. She said, "These exact bones walked the steppe, these joints bent to let the trunk twist itself around a tuft of grass. This skeleton has been to a place where none of us can go, no matter what we do."

Eve and Vera lay down on the tile floor and looked up at the bones as if they were the extent of the heavens. "Come here," Eve said, and pulled Jane and Vera to her. Beneath everything warm in their own bodies was a skeleton. A cold scaffold that would outlast the rest.

"I miss him," Jane said. "I feel like I have not been all the way in the world since he died. Like I don't have a living body either." Vera looked at her mother's chest and half expected it to peel open. Vera had always assumed that she and Eve had suffered the most. The children's loss somehow thicker.

Bones watched. Apes. Jars of pickled mutants on the shelf reflected moonlight and lantern light over the three humans on the floor.

"I keep trying to tell you that you aren't alone," Vera said. She would love Jane after Pearl died, whether that was next week or in fifty years. She would love her if she was famous or jailed or a regular mom with a boring job and the same thing for dinner every night. They would all be bones sooner or later but they were not themselves specimens. In the earth, unexcavated, of no scientific note. They would never be reassembled in a museum. They were human bodies in a world with too many human bodies. They mattered to one another, now, alive, and that was the whole gift.

Jane grabbed her daughters' hands. "You shouldn't have to be grown-ups yet."

"Then don't make us be," Eve said.

The tusks cast a shadow over their faces. A dark stripe, hiding them.

Nine

Vera woke at dawn, her head thick and dark. Jane was in Vera's bed with her while Eve, still in last night's dress, was in the other. Vera got up, washed her face and looked in the mirror at a person who seemed changed. She was a foreign self. Growing up happened in bursts, Vera understood now. There were secret chutes out of kidland.

Jane opened her eyes. "Good morning," she said.

"Hi, there." Vera did not know how to say that she understood her mother in a way she had not before.

"I should go to her," Jane said.

"Let's let Eve sleep," Vera said. Her whole body was thrumming. She had begun something that now needed to be completed.

. . .

WHEN JANE AND VERA APPROACHED, they saw no hump, no animal. When they entered the pen, they saw no animal. "Where is she, this is not happening," Jane said. The gate had been latched. Jane spun in a purposeless circle. There was no mammoth here. Everything slowed. Vera heard a fizzing sound like she was swimming through bubbles.

"Maybe Helen took her for a walk," Vera said, trying for confidence.

"Did we make it all up?" Jane asked.

"Make what up?"

"The mammoth. Everything."

"I'm going to wake Eve. We'll look on the east side of the property and you look on the west side. Meet back here."

VERA TRIED TO IMAGINE what was in her mother's head. Pearl walking off the property, crossing the road, arriving in town. Housewives would stop beating their rugs, fishermen would lay down their tangled nets. *Is that an elephant?* they would say, because that would be strange enough. With fur? Someone would shoot it. Or the fishermen would encircle Pearl, nets draped, closing in, until she was caught by them all.

Pearl must be afraid. Out of her known lands. The animal's size made it hurt Vera more, as if sadness in a bigger body was a bigger sadness. How much fear that melon-sized heart could beat into the blood. Branches cracked under Vera's feet and she heard her mother calling the name of the animal, her huge child. Leaves hushed, breeze gentled. A quail jagged across the ground so light its feet made no sound. The little feather on its head bobbed. Vera stopped, her lungs hot. She put her head back and breathed, breathed, breathed, the sky a geometry of blue between leaves. Though she knew better, it seemed possible that Pearl really had ceased to exist, a dream cracked by daybreak.

VERA WAS AFRAID AND, she thought, stupid. Little Vera, trusting Vera. In the most hopeful version of the story, there was still time to get away. She tried to be strategic. Though no one was watching, it seemed important for solidarity with her family that she perform the act of looking, that she participate in the stage play she was directing and pretend to look for Pearl before going to where she hoped Pearl still was. She ringed the rose garden, the cypress grove, checked behind the wall of jasmine, in the succulent garden, by the birdbaths. She walked the steep path to the water far enough to see the beach.

Vera imagined her mother searching, truly not knowing if the mammoth had been stolen or had wandered off. Jane would picture Pearl hit by a car on the highway. Picture Pearl raging through the village, knocking over café tables, spiraling a child in her trunk and carrying him away. Jane might have imagined the animal shot and bleeding in the piazza, how much blood that would be, the cobbles running red. The ending, known. The ending an accident. More likely, Jane would assume Helen had had Pearl carted off to an Albanian circus, sold her to a collector for millions of euros, reported it all to the police.

That was still a possibility. That someone with money on the line would chase them. Vera thought of the doge's palace in Venice, where they had been when she was a child. She thought of the Bridge of Sorrows leading to the dungeon cells. Shackles and stone. What would the charge be? Animal smuggling, but smuggled from where? Prehistory? Perhaps it was theft they would be charged with. The lab with its millions of dollars in research funds, the squiggles of embryos laid down in a red plastic cooler with dry ice.

Squirrels zigged up an oak tree. It was hot. Vera put her arm over her eyes for shade. "Are you ready, baby mammoth?" she whispered. Her head hurt, an insistent beat.

Vera headed for the cool dark, for the prize she had stashed late the night before.

Entering the museum, her eyes were helpless. The old room with its old things smelled halfway sour. Vera pressed her palms to her eyes to help them adjust. Please be here, she thought. When she opened them she saw the mammoth skeleton, tusks raised, its ancient shape unmistakable, and below that she saw an animal reclined against the great bones of its ancestor. Her ears flat in surrender.

Vera knelt down and put her hands out. "Kiddo?" she said, like this was a baby sister. "Are you okay?" Pearl was warm and breathing. Her trunk was wrapped around the leg of the bone beast. Pearl's eyes were watering, her fur matted in streaks. She was trembling slightly. "Love," Vera said. "You look so scared." Maybe it was the simple fear of being out of the pen, the bigness of the world. Or maybe it was this skeleton, the architecture of something familiar with none of the warmth. Or maybe the animal was just done trying to live on a planet to which she did not belong. And hungry, always hungry. "Are you getting ready to die?" Vera asked, reaching out. It had been a matter of days, but this animal looked empty of life.

Vera said, "I'm going to find Mom and I'll be back, okay? I'll bring milk and water. Okay? Are you thirsty? I know it's hot. You stay here."

Vera closed the big door and swung the latch across. A chant ran through her head: milk, water, family, escape, milk, water, family, escape.

THERE WAS A SPIGOT on the outside wall by the grape arbor. The water was cold, coming from a deep spring a thousand years hidden. Vera drank first, her face wet and the taste metallic and perfect. She wanted to put her whole head under but Pearl's bowl needed filling.

Up the path she heard footfalls, coming fast. Vera jumped behind the jasmine bush because this day seemed like a chasing day but the person she saw was her sister wearing the dress that Helen had worn the night before. Fairy tale red, bloodred, the kind of dress the innocent girl wears while the wolf devours her or takes her as his bride.

Eve did not notice her sister there, tucked in the thorns, but she did see that the water was running and the mammoth's bowl was there, spilling over.

Eve froze. Scanned. Vera watched her and understood that she was as afraid.

She moved out of her hiding place. "Eve," she said. Eve jerked at her name.

"What are you hiding from?"

"You," she said. "Just you."

Vera turned the faucet off. "I found Pearl. She's in the museum with the skeleton. She really doesn't look good."

"What is she doing there?"

"I don't know. I was getting water."

Eve's voice was thin with fear. "Helen must have hidden her. Or George. They have plans. We have to get out of here."

Vera did not know for sure what Helen's plans were. She knew, or believed, that George intended to sell the animal but when or how to or to whom were big black X marks. They might have weeks or some-one might be on the way with a suitcase of cash now. Her own plan, at least so far, was working. "I think you're right. We need Mom. I no-ticed that the keys are in the van?" This lie was clunky and she should have come up with a reason she would have known this but Eve did not seem suspicious.

The two girls brought Pearl outside into the shade, where she lay down, and Vera splashed her with cool water and she fell asleep and it seemed like she might not wake up and they waited while the sun rose higher and hotter and they both looked up at the top floor of the castle where Helen and George were either asleep or plotting or watching. Vera pictured Helen with a bow and arrow, ready to take them all out.

"You're wearing Helen's dress?" Vera said.

Eve shook her head. "You were gone when I got up and I went to look for you and no one was in the mammoth pen so I went to the castle and the dress was hanging on the door."

"So you put it on?"

"The witch was asleep. The girl did not belong in virginal white so she went to the red dress, slipped it over her head and ran away."

Jane, finally, appeared on the path. She was not running, was hold-ing her side.

The girls ran toward her.

"I found her!" Vera called.

"Is she all right?" Jane asked.

"Sort of."

Jane jogged, bent to the animal's face, put a hand beneath her mouth to see if she was breathing. "She's so weak," Jane said. "She looks like she's dying." Vera had felt this coming but had not wanted to say it out loud. To risk making it come true.

Every living thing has a length of time on earth.

"Can we take her away from here? Can we take her to the wilderness?" Jane asked. It was the very thought Vera hoped she would utter.

They were three humans with an animal that deserved release.

"The keys are in the van," Vera said, and Jane did not question how she knew this.

"Away we go," said Eve.

THE GIRLS WENT TO the cottage and threw all their things into their suitcases. "Fare thee well, little hut," Eve said.

Vera said, "I can't help but notice that you have the necklace on."

Eve touched the stones. She closed her eyes and said a silent goodbye, unclasped and laid the jewels beside the sink. "It was nice while it lasted."

"Good job, E."

"I'm keeping the dress. I'm not taking it off until this is all over." Eve ran to load their things, Jane went for hopeless elephant milks and bottle, a tub of mulberries, while Vera led Pearl into the van, which was parked where it had been parked all the while. The key glinted in the ignition, ready. No one woke up, no one stopped them. Vera led the sleepish animal up the ramp, big feet, dry riverbed skin, bristle tail. "There you go, sweet girl," Vera said. "Let's get you somewhere wild." She closed the door and stood alone in this good-life place, this buttery, sunlit day, summertime at its highest volume, flowers and water and boats and pastries on plates and thousands of tiny espressos on thousands of tables, all the hands reaching out for the first sip of this perfect day.

Pearl let her ears go flat.

All the noise of the week went away. The elation and panic and fear and electric hope. It was a peaceful drive, Pearl stretched out in the back of the van, girls beside her and mother driving. They did not snack or listen to music or talk. They had only the sound of rubber on road, the sound of movement. Toward, away.

To Vera it felt like carrying the world's own ending. They had tried to resurrect. They had tried for rebirth, but an ending, steady and true, was what they had made.

"Pearl? It's all right for you to go whenever you're done," Jane said from the front seat, eyes in the mirror. "Thank you for coming, and thank you for teaching us so much. You don't have to stay any longer than you want."

Pearl opened her eyes and looked around, looked for Jane, for her almost-mother, then closed them again, lashes like a fallen forest. She seemed tired. She had traveled far, though her life had lasted a matter of weeks.

Vera thought about the lab that had been Pearl's beginning. Steel and glass and spreadsheets and expensive equipment. How far away that was. She wondered if her mother would go back, once this was all over. If her hands would once again pipette and measure, log the data points on a decades-long journey to a never-before-seen place in which she happened to have visited.

"They're just animals," Vera said.

"What are?" Eve asked.

"Woolly mammoths. They happen to be extinct, but they're otherwise not any weirder than what's still alive."

Jane looked at her daughters in the mirror. "The fantasy is always better before it comes true. That's a life truth."

"Are you all right, Mom?" Vera asked.

"I'm kind of good, actually. In addition to being profoundly sad and tired."

"Yeah?"

"The invisibility of middle-aged womanhood has a lot of downsides but I probably wouldn't have done any of this if I was easier to notice. No one expects the girl to be able to pull off the daring deception. And when it's over, when it's time to go home, everyone will figure I've spent my summer doing menial lab work or menial mom work. I doubt the conversation will go more than three exchanges before someone hands me a list of numbers to transcribe."

"But how terrible," Vera said.

"It's totally terrible. What if it's also a superpower? What if it means that we can do whatever we want?"

"That's fucked up," Eve said, "but maybe also a little bit brilliant."

Jane laughed. "Thanks, kiddo. I think that about you all the time." Eve raised an invisible glass in the air and Jane raised another and they cheers'd in the mirror.

Eve said, "My plan is to go to college and take classes that someone in a small town is making fun of right this minute. Intersectional Feminist Weaving and the Ecstatic Poets. I want to mean it. I don't want to be invisible. I want to be loud and annoying and impossible to ignore."

"I want that for you, too," Vera said.

"What about you, Vera?" Jane asked.

"Can I just be a kid for a little while? Maybe take some horseback-riding lessons and apply to be a camp counselor?" She paused and looked out the window. She had grown up in the last weeks and she wanted to stop for a while. "I'd like to put a towel out in the yard and get an irresponsible tan. I wouldn't mind being irritated with my mom in a ploy to get a bigger allowance. That sort of thing."

Jane reached into her back pocket and took out a folded bill. She opened it and smoothed. "Fifty euros a good start? You've had at least that much irritation."

"Hey, I want to be bought off, too," Eve said, and Jane tossed her wallet back. "Go for it," she laughed. "Take it all."

"What about you, Mom?" Vera asked. "Big plans?"

Jane was quiet for a moment. She looked back at them, the beast and the girls, all that she had made. "I guess I have a paper to write. Maybe, just maybe, we'll learn enough about mammoths to someday resurrect the species." Jane winked at her daughters in the rearview. "Until the planet kicks us off we have to keep trying to do good."

"Where are we going?" Vera asked. She had orchestrated the escape but there was no possible destination that made sense, yet Jane was driving with confidence and purpose.

"I think I know a place," she said. "I hope."

THEY DROVE EAST FOR two hours, passed through Bergamo, Brescia, signs for Lago di Garda. "I wonder what rich-people mysteries are afoot there," Eve said. Because now they had a window into what money could get you, the secrets that could be housed in a great estate. Jane bought panini and sparkling water and chocolates at a service station before they turned northward. "Are we going to Siberia?" Vera asked. "Will you at least tell us that much?"

"We are not," Jane said, chewing.

They passed exits for Trento and Mezzolombardo and went through a long tunnel. Mountains rose deep green and rocky. A billboard appeared with a picture of the iceman, their iceman, more theirs than ever before, skins and beard and stringy hair and gentle smile. South Tyrol Museum of Archaeology, it said in English, then German, then Italian. "Are we going to him?" Their ancient uncle and the possible father of Eve's possible baby and their father's other love. The former organizing principle for their family.

"Later."

Jane did exit in Bolzano but wound through the city without looking at a map, spinning around roundabouts, and headed west on a smaller highway. On the hillside there was the ruin of a castle, one turret standing in a pile of stones. "A crumbling castle is nothing special," Vera whispered, remembering Helen's words. Specialness defined by rarity. Specialness defined by one person in possession and everyone else without.

In front of a long elementary school, Jane turned up a mountain road, two lanes, an angle that seemed more suited to a slide than an ascent. Jane said, "You know the story of me and Dad. How he was my professor and then hired me as an intern for his Kenya project and how we fell in love and he asked me to marry him in the old hotel, yes?"

Eve and Vera said, "Yes, yes."

"And you know that we came here for him to start what would become the iceman biography."

"We know," Vera said. These were the stories they had been raised with, the myth of their family's origin.

"That year was beautiful and we were in love but it was also really lonely for me. I tried to be confident and fine and not show how stupid and young I felt. We all went out to dinners, the whole crew and me and Sal and I worked so hard to seem like I belonged."

They made a hairpin turn and Pearl's head rolled into Vera's lap. Their eyes met and Pearl looked disoriented. "Shhh," Vera whispered. "It's just a windy road." She smoothed the fur between Pearl's eyes, which immediately calmed her.

"The night after they finished their big thawing and sampling of the iceman, Sal came back to our room so excited he could not stop talking. He described the way the body had relaxed when it thawed, the chemical smell in the room, the samples in the tubes. They were like time travel. He told me about the dried skin of the iceman's testicles and the little cube of flesh that had been taken. He told me he loved me. It was not a thing we said to each other often. I had been his student and then his fiancée. Saying this word out loud had been vaguely embarrassing at first and we'd never gotten in the habit. We had been together less than a year. I was twenty-two and he was thirty-four. That night we went out for dinner and then sat in the piazza. I remember everything extremely clearly. Someone in a car yelled at someone else in a car. A woman dropped change on the cobblestones and bent to get it. She had on tall black boots and oversized sunglasses. I wondered what the iceman would have thought of her. A magical beauty or a hopeless creature who had crippled herself with her own shoes.

"This feels terrible to say, but having a baby seemed like a strategic move. I saw how Sal's work on the past could make me a future. I saw how he could publish more, post more, take up space. He wasn't especially good at the business end of things, but I was. He would research and write and I would be his research assistant, his fixer, his first reader and his publicist. A baby seemed like a way I could tie myself to him. I got pregnant instantly. When I left the doctor's office after my first prenatal visit I was so scared of what I had done that I knelt in the empty alley and licked the cobblestones. I don't know why I needed to do that right then. I still remember pregnancy as the feel of cold granite on my tongue. The taste of dirt and mineral."

On the uphill side, sharp pines and rocks; on the downhill side, electric green valleys spread out like a storybook. A stone castle, a white church, a cluster of wooden chalets and a flock of pale gray sheep. In the distance: high granite peaks. A blue ribbon of a river far below.

"And?" Eve asked, her voice full of urgency.

"And?" Jane said.

"You had me to win Dad? That's my job on earth? Mom. I have some very unfortunate news for you," Eve whispered. Vera's mouth went dead dry. "The science experiment won."

"No. I got Sal and I got you," Jane asked.

"That's not what I mean. The vial. That got sent to Iceland."

Vera felt the iceman join them in the van—short frame, scrappy beard, kind eyes. His leather pouch, bearskin boots. His image was as familiar to them as any grandparent. He would have walked these ridges, these exact ridges. Hunting now-extinct deer, his feet on the stones, the same as any other human's feet on stones.

"I didn't dump it."

Vera held her breath.

Jane found Eve in the mirror. "You put it in your body." Vera let her head fall toward her chest. She pulled the air in and held it until her lungs hurt. She squeezed a handful of mammoth fur. "But you did have sex with Lars, right?" Jane asked.

"I did."

"Lars is the father. Oh, Evie. There's no way it was the vial," Jane said. "There's nothing in there. It's code, if it's anything at all. Code scraps floating in saline."

"No chance even a little bit?" Vera asked.

Jane said, "Even if there were sperm in there, which there really, really weren't, they think the iceman might have been sterile. He had markers of a condition that usually results in sterility."

Vera's ears thrummed. She dug her fingers into the animal's hair.

"Would he have wanted it?" Eve said to her mother. "Would he have wanted to believe in it?"

Jane shook her head hard. "It doesn't matter what he would have wanted. If he had wanted to have a say then he shouldn't have died."

Eve pinked up.

"Second," Jane continued, "if he had wanted it, he would have been wrong. You are not a science experiment."

Vera leaned toward the animal, which was reliably warm in her sleep. The rules for being a person were indecipherable.

"I don't want to be a mother," Eve told them. "Maybe ever. Definitely not now." Tears broke in her eyes and spilled.

They twisted and twisted upward. On some turns it seemed like they might easily slip backward if Jane slowed down too much.

Jane said, "I'm the one who should be admonished for trying to bring him back."

"I am a punch line of a long, unfunny joke," Eve said.

"Clearly, we in this family are susceptible to impulsive experiments."

Either Vera did not fit or she had not found the end of her own joke. She curled in with her sister-pet. "A woolly mammoth and a pregnant teenager and her boring sister walk into a bar," she said.

Jane slowed as they passed into a small town. Wooden chalets too perfectly alpine to be real. Chickens. Horses. A wooden church. The sign said SALONETTO. "Dad," Vera said.

"I promised you we'd come," Jane told her. "Do you still want to?" The silence grew very dense. Vera did not say that she wanted to because her throat was locked closed, but Jane must have understood that because she continued to drive. The mammoth rolled slightly. After a kilometer, Jane pulled over into a dirt track in a field. She turned the van off. "We better walk from here. I don't know if there will be another good place to park."

Jane opened the back of the van and kissed Pearl on the foot. She said, "Be good. We'll be back." Pearl did not open her eyes or cry.

"Should we leave her?" Vera asked.

"My daughters need to say goodbye to their dad in the place where he died. The animal will be fine."

This time it was Vera who held Jane's hand and Eve who shadowed. Red-dress sister, unusually quiet, following behind.

At the next bend, a wall of granite on the northbound side, only a meter from the edge of the road. A surface. An ending. Vera did not picture the car bursting into flames when it hit, did not picture the crumpled metal. She pictured the car carrying her father turning unsolid, driving straight into the earth, changing realms. Vera walked to the stone and knocked. She rested her forehead on it and listened. She could feel Eve and Jane watching. On another day she would have stopped so as to appear sane but on this day there was no such thing. She could afford to be honest.

Sal was absent and he was part of everything. He belonged to Vera and Eve and Jane and he was gone. Vera closed her eyes and tried to feel the force that was her father locked in that cliff, or the way he was in her, the way they were joined. She could not conjure him, though.

Sometimes he slammed forth, universe sized, absolutely everywhere, but Vera did not get to choose when this happened. She had to take him how he came, whisper or bang, and she had to learn to love his absence, too, because the empty space was also her dad.

Vera wasn't sure if her own fury—for her father's death, for the mistakes everyone else was always making—would come later, if she was coasting a good-daughter wave that would eventually break. Vera's fingers were prickly and her lungs felt tight and she reached for a jagged granite stone on the ground and put the stone in her mouth. She sucked the cold rock, felt the bumps with her tongue, earth and time and weather and matter.

Eve, red satin fluttering in the breeze, wiped her nose on her wrist, pressed her palms together.

"You are loved," Jane yelled to the mountainside.

A car drove past and sent a gust of air at the women. The driver would have tried to make sense of the scene—a woman with her forehead on the mountain, another in a red evening gown, an older one screaming into the abyss. Jane and Eve came close to Vera and each put a head on one of her shoulders. She spit the stone out of her mouth and the three of them looked at it, dark and wet in her hand. "You are loved," Jane said again, whispered, and when Vera looked up she saw that Jane meant it for her. She made a tiny sound, all she could conjure, and squeezed the rock in her fist.

Vera put the stone in her pocket because it felt like something she would always need.

FOR TWO HOURS they drove steep fire roads through alpine meadows brightened with wildflowers. There were no more churches, no more chalets, no more castles. Boulders and grasses, pines. Jane drove as if she had mapped this route the day they had arrived, Pearl still the full miracle. Now her breath was shallower. She was old. New, and already old.

When they had not seen another car for an hour, Jane pulled over on a pathless place, a stretch of hillside unwalked by human feet. She turned the engine off and everyone took a deep breath: they had not realized how loud the motor had been.

The forest was full of birdsong, beetle song, wind. It was cold, this high up. At the edge of the road was a patch of wild strawberries and Vera knelt to gather them, the tiniest gems, to tempt Pearl out of the van.

Pearl was weak. She did not want to walk down the ramp. She scuffed, trunk dragging, feet heavy. Her eyes stayed mostly closed as she exited the van and she let herself be led. When she stepped onto the soil, grass and loam, she looked up for the first time. Her posture brightened. She willingly walked and so they went into the woods, over a ridge to a valley sharp with columbine.

Pearl wrapped her trunk around bundles of grass and brought them to her mouth. Everyone held their breath and watched her chew. Jane said, "We gave you hay and milk but never grass." Pearl continued to graze, as if she had never not done this. As if she had been patiently waiting for a wild meadow. The underbrush was sun-soft. The air was clean. The woods were wild, guarded by pines. People and animal were enclosed, and in the trees, small. This was the gift—to be invisible and to be resized. Pearl was not mega-, just fauna. An animal in the wild. She ate and ate and ate and nothing could have been more beautiful. All this is yours, every shade of green something delicious, Vera thought. Tree cover, shade, ten thousand miles of mountains, of pine and granite, dark earth, the stars of purple flowers, white, yellow, blue.

A flock of birds rattled a tree. A rabbit tested the air. There were many sounds and it was so quiet. Nature felt full and it felt gentle. None of them wanted to disturb this.

After a long time walking, Pearl lay down. She looked satisfied and warm and content. She wrapped her trunk around a stick and broke it in half. Jane sat beside her, the girls, too. They had been moving since they woke up and Vera still felt rhythm in her cells like a sailor listing on land. Jane picked leaves out of the animal's fur. She looked like an ape picking lice. Jane reached for an ant walking Pearl's spine like a ridgeline. Vera almost expected her mother to bring the ant to her lips.

"I wish she could walk to Siberia," Jane said. Vera pictured Pearl climbing ever northward, winterward, until finally she would emerge onto permafrost thick with the bones of her ancestors. It was still summer in Siberia, white-lit all night and no end to the land, grasses and mud and the dark melting cliff to the sea, the steppe populated with musk oxen, bison, yak, reindeer and horses, all of them having made a journey across continents, sometimes seas. And the mammoth would stand there, fur and the pearls of tusks, and her silhouette would look exactly as imagined and as natural as the grass. As if she had been there all along, every year of the tens of thousands, and here still.

It was the circle, completed. Or would have been.

AND HELEN? Was she chasing them? Vera imagined Helen waking up late, her head heavy and blunt, and she would have put on her robe and a pair of sneakers, would have walked outside and seen the van gone. "Good girl," Vera imagined her saying. Helen might have expected that the van would be retrieved by the police eventually, parked for too long at some train station, and she would pay the fine and have it towed home.

Vera felt in her jeans pocket for the specimen tube with the sprig of mammoth hair that she had taken from the person who had taken it first. Later she would tuck this into her jewelry box, full of cheap, fake prettiness. For Vera, the secret would always be better than the telling, worth more held than dispersed.

THE FAMILY PASSED a bar of chocolate around and drank water from a plastic bottle.

"How do you feel?" Jane asked Eve.

"About what?"

"Do you feel sick? Do you feel tired? Do you feel, I don't know, pregnant?"

"Tired, yes. My boobs are sore balloons. Is general dismay a pregnancy symptom?"

"It's so weird how you can forget what something so intense feels like," Jane said. "I remember that beef tasted horrible and fleshy. I remember that I always needed a nap. How I kept name lists in my notebook and tried to conjure the Claires and Marigolds and Simones. But I cannot, cannot remember how it felt."

"I hope I also forget."

"Your general dismay," Jane said, "I believe you get from me."

Vera buried her hands in Pearl's thick fur and felt the dry skin. The animal moved slightly. Sighed. Her red hair was sun-warm.

Jane said to Eve, "When this is over we'll fly home and in a few days you will be yourself again, only yourself." That word, "home," came at

Vera like wind. Ordinary days in an endless line and their little family, as intact as it would ever be, traveling across them. Jane was not a scientist today, not an inventor. She was a mother. Eve was her daughter, not a carrier, not a piece of a project.

"I wish you had told me earlier," Jane said. "I'm so sorry you were alone with this. I'm sorry you thought I might want you to continue."

"I wasn't all the way alone," Eve said, and pride crawled up Vera's skull.

Now that the unsayables were being said, Vera asked, "Are we worried about going home? Is there any chance the lab knows what was taken?"

"I let myself worry about that for a while," Jane said, "but they wouldn't have believed me if I had told them. They wouldn't have believed me if I had sent photos and tissue samples. What happened is not, according to science, yet possible. I've got my invisibility lady cloak and a story that couldn't be true."

Vera took a breath that went all the way to her toes. She had never loved science with all its suspicions more.

Jane said, "We'll go back to California and you girls will go to school and I will write my paper about Veve and then I'll get a job somewhere and we'll buy a little house and everything will be so normal we almost won't believe it."

Vera said, "Can we learn to bake sourdough and hike by the ocean and eat soup?" She smiled and shook her head. "Somehow soup seems important."

"That's just what your dad would have said. All problems were solved with food and water."

To Vera Eve said, "Once I'm unpregnant can I come with you to your topless earth-savior protest?"

"What's that now?" Jane asked.

"I'd like that," Vera said. "I'd like to be responsibly irresponsible with you. For a good cause."

"I'm going to choose to not worry about whatever you're planning right now," Jane said.

They all turned back to the animal at the center of their circle. Her big warm body, strange and sweet and plain. Vera studied the cracked landscape of Pearl's feet. She was a whole world, all on her own. "The hardest part will be knowing what happened and never sharing it," Jane said. "I'll never do anything of this scale again. But I'm learning that we could do a better job of celebrating small and medium-sized achievements in this family."

Pearl had fallen asleep. She was a small hill, all fur and warmth, her trunk a spiral on the ground. Her breath was so shallow there was hardly any rise and fall.

"I wish we could bring her home with us," Vera said. "I like her. She's a nice beast."

"She doesn't belong to us," Jane said. "That's what I got wrong."

Pearl did and did not belong to anything. She was her own species, belonging in ways unimagined until now.

"Is she going to die?" Vera asked.

Jane said, "She was definitely starving and now she's full of grass and she's asleep in a meadow."

From her bag Jane took all her careful handwritten charts. She dug a hole in the earth with her fingers and laid everything inside. She made a neat pile, all the evidence, the whole story below the surface. Jane took a matchbook from the same bag, tore one stick and struck it on a rock. "What I do know is that I will never claim this. None of this happened," she said.

The paper burned. Jane started to speak and her voice was slow and soft. She said, "Once upon on a time, the white sky cracked open, all those atoms and particles crashing together and the universe was born."

Vera had gotten used to their mom's voice at a fast and urgent clip, small emergencies and panics, manic joy, exhaustion. It had been a long time, she realized, since they had heard her tell a story this way. Jane kept her eyes on Pearl. Vera let her mother's voice cover her like a blanket. She felt like a bedtime child. She bent and put her head on Pearl's belly. Eve, seeing this, joined. Two daughters resting on the family pet while their mother told them a story. What if it was that pure?

"The sphere that matters most is the one that turned into our own," Jane said. "The blue and green one, which wasn't yet blue and green. Its surface was hot and metallic at first, no topography, unmappable. It might have looked like a drop of mercury. It might have looked like a pool of fire. It might have looked like a big heart, beating and bleeding and coming to life.

"And after what seemed like forever was a kind of forever: water. And that was the magic, it still is. How do you go from fire to water? Ages passed, and in that water, because of the water, the squiggle of life began. Somewhere in there, time came into focus. The orb spun in space, and it was warmed and it was cooled. The squiggles grew tails. Darkness and light, darkness and light a million times."

Jane stopped talking and she leaned down, too, and rested her head next to Eve's. Vera could feel Pearl's shoulder joint beneath her. All was quiet. Air, trees and the sound they made together. Vera could almost feel the heat of her mother's and sister's bodies join with her own, like they were three chapters of the same story.

The silence became unbearable and Jane did not begin again. Then Eve's voice: "Life realized that no one else was going to throw the party it deserved. If the squiggles wanted to celebrate, it was up to them. They gathered in the warm spots, sloshed their bodies together until the water foamed. They celebrated all the news: algae, gills, fins, photosynthesis. The mood was incredibly cheerful, despite how difficult it was. The water was swarmy and gross. There wasn't enough room for everyone. Somehow their bodies sprouted short legs. You can't imagine how happy the squiggles were, and they thought of something else: the high five. That's how it went: planets, water, light, life, swimming, walking, the first high five." Jane smiled.

It was Vera who spoke next. "But they were afraid, too, because they knew nothing of the dry land, how big it was, if they would wither and die off, strewn out over the sand. They walked out slowly and laid their eggs. They watched as something huge and terrible called wind picked up and scattered the eggs in every direction. The eggs were tiny and they were lost in the dust. The creatures looked back at their warm ponds, wondered if they had chosen wrong."

The three family members dug their hands deeper into Pearl's fur.

Jane took a deep breath. "That's when the love story began. The love story that has continued all the way to now, pair by pair, finding each other. Two small creatures on the sand, nameless creatures, two of zillions. They pumped their arms, doing short push-ups to say, Hello, handsome. Hello, there. They were everything that had been and they were their own invention. From that act, everything became possible: whales, giraffes, chimpanzees, gazelles, mice, hawks, dogs, elephants, people."

Jane stopped talking, leaned over and pressed her face into Pearl's body and inhaled. Vera thought of the invisible bits of animal that must have rushed into Jane's lungs just then. Jane's voice changed and she said, "That's the story that made me fall in love with your dad.

He told it so well. I signed up for his class to cover a requirement and I left in love with evolution and the professor. I can hear his voice in that classroom still even though I can't quite remember it in our own house."

Vera and Eve had sat in their dad's office while he read his work aloud to himself, part of his writing process, his voice, this story, filling the room. Vera remembered how sleepy the words made her. She would have done anything to be warm and sleepy in that room again.

Jane rolled over and petted Pearl's face, the looping skin under her eyes. "I guess he's kind of your dad, too, kiddo. Sal led me to evolution and evolution led me to genetics and genetics led me to you. If not for him, no baby mammoth in the Italian Alps. What a twisty road."

"Is this the ending then? Life climbs out of the primordial slush, evolves into a jillion different species which slowly go extinct?" Eve asked.

Jane said, "We got too comfortable. We got too fat. We are lazy and greedy and bad at thinking ahead."

A small gust of wind rattled the pine needles. A cloud covered the sun and the forest darkened. Two birds called back and forth and Pearl breathed shallow breaths and the cloud passed and everything seemed sharp again and so bright.

It was Vera who told the ending. "Eventually, like all epochs, the Anthropocene will end. It will take a long time for everything humans built to be taken back by the earth. But time is endless and the earth is patient. It will overgrow, regrow and invent. The future doesn't have an ending."

Jane started to cry. "I'm sorry you didn't have a mom," she said to Pearl. "Of all the things, I'm most sorry for that."

Vera and Eve reached to their mother, whom they very much did have. Vera said, "She had a kind of family. Even if we were the wrong species. She was loved. You loved her."

"Thank you," Jane said. "You've been a big part of this project without anyone having asked your permission. I thought I had to get out from under being a mom in order to work, but in fact, you've made it possible. You rescued her. You rescued me. You shouldn't have had to, but you did."

Vera twisted the hem of Eve's red dress, which she hadn't realized she was holding, and said, "Can your next project not be a secret, though? And not dangerous? And can we skip the villains and the haunted castle?"

Jane put out both her pinkies and Eve and Vera hooked.

They were prepared for Pearl to die there in front of them. It was the story as they had written it, anticipation meant to inoculate against the sadness of that ending.

Instead, Pearl stretched her back legs out, uncurled her trunk, and stood up. She shook her big fur self, sticks and leaves falling off. She nosed the earth. She gazed up at the trees. She was like any baby waking from a nap and remembering the world, soft and cheerful. Without looking at the ones who had brought her, on whom she had depended, the baby woolly mammoth turned and walked, step, step, step, away into the woods.

There was no breathing, no speaking, as the women watched their creature retreat into the trees. None of them moved to follow her. Nothing had made sense all week, all year, longer, but finally, this image resolved into perfect clarity: a wild thing in a wild place, for however long it lasted. The planet, on this day, was weighted with the feet and body of a woolly mammoth.

Jane said, "You're a good mammoth," to the woods where Pearl was disappearing. "Happy trails!" Eve said. "Thanks for visiting," Vera said more quietly.

Vera squeezed Eve's hand, hand of her sister, hand she had held across streets, into oceans, rivers. Safety or comfort in every grasp. Eve's eyes were sorry, were forgiveness, were home. Everything belongs somewhere. Mother and daughters tangled all six of their hands together, fingers knotted, hands that had touched an impossible creature, hands that held a story no one else would ever know. They had been there, they knew Pearl was true. Soon the world would again be mammoth-less. No conjured prehistory, no magic. Except there was nothing *but* magic.

Everything that had ever been, life, light, the entire unknowable future, was in that hold.

IN THIS SPOT, this forest, on this ridge of this mountain range on the surface of the earth, a body would come to rest. Through summer it would be visited by worms and bugs and birds, foxes, deer, and the grass would brown and soon it would snow and the trees would turn to crystal. A thousand seasons more, ten thousand, the glaciers retreating as the earth warms, seas rise and slosh, the wreckage of storms, debris washing into the hills. Animals that were present now would be gone. Over centuries, ice will freeze, melt, freeze, the shape of the lakes will change, the shape of the oceans, the continents, everything that has ever lived given over to glacial time, to geology. Their old bones a reminder of the moment they had trampled, gathered, built, destroyed, imagined, loved.

Acknowledgments

Wild and woolly thanks to Sarah McGrath and Alison Fairbrother for their ultimate wisdom and vision and faith. To my whole Riverhead family, especially Claire McGinnis, Jynne Martin, Bianca Flores; and to Helen Yentus and The Riverhead Design Lab.

To PJ Mark. Thank you for thirteen years of reading and thinking together, and for friendship.

To Matt Sumell, Marisa Matarazzo and Michael Andreasen. First readers, forever. To Marie-Helene Bertino. Thank you for making room on your table for an early draft and for asking all the right questions.

To my amazing and generous students and colleagues at Colorado State University, IAIA, and Bennington.

To independent bookstores everywhere, especially those in all my towns for support and community: The Boulder Bookstore, Tattered Cover, Old Firehouse Books, Books Inc., Diesel Books, Collected Works, Garcia Street

Books, Chaucer's Books, Bunch of Grapes, Books Are Magic, Skylight Books and Book Soup.

To my grandmother Anne Ausubel, the best writer in the family.

To my uncle Jesse Ausubel: thank you for inviting me into your scientific projects from China to Panama to Russia and beyond, and for keeping me up to date on all things mammoth.

To my family and friend-families in Boulder, Berkeley, Santa Fe, Taos, Chockers Point, Los Angeles, and New York.

To Teo, Clay and Prairie: my home.